Zigzags
by Kamala Puligandla

Not a Cult
Los Angeles, CA

Puligandla, Kamala
First edition

ISBN: 978-1-945649-34-9

Edited by Safia Elhillo
Proofread by Rhiannon McGavin
Cover design by Kassia Rico
Editorial design by Julianna Sy

Not a Cult
Los Angeles, CA

Imprimé au Canada

To all the dykes who have loved me.

CONTENTS

Zigzags
by Kamala Puligandla

Prelude

It was no secret why I had come back to Chicago that summer. I could still recall the December night when I'd found myself slumped against Whitney at 3 a.m. in the Uptown Lounge, surrounded by dykes we had just met. One of them was a large woman with a bad platinum dye job and a leather wristband. She went by Peach Tea or Peach Tree or something I couldn't keep straight. She was trying to go home with us or maybe just Whitney, or probably anyone.

"You want another beer?" Peach Tea was offering me her Miller Lite. She had already plied Whitney with IPA and gifted me a pilly pair of fingerless gloves I didn't want. All of us seemed to notice that we were in over our heads.

"Aneesha won't drink that," Whitney answered for me.

Peach Tea shook her head and set it front of me anyway. Then she leaned toward the woman beside her—who I thought I recalled was an architect, which might have explained why she was carrying a briefcase at this hour. The two of them got up and headed for the bathroom.

"I think they're going in there to do it," Whitney whispered. "Good," I said. "She's given up on us."

"I like this," Whitney said. "Come stay with me this summer." Her left eye was at half-mast, but she seemed otherwise serious. "Don't argue with me," Whitney continued. She was extremely confident when she was drunk, and rather commanding. "You already know it's the right choice. You love it here. We have the best time together."

Whitney and I were always having the Best Time. I understood that this was the risky tip of a peak that easily dropped off into a Bad

Time. Once we had stumbled into the top floor of a leather dungeon called Jackhammer—it was the only place still open— and before our drinks were poured, we were approached by a woman in a leather vest. She had a grey ponytail flipped over the front of her shoulder, like a pet parrot, I remember thinking. These things didn't happen to me without Whitney, and it took me a while to understand why the woman kept pointing at her apartment across the street. "The two of you should come over," she finally said, and I felt her hand on my thigh.

At the time, I imagined this meant that Whitney and I looked good together—that my hawkish hair and tight jeans, her red nails and loose flannel provided a queer symmetry, but I'm sure, even on our better nights, we just seemed young and drunk, and it was always so late. I wasn't altogether opposed to the vested woman, but then she knocked my drink over with a careless elbow, and that was enough to suggest I wouldn't like what was in store.

Still, I wanted to think there were more nights like that ahead of me, and that one of them might lead to a place from which I would not fall, but fly off into some other dimension.

"You're thinking about the free pickle martini night, right? With that cute bartender?" Whitney winked at me in a way that looked, for a moment, like she might be going to sleep. "If you're not, you should be."

"Well, I am now." I decided I might as well have a few sips of Peach Tea's Miller Lite.

"I need your help dressing myself, Aneesha. I don't think real accountants wear cutoffs. You can write all day and hang out, summer bear style."

Whitney was wise to appeal to my practical side, and I was touched to know that I would always have a place with her. Though I was vaguely aware of how precarious it was to spend the summer with someone who threatened to haunt my heart forever.

Whitney had never quite decided what she wanted with me. She had, however, offered me an ideal way to spend the summer in Chicago. Under the silver beer lights in the bar window, the summer blossomed in my mind. I imagined the crisp of dried sweat and sand on my skin, heard the crowd of us gathered around the musty wooden bar at the Heartland. So I agreed. It felt good to have a vision for the summer ahead.

Whitney pushed the end of her beer toward me and pulled out her phone to find the best route to J.B. Alberto's for pizza.

"You don't want to catch up with Peach Tree in the bathroom?" I asked. "I'm sure it fits three."

"Shut up, she bought us beer. It wasn't so bad." Whitney eased off the bench. "Let's get out of here."

We hastily threw on our layers and scurried out onto the snow-packed sidewalk. I shoved my hands in my pockets, and we both ran screaming into the night. The air was so fresh and frigid I felt like I was going to cough up glitter.

That was the thought that kept drifting through my head as I tried to get comfortable back home in Riverside. I had moved to the desert east of LA to get my master's in creative writing, and each morning as the sky stretched out before me—taut and bright blue, like a sheet of plastic—I was reminded of where I was not. The arid climate had me rubbing lotion on my hands obsessively, and the radiant heat, which persisted well into October, felt thin and flat, as if I had been stuck under a warming lamp at a cheap buffet.

I was used to the constant shifts of my privileged youth, in which friends shuttled between coasts and schools, organic farms and countries without running water. We were aligned only for brief, golden moments, like popcorn kernels exploding together. "Everything is fluid," a melodramatic dancer friend of mine was fond of declaring whenever she felt like leaving in the middle of something. And I was fine with that as long as I had my writing, my little pieces of solid ground.

So I expected to be thrilled by Riverside. It was a small town with no distractions, where my only responsibility was to write. It was my homework. In exchange for my writing, the State of California had invested in paying my tuition and stipend. That fall, however, I came to my stories only in stagnant afternoons or late at night, always with a grudging sense of obligation. Instead I filled vast stretches of time with my new classmates, getting soggy with booze, dazed by weed, lost in malicious laughter.

Anything to stave off the terrifying starkness of the stubbled mountains that surrounded us, and the vastness of human experience we intended to share with the world.

One morning I was sitting at the kitchen table, avoiding my current story, when I got a call from Richard. We were nearing

Thanksgiving, and I hadn't heard his nasal Southern-tinged voice in months. "I won't lie, doll, it's been awfully quiet on your end. But there is plenty amiss out here in Chi-Town." Richard gave me the most recent Heartland gossip—that a veteran bartender had slipped booze to and then slept with the owner's seventeen-year-old son. Richard also let me know that he was back on again with his elusive girlfriend, Karen. She was a textbook cougar: fun, beautiful, owned a production company, and lived on the Gold Coast. The few times I'd seen them together, she put a touch of class on the inappropriate mutterings that regularly spilled from Richard's mouth. They had kinky sex and took fancy trips. I liked them.

"She really doesn't want kids," he mused. "She wasn't joking. She doesn't want a family at all."

"She's forty-five," I said in her defense. "I'm sure she knows exactly what she wants." I went on to describe the unlikely people who populated my new life and the exotic strip malls where I spent my afternoons. Richard cut in hesitantly before I was finished.

"You know, honestly, you sound lonely, doll. You don't have anyone to rub your knotted writer's neck and whisk you away for a day trip. You're on your own. Does anyone test your bike brakes before your drunk ride home?"

Nobody had ever accused me of being lonely before, and my instinct was to disagree with him. I was spunky, and fun, and constantly surrounded by people—it was a gift of mine—but Richard saw through me, and there was no point in pretending otherwise.

"Yeah, okay," I said. "I see your point."

"Come on back, Little A," he cooed. "I miss my number one lesbian. I still save a seat for you at the bar sometimes, and get angry when you don't show up."

From then on, as I drove the dusty roads to school, dodging tumbleweeds and waiting interminably for the trains to cross, it became clear that I wasn't just lonely. The ache that I felt was homesickness. It surprised me. I'd always savored a fresh start. I fancied myself a perpetual visitor, a woman who, in equal measure, did and did not belong in any given place. I took great pleasure in minor reinventions of myself: deciding on a "usual" pair of shoes, and whether or not I was dedicated to composting, and when to reveal my always-surprising ineptitude with women. Chicago had only been a year, a stop on the way to graduate school, but I could tell this kind of fun had been ruined. Despite my conscious focus on the fact that I was living the dream—writing fiction for my livelihood—when the sun started to set, I still felt myself preparing to finish up and head to the Heartland.

Part 1: Return

I hurtled out of the sliding doors at Midway and was greeted with the wet, sloppy kiss of Chicago in June. The thickness of the air caught me by surprise, the way my flannel stuck to my arms, and my hair to my forehead. I had to put down my bags to take off my shirt. I was stuffing extra items into my backpack when a familiar "Hey" cut through the rumble of cars. There was Georgie in her parents' green Prius, carefree elbow perched on the window, turquoise sunglasses sliding down her nose.

"Aneesha, you're back." "I am."

"I'm getting out," she said, and I waited for her to pick the right break in traffic.

Eventually her door peeked open, and she darted around to the sidewalk so we stood facing each other. It had only been six months since I'd last seen her, but I was happy to find the same best friend I remembered. Georgie had a long, thin frame, broad shoulders and an asymmetrical, chin-length haircut, which made everything look intentional and chic. Something about Georgie's posture reminded me of an elegant chicken. We looked each other over and nodded—hugging had never been a regular part of our rapport.

"You'll have to let me pluck your long blond face hair," she said. "Thanks," I said. "Just think of the damage that that one hair could do."

We settled into the car and slipped silently off into traffic. "So you want to go get a hot dog?" she asked.

"I said we'd have lunch with Richard. I hope that's okay."

Georgie sighed. "I don't mind. I'll prepare myself. I feel bad about cancelling our last few Two Person Bookclub meetings. He's just a lot to handle."

The strip malls slid past us and I inhaled a delicious waft of something fried. I knew what she meant, but that was also Richard's charm. He was too much and you were permitted to be too.

"In other news, you staying with Whitney for the summer is an interesting choice. Especially since I offered you the option to stay with me."

I glanced across the car at Georgie, whose pursed lips told me she was waiting for me to address this egregious insult.

"With you at your parents' place," I added.

Georgie had finished her MFA in poetry that spring and was temporarily living in her childhood home. The Summertowns' three-story townhouse in Andersonville was known for being lively and full of strange, international guests. Georgie had written me pages and pages of letters, detailing each and every annoyance of residing in a space over which she had no control.

"Alright, good point. But, for the record—"

"I know you think it's a bad idea," I said. "But for the millionth time, Whitney and I are good friends."

"Ugh, fine," she replied. "I am still so neutral about her."

We drove in silence for a while longer until we turned on to Lakeshore Drive, and the buildings of downtown sprang up around the bend. Every time I saw the Sears Tower, like a giant remote control, and the flat diamond face of the Smurfit-Stone building, I felt I had finally arrived. I didn't even particularly like downtown, but the skyline gave the impression that you were entering an elegant party, and I wanted to be welcomed like that. I rolled the window all the way down to let the hot breeze blow in.

Georgie did the same. She yelled something to me through the roaring wind. "What?" I asked.

"Fun!" she cried. "I hope we have fun!"

"You?" I screamed back. "You hate having fun!"

Georgie had professed herself, on a number of grumpy occasions, to be averse to fun. Though it wasn't entirely true, she did prefer to work anxiously and meticulously, even on pointless projects, like sewing new armpits into her old t-shirts, rather than simply relaxing.

"Maybe I've changed," she said. "Maybe I like fun now!"

Georgie's hair was a short lion's mane dancing around her face, and her loose grip on the steering wheel gave me the confidence to believe that in the year since I'd moved away, we had taken one step closer to becoming better versions of ourselves.

At Tank Noodle, Georgie and I sat across from Richard. He hummed as he flipped the pages of the menu. "Oh, I don't know, I'm not married to the spring rolls, but I do feel they're a good warm-weather choice." He looked up at me. "You know what, doll? You're the guest so you choose an appetizer, I trust you."

"Since when are you the boss of lunch?" Georgie asked.

Richard waved a hand at her. "Oh, you're around all the time, Georgie, and I know you'll pick those crispy wonton things."

"Those sound fine to me," I said. "Pick whatever you want."

"Thank you, I will," Georgie said, leaning toward him indignantly.

Richard had checked out and was watching the street through the window. "Do you think it'll rain today?" he asked.

"Maybe later?" I turned back to discuss the avocado smoothie with Georgie. It was an indulgent choice, but this was a celebration.

"I sure hope it does," Richard said. When I looked up, his face had melted into a leer, and I followed his gaze out to where a girl in a flowy blue tank top was unlocking her bike. "Because she is something, and I would love to see her shirt, soaking wet, flapping in the wind, maybe get a little wrestling—"

I stopped listening after that because she was cute, the smoothness with which she stepped onto the pedals, the bounce of her hair. I didn't want to imagine any of the scenarios Richard might possibly construct—the disaster, the calamity of him befalling her. She rode away and I admired the tiny flexes of her calves.

"Don't give me that look, Georgie. Aneesha is thinking the same thing," Richard was saying when I tuned back in.

They were both looking at me expectantly. I wanted to deny vehemently that Richard and I shared any of the same thoughts, because I was never hoping for a sudden thunderstorm to render a woman naked, but I had been watching her too. "What," I said instead.

Georgie threw her hands in the air. "It's not boner hour, you guys. Get it together so we can order, I'm starving!"

"Oh, Aneesha, I've missed you," Richard said. His pinhead was plastered with a smile. He had a long, sharp nose and a gentle chin, which only accentuated the girth of the grin.

"Oh, Richard," I said, and I did feel a sudden wave of affection for him. "You always bring out the worst in me."

Georgie shook her head. "I guarantee Aneesha wasn't thinking anything as nasty as you were, Richard."

"That is an unfair assumption with absolutely no proof," he said. "Just because she's a woman she's less crude? Give women some credit."

"It's not a man-woman comparison," I said. "It's a you-me comparison. I once heard you say aloud that you wished you could smell a girl's bicycle seat. I had never once thought of that."

Richard laughed. "That is pretty disgusting, huh?"

"Case closed." Georgie shut her menu and placed it at the edge of the table.

Richard reached for my hand. "None of this is to dissuade you from our baby. I promise you I'll find a way to keep from saying these things to our child."

For some time, Richard had been convinced that I'd find it convenient to have his baby one day. When the iron was hot—this was the actual phrase he used—he would donate his sperm to me and my hypothetical long-term partner. I wouldn't even need to ask. It was his solution for being involved in but not responsible for creating human life. "Lesbians are the most intentional parents" was one of his favorite aphorisms. As if I wanted a baby at all, let alone one with his DNA, to raise with a woman of my own choosing, who, based on my past, wouldn't be fit to mother a succulent. This should have made it perfect joke material, but instead it was Richard's open desire for fatherhood and its dependency on me—not his repertoire of certainly more crass behavior—that was starting to grate on me.

"I'm never having your baby," I said. "But don't think I'm not flattered in a disgusted way."

"Just think about it," he said cheerily. "My son with your hair. It sticks straight up all on its own. He'd be the belle of the ball. Georgie? Maybe if you and Youngsu break up, you'll consider it? We could expand the Two Person Bookclub. Kids love reading."

"We've been over this, Richard. Never going to happen." Georgie waved over one of the ladies in camouflage to take our order.

"We'd like to start with the spring rolls, please," Richard interjected. "And the fried wontons," I added.

Richard rolled his eyes. "Fine, yes, and the wontons too."

When we had placed our order, Richard put his palms flat on the table. "I'm glad we have the gang back together for a while. I'm already looking forward to Iowa this summer."

"Oh yeah?" Georgie asked warily.

It was amusing that Richard thought he had ownership over this trip. The Summertown Farm in Marshalltown, Iowa was where Georgie's grandpa lived, where her dad had grown up, and was her proclaimed favorite place on Earth. When Georgie and I met in our first year of college, she told me I had to visit her there in order to really know her. So I did. We had been taking blissful getaways to the farm ever since. She and I sped down dirt roads blasting Billy Idol remixes on cassette, drank beer in the pond, and ate neon popsicles in the cornfields. I'd never experienced the freedom and privilege of doing whatever I wanted on acres of land that belonged to a person I knew, and it blew my mind. The past summer we'd invited our friends to join us at the farm, and though it was a ball for everyone else, it had caused Georgie great stress.

"I hope you decide to invite us back," I said to her.

Georgie sipped her water and crossed her arms. "It does feel good to have everyone here. I thought we'd lost you to California forever, Aneesha."

"Really?" I asked.

Richard adjusted the napkin in his lap and sipped his water. He was gracing us with an uncharacteristic silence. I watched their faces and felt a sudden, fluttering panic. It occurred to me that my little corner of the world had been perfectly prepared to continue on without me. It seemed I was the kind of person who would draw up a neat ending and blithely walk away.

"Well, I'm not gone yet," I said lightly.

᷍

After Whitney finished work, she met me at her new apartment building. She was wearing a navy blue blazer with a silky salmon blouse, and I felt an unexpected surge of pride at how smart and professional she looked. She had a jaunty walk and tight, long curls, which made it seem that she was always bouncing.

"Your outfit is great," I said.

She tossed her hair and pointed down to her tan Top-Siders. "The dyke shortcut to business casual. And they're even women's shoes!"

"You're so classy."

"Duh. So this is the new place," she said, pointing upwards. "What do you think?"

It was a red brick building with arches above the windows, old-fashioned streetlamps and short posts in the front, as if somebody might want to hitch up a horse. It was intended to be impressive, but without making a complete effort, and for that I docked it several points. Though it was still nicer than anything I'd ever lived in. "It aims for majesty," I said.

We walked toward the door, and I found Whitney's placard in the shiny, silver callbox: Ash/Winters. Logan Ash was the boyfriend. Whitney was not known to date seriously. It was more than a little shocking that she had suddenly moved in with a 23-year-old med student. She had met Logan at a fundraiser for a youth nonprofit where she was also a member of their young professionals board. All of which sounded like an elaborate joke to me, something the real Whitney Winters would have invented to make people laugh at a party.

"You're moving up in the world," I said. We took the back stairs, past a series of porches that her neighbors had decorated with paper lanterns, potted plants, and neatly fanned copies of *GQ*. "Something tells me you do not have a drug dealer landlord anymore."

"You know, my drug dealer landlord used to give us free Internet. I kinda miss Rogers Park already. But Logan and I spent forever with the apartment lady and this place has in-unit laundry. Can't beat that."

I nodded and imagined an apartment lady. She would wear a knee-length skirt and reasonable pumps, and know to mention selling points like in-unit laundry. Apartment ladies were for serious, busy people—which I supposed Whitney was now. I remembered what a kick we'd gotten from setting up a fake office in her living room, complete with plants, a dress code, and mandatory office parties. I took a moment to examine the watering can on her deck and recalibrate my concept of reality.

"What are you thinking about?" Whitney asked. "Do you think you're an adult now?" I asked her.

"Do you think you are?" She opened the door into her kitchen. "I'm sleeping on a cot in your craft room for three months," I said.

She laughed hard and went to the fridge to pull out beers. "Somebody has to enjoy the fruits of my labor and you're the best candidate. Magic Hat or Two Hearted?" she asked, and I grabbed the nearest one.

My room for the summer had French doors with cream shades that opened into the living room. There was a door that led into the kitchen, but it had been blocked by a set of black bookshelves, lined with Logan's manga and public health textbooks. Whitney's old bedroom had been covered in drawings and posters made by her friends in Knoxville—bears in overalls, bearded men on bikes, portraits of gawky mermaids—and these now adorned my room. On the wall across from my cot was a pen-and-ink of a screaming Courtney Love: the patron saint of making bad decisions look good. I imagined that she would watch over me and offer me guidance in all of my questionable endeavors that summer.

Hovering in the back corner was Whitney's headless mannequin, in a boxy floral dress that had remained unfinished for years.

"She doesn't have anything new and trendy?" I asked.

"She doesn't get much attention anymore," Whitney replied. "She stopped trying."

"Well that's just sad. I'll be happy to take her out one of these evenings. I've always admired her figure."

Whitney walked over and adjusted the floral dress. It needed to be sewn up the back and could have used some straps, but it wasn't far from finished. "It's been so long, I wouldn't even wear this anymore. Not like it would fit," she said, fingering some tiny lace ruffles.

Whitney had been more muscular— her thighs were once tight clamps around mine when we spent the night together—but something about her looked less sturdy now.

"Isn't that hip these days?" I asked.

"Right, sure, my withered, tax-season body is hip," Whitney replied. "You're not helping, Aneesha." She smirked and pointed to what appeared to be a hammock with chrome legs. "This is Logan's cot that you'll be using."

"Is it going to hold my husky and unhip home-office physique?" I asked. "Oh, definitely," she said. "Dogs have slept on there."

I laughed to myself and checked to see if she was joking, but she was already at the closet, pulling out blankets and telling me where I could put my clothes. So I began to unpack my shoes. I really liked the idea of using dogs as a measurement. "Today I'm feeling the excitement of eight dogs," or "Oh no, not Uncle Henry, he's three dogs' worth of trouble."

"I know it makes no sense. Don't make me figure out what I was thinking," Whitney called over her shoulder.

I waved a hand at her. "I always enjoy the nonsense, don't worry one dog about it." The room was lit by the soft glow of lights strung above the windows, and I thought I could get comfortable here after I set up my computer and lined up my shoes. "I honestly can't thank you enough for letting me stay."

"I'm sorry, I know it's not our original plan," Whitney said. She piled more blankets and pillows than I'd ever need at the end of the cot. "It's just with Logan and my accounting work—"

"Don't be ridiculous," I interrupted, but I was touched by her apology for the change, by her recognition that something might be lost. "This place is perfect," I said. Which it was. For her. I was going to have to reconsider what I thought I was doing here. Whitney and I had talked about Logan and her job, but she always sounded like the exact same Whitney. It wasn't until I was here, amidst her bougie life, that I saw how stupid it was to believe that we could just run around, exploding together through the night.

"It'll be more perfect if you find something good to watch on the Internet." Whitney never lingered in a moment too long. She sank into the couch in the living room and opened up her laptop. "Logan's usually in charge of that since you're no longer my Download Manager."

I took this small dig in stride and found some reruns of *The Real L Word*. In between Kelsey and Romi's drunken fighting scenes, Whitney gave me a complete and somehow impartial update on her life. "You'll meet Logan this weekend," she said. "He's entertaining and you'll like him, he'll make sure of it." During the week, Logan was doing an internship at a hospital in southern Illinois, a Catholic hospital where he gracefully accepted their refusal to acknowledge that he was trans. There was something so responsible about this, so insanely disciplined and unfalteringly good, that I already keenly admired and disliked him.

"Mostly it'll just be me and you," Whitney was saying. "Kind of like old times." "Right," I said, "but with you going to an actual office, Logan coming here on weekends, and me eating your entire CSA box while I stream *The Jersey Shore* from my cot."

"Feel free to use the couch for that," Whitney said. She sipped her beer, eyes glued to the screen, and I wondered which one of us was bringing more sarcasm to the table. I must have looked too grave for the pure, empty dyke drama unfolding in front of us because Whitney threw a pillow at me. "Come on, I'm joking, you're supposed to laugh and be silly with me. I've missed you."

I did laugh then. I pressed the pillow up against her shoulder and rested my head on it. It was comforting to feel her there right next to me. "I'm planning to remind you of that sentiment," I said. "I have plenty more downloading tricks for when it starts to wear thin."

Richard called, and we decided to meet for drinks at the Heartland. I wanted to catch up with our old haunt—it was the other reason I'd come back—and I knew that if we played our cards right we'd drink for free. Or I would anyway, and that seemed important to me. I might never be successful or famous, but I wanted to be the kind of person who could show up at a dive and know that my company was worth the price of my booze.

When I invited Whitney she looked at me like I was crazy. "Fun on a school night?" But then she glanced back at the women on screen, rolling down the sidewalk in office chairs, and I saw that familiar glint her in eye. "I'll regret it tomorrow, but what the hell. Let's go!"

If I'd had a bike, which was high on my to-do list, we would have ridden. Instead, Whitney and I took the Redline to Morse, ran down the urine-splashed stairwell and pushed through the turnstile. *General Store, Buffalo Bar, Heartland Café* read the chipped purple sign painted high on the wall. The screen door still flapped in the breeze.

According to legend, the Heartland Café in its full glory was a hub for artists and queers, vegans and radicals—it was a cornerstone of Rogers Park. By the time I got around to it, however, it struck me as a dysfunctional co-op. The tiles on the floor tilted or fractured when you stepped on them, and on hot days the unmistakable musty smell of dead rats emanated from the long wooden bar. The food was inconsistent and haphazardly thrown onto plates. On paydays, employees knocked hard on the door of the back office so they wouldn't catch Gary, the volunteer accountant, mid jerkoff. But the Heartland remained popular, beyond expectation, because of the unmistakable feeling that when you were there, you were a part of the neighborhood. The place was owned by Lucy and Tom, a pair of generous aging hippies, and staffed by young kids who seemed capable of something big. There was always a regular huddle around the bar, and though I'd never worked there, I'd been welcomed by the Heartland family all the same.

When we walked in, Richard was sipping a Miller High Life from the bottle. The same bulky buffalo head stared down on him from the wall. "Hey, Youngsu, this isn't particularly cold," he called across the bar.

Youngsu's wiry body whipped around. "Really? I put them in so long ago."

"Hey now," Whitney said, putting a hand on Richard on the shoulder. "You were the guy behind the bar not too long ago."

"But that's why you and I became professionals," Richard said to Whitney.

"You get a credential and you can forget everything that came before. I have no sympathy for this plebeian plight." Richard smiled and patted the bar, but Whitney just looked at him.

"Oh come on, I'm only kidding, stop staring at me like I'm a Republican. I think we need some drinks here in the humorless corner. What are we having?"

Youngsu's face lit up when he saw me. He was known for his cartoonish expressions of surprise, which lifted his eyebrows into one tight arc. He had a high forehead and neat black hair, and I had an easy time picturing him as a Muppet.

"Aneesha!" He ducked under the bar, and we exchanged a tight hug.

"Hey, welcome back," Ben popped through the doorway from the kitchen. He had a long, chiseled torso and had been dreamily compared to Michael Phelps by many bar-goers. I thought it was more of a waspy Vin Diesel look myself, but same difference.

Whitney and I glanced at the specials board and then ordered IPAs.

"On us," Youngsu said, motioning to Ben. "Your money's no good here tonight."

"Are you sure?" Whitney asked. "We don't drink much less than we used to."

"Let's hope not," Ben said. "We can probably close early and have a dance party."

"Ohhh," Youngsu said grabbing my arm. "Good idea! Tell Georgie to bring my iPod."

"Why don't I get this kind of fanfare when I come in here?" Richard asked.

"It's plebeian treatment," I said. "It's not accorded to credentialed professionals." Georgie showed up an hour later with Jurate. They were both long-legged and wearing their bike helmets, and moved with such a slow ease that in my tipsy state, I thought they would make fabulous helmet models. Which I told them.

"Hmmm," Georgie said. "Youngsu, give me whatever Aneesha's having. I want to be delusional too."

"But you could be a model," he said, and I felt certain there was nobody on earth as earnest as Youngsu.

"Ah jeez, just pour the drinks," Georgie said. She dug around her in backpack and placed his iPod on the bar. "For later."

"Shots!" Jurate shouted above my head. She grabbed me by the shoulders and bent down to whisper, "I have a new one, you have to trust me." Jurate was from Lithuania, which originally seemed like the root of her strange habits. It explained her preference for flavored, flaming shots, and her addiction to trashy euro-techno. It wasn't until now that I considered Jurate might just be weird. I must have looked at her in an off-seeming way because she frowned.

"If we're so serious tonight, there is always a scotch," she said.

"What? No!" Whitney grabbed Jurate by the arm. "We're having shots, that's what you do."

"Aneesha looks at me like she's caught a bad mood, and I'm just saying we don't have to do shots if—"

"Stop," I said. "Of course we're having shots. I was just preparing myself, because you know how pleasurable shots are, so light and relaxing."

Jurate beamed with her prominent cheekbones and patted my head. She always liked my dry humor. "Okay, it's the real deal Aneesha, please continue."

Amanda wandered in and dropped her bulky photo bag on a chair. "I heard there was a celebrity sighting at the Heartland. I couldn't miss it." We threw our arms around each other and

giggled. "I was afraid I wasn't going to finish my upload in time, but sometimes, hard work and positive thinking pay off."

Amanda worked as a photojournalist for the *Chicago Tribune*, which primarily sent her around the suburbs of Chicago to document pumpkin festivals and high-stakes youth sports events, though the job had also given her the highlight of her career to date: shooting a Bears game at Soldier Field alongside John Cusack, her number one crush of all time. The event that blew me away, however, was when Amanda had been driving through Rockford, Illinois, and stopped at a hotel because she saw a group of cars with Wisconsin plates in the parking lot. She decided to take her camera into the lobby, and walked into a very early discovery of the missing group of Democratic Wisconsin lawmakers, who had fled the capitol to prevent voting on a bill that severely cut union rights. "I just had a feeling something was up," she reported, when I asked what made her stop.

As the only two members of our friend group who had not worked at the Heartland, Amanda and I had a special bond. We spent many evenings together verifying the social nuances that we'd picked up on separately, and marveling at the intricate balance that kept the place going. Now, she pointed her finger at the tap she wanted. She had thick fingers and a very emphatic way of pointing.

"You think that's a good choice?" she asked me of the Hennepin, and I nodded. I liked that Amanda asked what I thought of her choices, even if she wasn't planning to alter them in the moment.

By 11, a few more regulars had trickled in, and a decent crowd of us roared around the bar, slamming our glasses down. Ben went out to lock the doors and Youngsu played electro-pop hits over the sound system.

"Hey, Aneesha, you recognize this one?" he asked. People had the idea that I was on the cutting edge of music, but I just subscribed to newsfeeds and took suggestions. I couldn't even claim to have discerning taste. I liked anything I could jump along with that sounded like some kind of altered state: blown-out tinkly hazes, relentless building storms, overproduced crystalline bliss, all of it.

"Yes," I said and pushed a few tables against the wall. "I love it!"

"See," Youngsu said, "I keep up with the young people."

"You're only 28," Georgie protested.

"And already I'm uncool," Youngsu said. But then he hopped up on the bar and raised his arms. "The people will dance!" he called. He jumped down to the floor, bursting into a spastic running man, and the rest of us joined in. Jurate skipped side to side, swinging her arms over her head, and Georgie bent her elbows at sharp angles, shooting up and down from the knees. I shuffled my feet in quick, tiny steps and spun back and forth. Whitney and I liked to employ stiff robot arm movements and the occasional kayak paddle, for some flair. It was all so familiar, the group of us bobbing and kicking and weaving together freely. The dancing revved up to a point when Jurate was allowed to play her throbbing techno, and soon enough Richard and I were sloppily waltzing in uneven diamonds, trying not to catch our toes on the tilting tiles.

"What's so funny?" Richard asked as we tripped along.

I realized that I was laughing. "Nothing, I'm just happy."

Richard winked. "What a coincidence, me too."

At some point, Youngsu and Ben turned on the lights. After listening to several minutes of loud, unreasonable dissent, they thanked us, collected their tips, and ushered us outside so they could close up properly. On the patio, Georgie rested her elbow on my shoulder and leaned her head up against her fist. "That was awesome."

"Very awesome," I agreed.

Her face was pulled taut into a crazed smile, and she was smoking a cigarette, which meant she would stay out all night if I wanted.

Whitney was saying goodbye to Jurate, the both of them making accounting jokes that I didn't get.

Georgie coughed. "Whitney? Home so soon? How unlike you."

"Yeah, well." Whitney squeezed my arm and shrugged. "This is when I turn back into a pumpkin. Is that how it goes? It's a work night," she said, and headed for the train.

"Aww, too bad," Georgie said quietly as Whitney walked away.

"You don't even dislike her, you just enjoy being mean," I said.

"She's a snake in the grass," Georgie whispered sharply. We were both silent for a moment, and then we doubled over with laughter.

"Oh God, I do love being mean. Let's go be mean to more people somewhere else."

"Duke's, let's go!" I called and the group began migrating down the street. "Hey, Georgie," I said as we skipped along. "Guess what? We're having fun."

"I know!" she said brightly, and then stopped. "Man, Aneesha, you always do that. You know I can't consciously have fun!"

I opened my eyes wide at her and punched her shoulder. "Just kidding. We're having a miserable, insufferable time. I hate you and I hope you die in an unfortunate encounter with a meat grinder."

"Thank you," Georgie responded. "I'd be forever lonely without you."

I pushed into Duke's and held the door open as my friends streamed through.

✦

I awoke on the couch in the living room, still in my clothes and with a terrible ache in my shoulders. My mouth tasted sour. "Bleh," I croaked.

"Hey, you," Whitney said. She pulled a shirt out of the dryer and began to button it. "Good night?"

I nodded and sat up. "Good night for you?" I asked.

Whitney patted at her cheeks with her open palms. "Yeah, we haven't all gotten together like that in a while. But I do have little hotface going on." It was one of our shared hangover symptoms, only hers was also accompanied by a pink tint that my own brownish-reddish complexion hid. I patted my cheeks to see how I was doing. I felt her eyes on me as I got up and shuffled through the French doors.

"I'm jealous of you," she said. "You're reminding me of the person I really liked being."

I shook my head and collapsed onto the cot. There was probably an appropriate joke about beds and lying in them and dogs on a cot, but I couldn't pull one together. "I'm just a bum," I said. "You're doing things with your life. You can be a bum too, after work."

I went back to sleep and awoke several hours later to my phone buzzing in my pocket. "Hello?" I answered without looking to see who it was.

"Get up, Aneesha! We're going to the beach!" It was Heather.

I'd planned to write that day. My project for the summer was to complete a collection of stories for school and I had some serious revising to do, but I was already distracted by new stories fluttering anxiously in the wings of my mental theater.

"Sorry, I need to write," I told Heather.

"Wrong. I'm standing outside."

I rolled over and stuck my head out the window. Sure enough, there were the familiar hands on hips, the red visor cocked to the side, the faded green towel over one shoulder.

Heather always stood with her legs far apart so she looked like an A.

"Hi, Heather," I called.

"Put on your swimsuit and bring your visor." Heather had been a middle school teacher for a few years and all of her directions were authoritative.

"My work," I said, in an insincere attempt at responsibility. "Aneesha, get down here so we can pick up where we left off!"

Last summer, Heather and I had gone to the beach daily and she would share installments of her life story. In return for every three of four episodes, I would tell one or two of my own. It was a ratio that fit our natural inclinations and Heather had better stories—always off-kilter, but permeated by a wholesome Wisconsin innocence that was partly a result of her accent.

"Did you know I was addicted to Benadryl for three months?" she asked me once.

"No. I did not."

"I was. I took it every two hours or I went crazy because I lost that hazy mind balloon. Then it was too expensive so I switched to coke, which was also bad. But I do love a Cherry Coke every so often, it's still my favorite drink."

I leaned further out the window. "I missed you last night," I called down, feeling like a real-life Juliet.

"I know, I know," she waved me off. I'd heard that Heather was selling her eggs again. They got her an even $8,000 at a clinic in Milwaukee, which gave her the freedom to spend the summer as she liked, but toward the end she had to inject herself with hormones every day and abstain from alcohol and caffeine. It often put her in a bad mood.

I rolled off the cot, put on my suit, and grabbed the visor, which I purposely packed at the top of my bag. It had a white terrycloth headband and built-in Terminator sunglasses that flipped down. Heather and I had come across the visors at a dollar store on Clark and purchased one for each of the girls we hung around with.

Outside, Heather and I walked along Sheridan, past ritzy condos and apartment buildings that opened right onto the beach. Cars went whizzing by us. Every now and then a well-dressed couple descended the granite staircase of an elegant building and took a second glance at me and Heather. "Calm down!" one man called to us.

"Was that a compliment?" I asked Heather.

"I'm guessing yes," she said. "So, you're the one with the brand-new life, tell me all about it."

"Well, school is fine," I said. "I live in a house."

"Okay, sure," Heather turned to me, waiting for more.

"With a girl I knew in college and one of her friends. It's been fine. Kinda dirty, but fine."

"Dirty how?" she asked.

I pictured the house on Cedar, the thin mat of cat hair covering everything, and the crust that grew over the piles of dishes in the sink. I wasn't sure how to explain that these were not things that mattered. That what people saw when they came over were the vibrant record collection that my housemates kept, the mid-century coffee table, and the lush garden beds in the backyard. Still, the lumpiness of the couch and the slant of the plastic-topped counters in the kitchen bothered me.

"Maybe dirty isn't really what I mean. Do you ever see something nice?" I asked, trying to explain. "Like a nice sharp knife. You watch somebody use it, and they don't seem to notice its excellence. They use the knife to cut butter or they throw it in the dishwasher or take it camping and split branches into kindling. And it's not because they're dumb, it's just that they measure the value of something by what it can do right now, in this moment, and right now, the sharp knife can make kindling. Every time I see someone using that great knife—like it's a regular old knife—I feel its sharpness dulling and I know it won't be long before it's just like any other crappy knife, all of its potential squandered. Because the people using it don't have an attitude of 'this knife is special, what can I do to maintain that?' You know? Instead the attitude is all 'no knife is too good for any kind of cutting.'" I realized I was talking mainly to the small puffs of cloud that hung above the lake. I wasn't quite sure where I was going with this.

Heather picked out a spot on the beach and spread out her towel. "Hmmm," she said. "I don't think I understand. Explain again." She propped her heart-shaped face on her hand and squinted hard at me. "Are you the knife? What's the knife?" she asked.

"I'm not the knife." I sat down hard on my towel. "The knife is mine, though. Well, maybe I am the knife." What I was trying to say was that nothing was wrong, but it wasn't good either.

"If you are the knife, Aneesha," Heather said, "I think you'll still be a pretty sharp one, even after all the improper cutting. You're working with a lot of potential." She tossed a bottle of sunscreen at me. "Does this have anything to do with you and Whitney? Are you feeling out of sorts now that you're here?" she asked. "And will you please do my back?"

I squirted a pool of sunscreen into my palm and smoothed it into her shoulders. Yes, I was feeling out of sorts. It was surprising, a little disappointing, to see how quickly Whitney could integrate her life with someone else's. It made me think of the Gin Blossoms song about the girl hanging around a playground with someone else. This would have been easy for Heather to discuss without defensiveness or embarrassment, and I admired her for that. But I couldn't do the same without several drinks, and a lot of coaxing.

"Oh, I don't know," I said. "I just got here, we'll see." "It's weird, you know," she said.

"What is?" I asked.

"That none of you think it's weird to live together."

I made sure to get a little sunscreen beneath the string of her bikini and beneath the elastic waist of her bottoms. "So doesn't that make it not weird?"

"I guess we'll see," Heather said, flashing her uneven smile. "You're a very sharp knife with the sunscreen. Thank you."

"Calm down, Heather," I said.

"That man was calming down at you."

"Really? Because I'm the one in a zebra-print bikini with my perfect boobs?"

Heather just laughed. "Which reminds me!" She launched into a story about a one-night stand on the roof of her apartment building with a guy who asked that she punch him in the face and let him strangle her a little. "It wasn't very safe, I'll admit, but it was very hot sex," she added in closing.

Heather was unexpected, which wasn't an easy quality to find, I thought. Here was this wholesome woman who taught children and was addicted to Cherry Coke and had rough roof sex. Though he would never say it himself, I knew this was why Richard was in love her. "Who isn't a little in love with Heather?" Georgie had said dismissively when I brought it up before, but I knew it was more than that. It was why Richard decided to join us at the beach, even though I knew for a fact that he hated the beach—I had never once seen him in a swimsuit. He generally sat erect on his towel, brushing sand off himself and aggressively suggesting that we move inside to play cards.

Which was exactly what he did when he arrived. "Hey, H, how do you feel about finding a less fly-infested area to chat? Look at that lush grass calling over there," he said. After a few minutes of chatting with us, he pulled a deck of cards out of his pocket and shuffled them absently.

Heather was in the midst of telling us about a new guy she was seeing, and how she never imagined herself interested in a man with long hair before. "His name is Remi."

"Heather, tell us more!" I said, but when I saw Richard shift uncomfortably on his towel, I was sorry for my enthusiasm.

After a while Heather and I went for a dip in the lake, and I looked over my shoulder to see Richard sitting up, alert as the scattered seagulls. Years ago, he and Heather had made out on her couch, an event of which he said, "you know, it wasn't bad. It was entirely heavenly," and which she described as being like kissing a brother. "I came home and I thought that Heather was giving him a blow-job right in the middle of our living room!" Amanda still liked to recall with horror.

I returned to my towel before Heather was done with the water. "Richard, listen, we can go somewhere else, I know you're not the biggest beach—"

He cut me off with a curt wave. "Oh, believe me, it has its perks."

I turned around to see Heather emerging from the lake. For a moment, I saw her the way I imagined he did, or maybe the way he once had: her round hips, the water dripping off of her body, the bounce of her wet curls, and that skimpy zebra-print bikini.

"Oh god, no," I said, "don't start."

"Yes," he said. "I have held those breasts in my hands. And you know what, doll?"

I buried my face in the sand. "I know, I know. Nobody can take that away from you, not even some guy with long hair and a French name."

Richard snapped his fingers at me and smiled. "That's right."

"Maybe you could donate sperm to Heather?" I asked him. "Do you think Karen would go for that?"

"Karen is so awfully wonderful, she'd never have an issue with it, I'm sure. But aside from my feelings on the superlative qualities of lesbian parenting, Heather wants to make babies on her own."

I looked up to see what was happening on Richard's face, but in place of the glint I'd expected, there was something soft in his gaze. I thought I recognized that look of nostalgia: the hopeless-ness, the helplessness. Richard and I were both the kind of people who would fly directly into the sun because it was mesmerizingly beautiful. Heather was right, I thought. All of this was weird.

The Obvious Combination of Beef Stew and American Cheese

Richard had seen himself in me since the day we met, which was something I had never been able to shake. At the time, Georgie and I had just moved into an apartment together in Edgewater.

"I've got a job as a cashier!" she came home and announced one afternoon. It was Halloween that day, and the job struck me as a trick. "How?" I asked. "Where?"

"It's a hippie-dippie restaurant with a store and a bar. They were totally impressed that I lived in China, and they said they liked my scarf." Georgie fluffed her hair up in front of the mirror and adjusted her pashmina. "I start tonight. Everyone's so nice. They invited us to a Halloween party, can you believe that?" she asked. "I need to wear an exciting costume that will also hide my excessive amount of nervous sweat." We eventually settled on Waldo's Pregnant Wife, and Georgie told me to stop by the bar at 10 when her training was over.

"Friend potential?" I asked her.

"Oh yeah. High potential," she replied.

I liked the sound of that. I'd come to Chicago in the first place because of Georgie. When she returned after a two-year fellowship in Kunming, China, I wanted her to move out west with me but she wouldn't. "The fam is in Chicago and I can't leave the Summertowns," Georgie insisted. This surprised me. My family had good taste, and we generally enjoyed each other's company, but since we were kids, the idea was that my sister and I would strike out on our own, to discover the world for ourselves and make our own place in it. My mom had made it clear that only in a severe pinch could I live at home after college.

Georgie had grown up in Chicago and knew plenty of people, so I decided to move in with her. I didn't know anyone else. I spent my days on the computer, editing and writing inane articles about the kinds of skills one could expect to acquire with a vet tech degree or where to find online courses in soil science. It was both comical and depressing to break down every career into a series of concrete steps so web readers would believe that if they just stuck to the prescribed path, they too could become successful neurosurgeons and film directors. "5 Steps to Becoming a Successful Writer" was the name of one article I'd been assigned that day. I'd had to put down my coffee mug in order to laugh maniacally for a minute.

That night around 10, I showed up at the Heartland Café in my best rendition of beef stew. I'd taped construction paper vegetables to a brown shirt and fashioned a foil cap to look like a pot lid. As soon as I walked through the screen door, I was confronted with Georgie, in her blue knit cap and striped shirt. Her palms were pressed into the counter, and she was blowing at the longer side of her bangs. I was impressed that she'd managed to keep her pregnant pillow in her shirt for the entire shift.

"What's going on?" I asked casually.

"Oh my god, you scared me!" she said, jumping back. "I thought you were another customer and I was going to have to tell you we were closed or that we can't do the ginger dressing gluten-free. Hey, Nikki?" she yelled over her shoulder and a skinny woman with frosty blue eye make up appeared. I wondered if it was a costume or if she always looked that way.

"Georgie, don't forget to take out the cash for tips. That's what this stack is doing over here." She pointed with a pen that she stuck in her mouth and wandered back over to the bar. "And don't forget that you have to do all of the credit card transactions too," she called, and picked up her blue drink. "That's the stack on the other side."

Georgie stared at me with wild eyes and I knew that I would be going to this party alone. "I'm not doing well," she confirmed. "I'll join you later."

I walked over to a stool at the bar, and Georgie addressed the young servers who were taking off their black aprons. "Hey guys, this is Aneesha. We live together," she added.

I ordered a whiskey ginger and looked up at the large dusty buffalo head on the wall. The bar seemed like a standard dive. The vast beer selection was scrawled on a chalkboard, and an empty stroller sat idly in the corner. The wall behind the bar boasted a fantastic clutter of license plates and photographs of the Heartland across the decades.

My dollar bills stuck to the surface of the bar when I paid for my drink, and I realized this was exactly the place where Georgie was qualified to cashier.

"Hey, I'm Whitney," said a girl with very curly hair. She was writing in her receipt book and accidentally brushed my boob with it as she walked past. "Oh!" She grabbed my shoulder. "I'm so sorry." I was struck by the contrast between the firmness of her grip, but how lightly her pen rested between her fingers. She paused to take a better look at me. "Are you beef stew?" she asked.

"Yes," I said, excitedly. "I am. I'm so glad you could tell."

"Great costume. I'm American cheese." Whitney gestured at the piece of yellow foam she was wearing over her shirt. "I made the flag bloomers myself, so they're a little funny. You're coming to this party, right? The foods should hang out together."

"Naturally," I said.

"Good." Whitney added her receipts to the pile Georgie was working through and took the stool next to me at the bar. "What are you drinking?" she asked, which led to a conversation about our shared love of whiskey, temporary tattoos, and the boys' section at Target. Whitney was the kind of queer who didn't look especially queer unless you were queer yourself, and that was something I always liked.

She took me with her when the group headed down the street to an apartment, where someone named Heather was going to give us a ride to the party. I found myself standing at a granite island, watching a girl divide the last of a bottle of gin into a dozen plastic cups. She was wearing a glittery leotard that I very much admired.

"Hey, do you know who Heather is?" I asked.

"I'm Heather," she said. "I live here. You must be a new person. Why don't you take one of these drinks? Nice touch with the foil hat, by the way."

That's when Richard walked in, sporting slippers and a bathrobe. He nuzzled the hell out of Whitney's hair, picked up one of Heather's gin and tonics, and sipped it elegantly, pinky in the air.

He cocked his head to the side and watched me watch him. "Who are you?" he asked, as if I my presence were a mild insult.

This reaction was closer to what I had expected of the night. I'd tagged along to my share of parties, and mooched off a number of friend groups, but I had rarely felt so welcome to do so.

Whitney reappeared just in time to offer an apologetic introduction. "This is Richard," she said to me.

"Aneesha," I said, shaking his hand.

Richard raised his eyebrows at Whitney then grinned at me. "It's a pleasure.

Everyone's been saying there's a cute new cashier at the Heartland, and you're about as adorable as a koala."

"Oh, no. That's my roommate, Georgie," I answered.

He motioned between Whitney and me. "So that means you two are new friends."

"As of two hours ago," I offered.

Richard looked amused, and smugly drained his cup. "Alright, well done." Then he moved on. "I can't decide what to be tonight, hence this horrific nightmare." He gestured to his loungewear. "I have some options, but I'm not married to any of them."

In the end, Richard decided to dress up as a coke addict from the '80s. He wore an over sized thrift store suit, which Heather and her friend Amanda had apparently bought for him, and spent an unbearable 20 minutes applying Vaseline and baby powder to his upper lip. Right as the group was about to leave for the party, he ran off to his apartment, saying that he just couldn't bring himself to go out wearing a silver belt buckle and gold watch, that he needed to change. The car ride required us to jam into the back of Heather's car, but nobody seemed bothered.

"Make room for me," Whitney said, as she climbed onto our laps in the backseat.

I had no idea where we were going or what kind of party we were in for, but I had to admit I felt I was in solid company. Heather was dressed as a glittery Jazzercize instructor. Amanda was going as a businesswoman with an oversized cellphone. Amanda's boyfriend, Sam, had made a cardboard and long-underwear Batman outfit, and Whitney was wearing the foam cheese pull over with homemade American flag bloomers. Then there was Richard. He annoyed me. His pinched face, his brashness, his grabby comportment, and his less-than-inspired costume. I never expected to be friends with Richard.

At the giant loft party, I watched Amanda and the cardboard Batman get close, while Heather flirted with an Alex from *Clockwork Orange*. Meanwhile, Whitney and I downed drinks and chatted up strangers. She also hardly knew anyone there. We jostled on the dance floor, side-stepping loud girls in roller skates, and I sensed a playful glowing chord being struck between us. Her touch on my back was gentle when she asked me to get her a new drink, and there was a loose "baby" tacked onto the end of her thank you. In a haze, Whitney and I took a cab home together. I sat in the back seat, my hand on her thigh, her head on my shoulder, when suddenly, Richard materialized in the front. "Play nice, girls," he called and winked as the two of us slid out of the back seat.

Even as I followed Whitney into her apartment, I hadn't seriously considered that this is where the night had been leading. So often, these were the kinds of interactions that meant I'd made a new best friend. Richard, however, had known all along, and even Whitney was cool and casual as she poured me a glass of water. "You're welcome to spend the night if you'd like," she'd offered.

Richard still brought up his presence in that cab from time to time. "I knew something was happening there."

"Nothing even happened that night," I'd told him time and time again. "I had a glass of water and walked home."

But he knew I was lying, and I think he preferred not knowing exactly what to picture. "Of course. How polite and gentlemanly you are, Aneesha."

The truth of that night, I kept to myself. It wasn't pretty and it wasn't original.

Not even Whitney would have remembered that she took both of my hands, led me to her bed, and pulled me on top of her. We were both still wearing our coats and bags and even though I was straddling her, our fingers on each other's faces, I recalled the sensation that we were still so far apart. I was exhilarated by how sharply her lips tugged at mine. But as quickly as it began, Whitney's gin-soaked mouth went slack and lazy, and I pulled away from her.

"Hey, Whitney," I'd said, holding her cheek in my hand. She'd mumbled and turned her nose into my palm. I jumped off of the bed, and chuckled to myself as I unlaced her boots and pulled them off. Then I adjusted my scarf, pulled up the collar on my coat and left her to sleep. It was too unexpected to take seriously, but on my walk home I purposely attempted not to replay anything in my head, to keep the details fuzzy. I had an active imagination and a bad habit of falling in love faster than was comfortable for anybody.

It was then I had to acknowledge that Richard, the crass stranger with a goopy upper lip, had seen something familiar in me, some part that I hadn't entirely recognized myself. He would never be able to fully explain what he was doing in that cab, but I got the impression that he'd been in my position before, and I wondered what else about me he knew that I didn't yet.

᛭

I wanted to check out my best bike finds from Craigslist, so I headed over to Youngsu's place near Lincoln Square. His mom was in Korea for the month, and since he was borrowing her car he agreed to chauffer me around. This was a big luxury for us— even more so for him because he was a guy whose back bicycle wheel had been stolen four times in the past six months, who lost his phone every few weeks, and had spent a number of nights in the hallway outside his apartment after misplacing his keys. Youngsu was not prepared for his own car, but driving around Chicago was one of his favorite activities. I wasn't quite sure why. Most people found the narrow streets and extreme weather conditions off-putting. "I like to see what people are up to out there," Youngsu said when I asked if he would do me the favor.

"It's always a surprise with him," Georgie said, shrugging. "I'm not going. I've got my own errands and I don't want to sit inside a car all afternoon."

"Come on, it'll be fun," I said. "We're looking at bikes and meeting strangers!" "And guess what?" Youngsu looked at me and then back at Georgie, the arch of his brows peaked. "Well, actually, it was going to be a surprise, but now I should just tell you."

"What?" we both asked, my voice excited, Georgie's annoyed.

"Jesse has one hour to get beers and we're going to meet up with him!"

"Alright, yeah!" I said.

Jesse was one of Georgie's best friends from high school. I'd known him for years, and he was now managing a small organic farm in Michigan. Three days a week he came to do farmers' markets in Chicago, and these were the only occasions when he could sneak in time to hang out.

Georgie narrowed her eyes. "Oh, so now that Aneesha's in town Jesse suddenly has an hour to pound beers?" She straightened the papers and books on Youngsu's dining room table in a careful way that suggested restraint.

I thought I could jolt her out of her bad mood. "Quit it with the funk, Summertown, and just come with us," I said. "The books can wait."

Youngsu seemed to find this move risky and he stood behind me, gripping my shoulders tightly. "That's okay, Georgie, don't worry about it. We'll find you later."

Georgie released a stack of books and sighed. "I have a stupid electrolysis appointment my mom is making me go to. She says my face is too hairy again."

Youngsu's hands were outstretched in a manner that showed his loss for words. "Hmm. Alright," I said, and ushered Youngsu out to the car.

Youngsu fiddled with his iPod to play the Foo Fighters, and once we were on the street he squinted far out into the distance.

"So what's the deal?" I asked.

He was quiet for a moment, and I wondered if he was deciding how much he should say. "I think the deal is that Georgie is restless." I waited for him to say more. He continued looking off into the unmoving traffic on Western. "I think she wants to establish a way to move forward, something serious and important, and I think maybe she's frustrated," he said.

A woman on a bus stop bench was wearing sweatpants that had

fallen too low, exposing her bare ass. People were trying to survive, that's what they were up to out here, I thought as we drove by.

"I think maybe she's frustrated with me." Youngsu turned to me. "You know anything about this, Aneesha?"

I considered Georgie and the wealth of information I carried on her. The truth was that Georgie had never not been frustrated by someone she loved, and Youngsu was her first real boyfriend, a man in whom she actually invested. She agonized over his agony, attempted to solve his myriad of logistical snafus, and took his happiness as seriously as her own. Caring about him took a toll on her. I tried to identify the most constructive way to explain this to him, but Youngsu went on.

"You know, I thought when I came back from Alaska, when we could see each other all the time again, that it would be easy. Now I can't seem to do the right things. I think I'm worrying her."

I knew it wasn't Youngsu, exactly, it was the pace of his life. "Georgie just wants you to finish college," I said. "You know, stick with a major and finish it." This was something Georgie had expressed to me a number of times. "How can I build a life with him if he doesn't finish things?" she would ask.

I thought Youngsu might take this poorly because he certainly wasn't lazy. He did start college the traditional way. With no guidance out of high school, he had accepted a scholarship to a state school in Missouri, and fallen into serious depression. He missed his family and couldn't handle being the only Asian person around. Since then, he'd started and stopped taking classes at community colleges in Chicago a few times. I didn't know what kept him from finishing, but I had an inkling it was located somewhere deep in his psyche and family history, where he didn't have full control.

Youngsu, however, was unruffled by my comment. "Hey, well, I'm taking a class right now, a philosophy class," he said, slapping the steering wheel excitedly.

He wasn't getting my point. "Whatever happened with the EMT thing?" I asked. Youngsu winced. "It's bad. I failed the licensing exam." He fished for a cigarette. "I was busy around then, too many serving shifts."

"Maybe you can try again," I offered.

"I don't know, I'm thinking maybe international relations or something," he said and resumed squinting into traffic.

I couldn't imagine where international relations had come from or where exactly it would go. "Maybe you should stick with a major that gives you credit for the classes you've already taken? You've put in a lot of effort already," I said. "You can probably do something in health."

"You think?"

"I do."

"That's what Georgie wants?" he asked.

What Georgie wanted was for Youngsu to show that he could be an equal partner in their relationship. I just hoped he wanted something for himself that was more than Georgie, otherwise it would never be equal. "You work hard, Youngsu, and I think Georgie wants you to get a degree so you can have more choices. So you don't have to go to Alaska to fish. I don't think she cares what else you do."

"As long as I don't work at the Heartland forever," he said.

"Definitely." I pointed him to the corner on Lincoln, where I saw Jesse's massive white box truck parked illegally in front of a fire hydrant. Even though it was a fancy neighborhood, Lincoln Park always charmed me with its small-town feel. The tree-lined streets were narrow, all of the brick buildings were different shades, and signs for bars and shops hung low over the sidewalk.

We parked in a side street and then got out to receive our man-handling from Jesse. He had become burly since working on the farm, complete with a thick neck, bushy beard, and a formidable garlicky body odor. He was Gaston from *Beauty and the Beast*. What saved him from repulsing me completely was his beautiful, wavy head of hair. "You're just in time!" he called, as he saw us walking up the street. "I sent off my interns to run around the city, they should be back in an hour." He smashed me with a hug and lifted me a few inches off the ground, which resulted in a satisfying back crack. Youngsu was given the same treatment.

Jesse instantly located the nearest Irish pub, and Youngsu and I watched in awe as he casually threw back a few Irish car bombs.

He bought whiskeys for us with some flirty flourishes for the waitress, and launched into his sped-up abridged version of normal conversation.

"Been reading *n+1*, good stuff, love literary criticism, totally agree it's been underrepresented in the plethora of shit being published on the Internet. But," he paused to down another whiskey shot, "read that baseball novel of the summer. Great opening, sure, but fucking obvious character arcs, ham-fisted Melville themes and shit ending. Aneesha, thoughts on the ending and overall reactions to representations of race and sexuality." He motioned towards me.

I'd recently read *The Art of Fielding* and had been struck by how far removed I felt from the suffering of the men in the book. I gave Jesse a quick summary of my thoughts: not bad, but still lacking nuance and personality. We agreed that the "geezer," as Jesse put it, shouldn't have had it so easy by dying. It was a strange thing to agree on at 3pm, while drinking whiskey in a pub.

"God, I can't fucking tell you how long I've been waiting to have a conversation about literature," Jesse said burying his face in Youngsu's shoulder. "This doesn't happen on the farm. This is gold, it's pure gold."

I brought Jesse down the street with us to go look at the bike because I thought he might have some useful knowledge. Its owner was a man with a European accent who had asked me to meet him at his engineering firm. Over the phone, he had tried to tell me that it was too small for an adult, that he already knew from the sound of my voice that it wasn't going to work, and I had to wonder how this man had come to own this bike. Instead, I assured him that I hadn't grown since the seventh grade, and that I needed a small road bike.

"Is that the guy?" Youngsu asked.

Ahead, a man in a brown cutoff t-shirt was standing at a doorway with a small blue bike. He was tall and muscular with a bandana tied around his stringy blond hair, which made my re-evaluate my image of engineers.

"You're too big," he said as I waved to him.

"Let me try it out." I said. It was a little small—the seat barely came up to my hips—but I wouldn't need it for too long, and he was selling it for forty dollars, which was exactly my price range.

"You're letting your sister ride this child bike?" he asked, gesturing at Youngsu. "You're mistaken, sir. Aneesha's not my sister," Youngsu said. We exchanged our practiced, "that was so racist" look, the exaggerated, unsubtle one meant to elicit a reaction from observers. The Nordic hippie engineer was not moved.

Jesse inspected the brakes, and lifted the bike with one arm to see how the gears and wheels spun. He tightened the screw on the quick-release bolt, and gave me the thumbs up. I hopped on and rode down the empty street, pumping the pedals until I felt a breeze in my face. At the intersection, I pulled a tight turn that I'd never be able to manage on a regular-sized bike and decided that bad idea or not, I was sold. I wanted to prove the man wrong.

"You're like a clown," Jesse pointed out upon my return.

"So no?"

"Clown works for you," Jesse said. "The more serious you are, the more funny, the more funny, the more serious. You can't lose."

"You can always take it and resell it if you find better," Youngsu weighed in with a helpful comment.

After I handed the man my money, Jesse smashed us goodbye and ran off to find his interns, who were generally responsible for driving the truck back to Michigan. "Come out to the farm, you fools!" he called as he ran towards his truck.

We packed the clown bike into the back of Youngsu's mom's car and I considered Jesse's comment. I had always prided myself on my clown-like qualities, though a part of me, the part fueled by Jesse's whiskey gifts, was insulted by the idea that I couldn't be taken seriously. After all, wasn't humor an allusion to seriousness, to small tragedies that you preferred to laugh at instead of crying over?

I looked at the bike with its front wheel turned up against the window of the hatchback. The word "Caliente" was printed in red on the crossbar and it made me think of Don Quixote's Rocinante. It was fitting. I was happy to ride this workhorse around town believing she was, in fact, the finest stallion. Maybe I was a clown and maybe there was a certain value in that.

"Did you change your mind?" Youngsu asked. He was smoking

a cigarette in the drivers' seat. "I'm sure he'll take it back."

"No, Caliente is mine," I said and climbed in beside Youngsu.

"That was easy," he said and I nodded.

But I wished Georgie had come along. I was upset by the idea that she was running around getting her facial hair removed instead. It made me cringe that her mom still held such power over her, and that they hadn't figured out that variance and flaws were what made women beautiful. I had a hard time believing this was the Georgie I'd left behind. Years ago, when I cut my hair short and started shopping in the men's section, I had accepted that my own family might not fully understand my beauty, but in our family, physical beauty had never been all that valuable to begin with. My dad was a doctor and my mom worked in public health, so we talked about bodies as intricate machines, and it was always the mind that we worked to make beautiful. I supposed I tended to ignore the more traditional set of conventions that came along with being a Summertown because to me it always seemed that the real Georgie was mine— that she was only pretending with her family.

"Georgie will be impressed that we took care of this in one go," Youngsu said. "She'll wish she'd witnessed this efficiency instead of losing her mustache."

I smiled at Youngsu. I thought he must have felt the same way about Georgie.

—

I had a lot of questions about Logan. I still hadn't met him in person, but we had waved to each other on video chats and, after Whitney brought him as her date to the Heartland Christmas Party, I received a full report from the gang. Unlike everyone else, I was not concerned with his gender nor its "effect" on Whitney's sexual identity—all of which was captured by regular queerness in my book. Instead I was entirely consumed by what a more straightforward person would call jealousy. However, jealousy wasn't an emotion I allowed myself to experience on its own—I considered it an unconstructive weakness. So I, always the rational thinker, sought to learn from Logan what kind of person got to be in a relationship with someone whose heart was as slippery as Whitney's. And more importantly, whether I was, or wanted to be that kind of person.

Whitney was not the first woman—I both hoped and feared that she would not be the last—who wasn't able to explain why she wanted to keep me so close, but couldn't say she loved me, not in a romantic way. While I had always been adept at figuring out how to move gracefully through most parts of the world, the three or so times this situation had repeated gave me the very real idea that there was something wrong with me. I was proud of my self-aware-ness, and I wasn't sure whether it was a bigger blow that I was not quite lovable or that I couldn't see for myself why not. Regardless, I figured this was the perfect opportunity to gain insight from close observation of someone without my fatal flaws.

I wasn't expecting to meet Logan until Friday evening, when Whitney said he generally came home. So I was surprised when I heard a key in the front door on a Thursday afternoon. I was in my cot, re-reading my new favorite story, an Annie Proulx creation called *Wer-Trout*, and I leapt up, as if I had been caught someplace I wasn't meant to be.

"Hello?" Logan's voice called from the entryway.

I stood up and went into the living room, where a slight, wavy-haired boy was carefully setting down his bags. He was wearing a lavender polo shirt with khaki shorts and some locks of his auburn hair stuck to his forehead. "Hey," I said.

"I'm just so sweaty all the time," Logan replied. "Otherwise I'd give you a hug. Have you made yourself at home? Are you getting settled?" he asked. He looked me in the eye and seemed to care so genuinely about my answer that I felt I'd always known him.

"Oh yeah, I'm doing well. Back into a groove of sorts. You guys found a great apartment," I added.

"Well, it wasn't without some hard work." He patted the wall beside him. "Surprise, I didn't have to work today." Logan adjusted his tortoise-shell glasses, nearly identical to mine, and turned to show me the sweat stain on the butt of his shorts. "That's what I get for driving without stopping. Gross, right? Let me change." His head moved with an exaggerated comic motion toward the bedroom.

I laughed and settled myself on the couch.

"Did Whitney pick up the CSA box this week yet? I was thinking of making dinner before she got home," he called to me through the short hallway.

"Yeah, we picked it up yesterday. I can help if you want," I said.

"Maybe you can help me figure out what to do with all these garlic scapes we've been getting. It seems like there are only so many ways to cook them." He emerged again in a t-shirt and cutoffs. I had to hand it to Whitney, Logan was adorable. Plus this dinner idea was sweet and I knew exactly what to do with the garlic scapes.

"Pesto?" I asked, getting up from the couch.

He pointed enthusiastically at me. "Oh, I haven't tried that one yet. Great idea."

Logan did the pasta and kale while I wrangled the tangled green mass of garlic flowers and stems into the Cuisinart. We both decided that some actual cloves wouldn't hurt either, since we'd already be breathing garlic fire anyway. Logan smashed a segment with a large knife and carefully peeled the skin off with just his fingernails.

"I know it's ridiculous since we're going to be ingesting it, but—"

"You don't want to get it all over your hands," I finished for him. "I do the same thing."

"Then at least you won't think I'm crazy," Logan said, opening his eyes wide. I added olive oil, pine nuts, basil, and Parmesan to the Cuisinart while he checked the pasta water, and then added more salt. Logan moved jerkily around the kitchen, but when he came to the stove a nimbleness took over his limbs, and it was with a light touch that he tossed the kale in the pan, and slid the pasta into the water without a splash. It was like cooking with another version of myself. "I don't think you're crazy," I confirmed. "You seem regular to me."

"Oh, thanks," he said sarcastically. "You just got here and you've already decided I'm boring."

I laughed. Perhaps I was more transparent than I thought. "Not boring, just not crazy. Yet. You have time to prove otherwise, no need to rush into it."

"I have heard from Whitney about the stunts you two used to pull."

He stirred the pasta with one hand and adjusted the heat on the kale with the other. If Whitney had told him anything at all, I was sure she skipped all parts possibly uncomfortable or difficult to explain. "Like what?" I asked.

"You trying to ride a stranger's scooter, the two of you spilling candle wax all over a bar, the Republican Whitney went home with because she said she'd make her waffles in the morning. General drunken mayhem," he said, waving a hand.

We had spilled candle wax on each other in a bar, and the Republican was Whitney's boss, and they weren't entirely innocent stunts. I wondered if Logan knew about the dark undertow at the heart of those early adventures. Whitney and I still had a bad habit of gathering momentum in the wrong direction, even when we knew we'd regret it, because it always seemed that we were on the brink of something different this time. Or maybe it was only me. Whitney always landed on her feet. It was one of her more attractive and hateable qualities.

"All sounds familiar," I said. "Who can turn down Republican waffles?"

"I'm pretty embarrassed to be dating someone who couldn't," he said. "But don't tell Whitney that."

"I think she's well aware. I gave her hell for that one. Here, taste this," I said, holding out a forkful of pesto to him.

"Delicious," he declared. "Who knew there was such an easy way to deal with all of this garlic?"

Whitney came home, and I heard her giant bag being dropped on the floor. "What's going on in here?" Her gold earrings swung back and forth as she peeked into the kitchen, and I waited to see what kind of reunion she and Logan would have.

"Dinner," Logan replied and held up a plate with servings of pasta and kale. "I got back early this week."

She was clearly delighted. "That's such a great surprise. You guys!"

"Logan knew you'd be tired," I said. "And stressed about using all the vegetables this week."

Whitney leaned in and gave Logan what I could best describe as a friendly kiss on the lips. "Mmm, garlic," she said, kissing him again, and I had to look away. I ripped up some basil leaves and sprinkled them over the tops of our plates.

Whitney took her plate out to the living room. "Want to watch something while we eat?"

"We've been watching *United States of Tara*," Logan explained to me. "Is that okay with you?"

I nodded and sat down at the far end of the couch. "I've only seen the first few episodes, but I'm sure I can catch up."

"She has something like multiple personality disorder," Whitney added.

"I'm pretty sure Aneesha got that if she saw the first few episodes," Logan replied. "It's the main point of the show."

"I just wanted to remind her. In case she forgot. I would."

"Only you would forget something like that." Logan said this with a hand on Whitney's thigh, but I didn't like the dismissiveness in his tone.

I glanced at Whitney to see what this exchange was about, but she seemed unaffected. She shrugged and lifted her fork to her mouth. "Great pesto, nice job, team."

"It was a joint effort," Logan said. He held up a high five that I returned. "It's really nice to have Aneesha in the kitchen. I think we'll make some great things together."

Whitney's mouth was full of food, but she spoke anyway. "Total win for me. Knock yourselves out."

Logan caught my gaze and rolled his eyes. He smiled, and I had to admit that I felt a kinship with him. I'd only ever loved difficult women, who didn't particularly care how I felt, and there was something reassuring about this wholesome young man having fallen for the same charms and tricks that I had. As we ate, I watched Logan and Whitney because I wanted to think that I was starting to understand them better, but it didn't really look remarkable from the outside.

The next morning I went down to Metropolis. It was a coffee shop two blocks south of Whitney and Logan's apartment that featured balding couches, giant windows and two open rooms filled with tables. I could say that I wasn't looking for a cool place to do my work, but I was. I liked that my coffee was made and served to me by hip college students from Loyola, many of whom were brown and queer, all of whom adored my hairstyle. It was a fabulous way to start my writing sessions, which, though satisfying, generally included a thorough questioning of the value of my own perspective on the world and an unencouraging estimate of the meaning of life.

My usual table was against a wall with a window into the kitchen. They baked their own pastries at Metropolis, and it felt good to have people in constant motion beside me, kneading dough, running the Hobart mixer, thrusting pans in and out of the oven. It created a sense of drama and accomplishment that I wished could be present in my own work.

My task for the day was to rewrite the opening scene of a story called "The Ocean." One of my professors had pointed out that I liked to start all of my stories with what were their middles or endings: "On Wednesday Claire went to the zoo and fell in love with a polar bear," or "The Little People had taken up residence in Nathan's sink and were ruining his life," or in this case, "Gloria was no longer afraid of the ocean."

At the beginning, they sounded like the beginning, but there was always some history I had to return to later, and it tended to expand well beyond a flashback until it became the actual body of my story. In my spring quarter I had taken a seminar on neoliberalism and literary aesthetic in post-colonial literature, with the hope that one of these lenses would help me perceive time differently, and better connect events in a timeline. But as far as I could tell, I was still off by an act or two.

Today, Gloria, my middle-aged heroine, was about to quit her job, leave behind all the good-for-nothings who constantly gave her shit, and go confront her fears at the ocean. She was in the midst of the insurmountable task of cleaning a giant fish tank in a fancy hotel lobby, and I needed to whip her up to her breaking point. So I considered the stench of fish tank grime, the texture of a maid uniform, and the differences between "slosh" and "splash." I drank espresso until my mind buzzed and my fingers chattered over the keyboard. Soon Gloria fell into the tank, panicked, and then submitted to its dreamlike quality. I had hesitantly gathered the start of the scene's final sentence, when I noticed a figure pause before my table.

"Aneesha," a playful voice announced.

I looked up and there was Zoe. Tutor Crush. Her ponytail was the rich color of pecans and her nose was a loose check. "Zoe, Zoe," I said, subduing the giddy wave rising inside me. "What brings you up to this neighborhood?"

She presented her winning smile, all dimples and eye sparkles. "Big news, I live in Edgewater now." She sat down across from me. "I'm not intruding?"

I shrugged. "Could be worse."

She eyed me and my computer. "You're about to become the next John Grisham, aren't you?"

"I wish," I said. "Didn't you get a real teaching job? Shouldn't you be ruining some students' lives with Shakespeare?"

"Normally, yes," she said, crossing her legs. "But I'm not teaching summer school this year. I'm a free woman!" Zoe waved her arms in the air and then sipped from the straw in her iced coffee. Her lips puckered gently. There was suppleness around her features, as if a severely angled face had been covered in a sheet of fondant. It gave her a deceivingly soft and innocent beauty. Her mouth released the straw, and I imagined her bottom lip like a firm caterpillar in my mouth, and then I wondered from where I thought I knew the firmness of caterpillars in my mouth, and then I feared I was being a Richard-caliber lech, so I looked at her coffee instead.

"I get a real summer vacation, which is nice," she was saying. "Though I've been reworking my curriculum over and over. I'm not used to student-free time."

"Well, congratulations. On both the job and the vacation. Way to educate the youth," I said, and closed my laptop. "I do mean that. I'm not just being an asshole," I assured her.

Zoe's jaw dropped and she looked wild-eyed at me. "And the whole time, I thought you volunteered at that tutoring center for the prestige!"

I had actually begun volunteering in order to meet new friends, but it didn't take long for the smart-ass kids I tutored to grow on me too. "I was there for the prestige and to see your beautiful, shining smile." I gave her a cheesy grin.

"Well, that's a relief. Now I can quit pretending to be funny and smart. You can't imagine how exhausting it's been."

Her sharp reply sent the wave rushing up again. "You had me fooled, so we might be on the same level."

Zoe laughed and shook her head. She recrossed her legs and her foot brushed my shin. "Hey, I don't want to keep you from your masterpiece, but I'm going dancing tomorrow at Danny's. Soul night. You have to come and show off your moves."

"Didn't you just say you moved up here?" I asked.

"Yeah," she said. "So what?"

"Bucktown is kinda far," I heard myself whine.

Zoe shrugged. "Uh, so get tipsy and take a little bike ride. I get to pretend I'm young for a couple months. Work with me, Aneesha. I'll text you to remind you." She picked up her bag and stood up. "Your summer look is wonderful, by the way, love your bright colors."

Bright colors were not seasonal for me and she knew that. "I'm not that easy," I said.

"Neither am I. Be there. No excuses about getting drunk too early at the Heartland." She started to stand up and then stopped. "Oh," her tone dropped. "Did I tell you that Julian and I broke up? So you won't be burdened with his oppressively brutish presence. Ever again. And I'm sorry that you were before."

Zoe and her immaculately dressed boyfriend had been planning to move to Portland when he'd finished at the Art Institute. He'd always struck me as a little uptight, but I guessed he must have done something terrible. Her eyes wandered from mine down to her coffee. I'd never seen her this serious before, we were always playing. "I'm sorry," I said, trying to find an even, earnest tone.

She played with the triangular pendant hanging around her

neck. "Hey, Zoe, I'll be there tomorrow," I said.

Her vacant stare lingered for a moment and then a smile snapped across her face. "Not easy, my ass," she said, winking.

"Oh god," I said. "So, so not fair."

She stood up and pushed her chair in. "But really, please come."

I nodded and watched her leave. She was short, like me, but her walk was smooth and her hips rolled gently. I pulled a notebook from my backpack and flipped to a blank page. "Diff btwn good/ bad choices" I wrote and drew a box around it. There were still 45 minutes left in my computer battery and I needed them for me and Gloria. I could savor and condemn Tutor Crush later.

Georgie's current job was giving food tours around the city so I figured she'd be out and about. After writing, I called to see what she was doing, and she answered with a sigh that sounded like heavy wind. "Will you please meet me at that stupid ice cream place you and Rachel like?" she requested. It was a gelato shop called Black Dog, and it was in Ukrainian Village, a 45-minute bike ride from me, she knew, though I could tell she was not in the mood for hesitance or argument. I was sweaty when I arrived, and gelato wasn't what I wanted in my dry mouth, but as it turned out, Georgie didn't want anything either, and it seemed like a waste to get nothing. So I ordered a salted peanut and sat next to her outside on the aqua bench.

"Is Rachel coming?" I asked.

Georgie looked at me like I was an idiot. "No, of course Rachel is not coming."

"Oh."

"We're here to talk about Youngsu." She crossed her arms and leaned against the bench.

"Oh no." My mind slipped back to our conversation in the car, and I tried to decide which was the most disagreeable part. College, I thought, that had to be it.

"'Oh no' is right." She was calm, composed. "What exactly did you say to him?"

I dragged my spoon around the mound of gelato in my cup. There was an indignant part of me that wanted to remind her that none of it wasn't true. However, that would be cowardly, and it wasn't how Georgie and I conducted our friendship.

"I told him he needed to graduate from college and make more money so he didn't need to go fishing in Alaska again."

"*And* that I thought it was stupid to work at the Heartland?" she asked.

I took a bite and pointed my spoon at her. "That was his own addition, though I didn't disagree. Georgie, you worked at the Heartland. You and I both know that it's a way station where some people get stuck. It can be like the Bermuda Triangle."

Georgie uncrossed her arms and sighed. "Yes, well, Youngsu, doesn't know that."

"Yes, he does," I responded. "If he didn't, he wouldn't care. What was he upset about?"

She picked at a hangnail on her thumb. It was such a helpless action. "He was mad that it was you who told him and not me. That you knew all of it already.

It was a valid point, unrealistic, but valid. "I'm sorry," I said. "I was trying to help. I should have kept my mouth shut."

She shrugged. "I guess, to your credit, you were being honest."

"I really like Youngsu," I said. "He's an awesome man. Plus he gets you, and he makes you happy."

It was late afternoon, and the sun was falling lower in the sky so that we both had to look down at the ground. There were crisscrosses of brick laid into the sidewalk, and it made me feel old-fashioned, sitting on a bench, with an ice cream treat, talking about who said what to a boy. Like I imagined a Jane Austen book would be, if I ever relented and read one.

"You really think that?" Georgie squinted at me.

"Yeah." I so rarely felt that the people I loved had worthy significant others. "It's a little surprising for me too."

I offered Georgie a spoon of gelato and she accepted. She nodded her head with approval, and then brushed at her far shoulder with one hand. "Is there something on my back?" she asked, turning away from me.

Attached to her bare shoulder blade was a prehistoric-looking bug the length of a thumb with yellow and orange armor, and two sets of tentacles. It was the most frightening bug I'd ever seen, and I jumped off the bench immediately.

"What is it?" she asked, now flailing her arms. "Get it off, get it off!" she shrieked.

"Don't worry, it's not so bad," I lied and picked up a leaf from the ground. People inside the gelato shop were watching our little drama unfold, and I suddenly felt pressure to get the bug off cleanly, in one go. I swiped at it with a leaf, but it didn't budge.

"What's going on?" Georgie hollered.

I decided there wasn't a delicate solution, so I dropped the leaf, took a deep breath and pinched the armored body between my thumb and index finger. It began to flap its wings in a spastic fashion, and I ignored the drumming of panic in my chest.

"Is it off? Did you get it?" Georgie's shoulders were hitched up, her back tense.

The rubbery skins of the bug's wings brushed against my fingers and I dropped it on the ground, backing away.

"Thank god," Georgie said, returning from her hysteria. She bent down to take a closer look. "Wow, that thing is huge. And really ugly."

"I know," I said, wiping my hands on my shorts.

"Did you just pick that off me with your hands?"

"Yep."

Georgie stood up again. "Well." She adjusted her tanktop straps. "Look who's the fool now."

"Nobody's a fool," I said.

"Thanks for taking that hideous thing off of me." She slipped her phone out of her pocket and took a picture of it.

"Thanks for meeting me at a gelato place to tell me you're upset with me." I smiled, and spooned out the last bite in my cup.

Georgie shrugged. "Right. Well, it was far away and I wasn't sure you would come otherwise."

"What are you going to do about Youngsu?" I asked.

"Who knows," she said. "I don't know what I'm supposed to do." She walked toward her bike and I followed with mine. "I don't know how we really be together."

"I don't think anybody does," I said. "I think they just pretend. Or they just decide to be together, and then try really hard to make it stay."

Georgie bent down to put the key in her bike lock, and we walked beneath a line of trees in the shade. "You don't think it's just that you and I don't know?"

"Maybe," I said. "But that doesn't make it any less mysterious. It's not like there's one secret we can learn to make all our relationships work."

"Yeah, too bad, though, huh?"

"Hey, you wanna go to a soul night in Bucktown tomorrow? I ran into Tutor Crush at Metropolis and she invited me. I said I'd go."

Georgie eyed me. "Ol' Tutor Crush again, eh?"

"Yeah, why not? It'll be fun and you love soul."

"It's true, I do love soul." Georgie looked up at the sky, and seemed to consider the invitation. "You shouldn't be surprised, Aneesha, when your bruised little raisin heart gets smashed into jam."

"Jeez." It was apparently not the invitation she was considering. "Smashed into jam? It's dancing, Georgie, it's just for fun! Are you serious?"

"There is no such thing as 'just for fun,' and you know that very, very well." Georgie hopped onto her pedals and glided onto the street. "I'll think about soul night. Come over tomorrow and eat dinner at my parents'. They've been asking about you."

"Ugh, fine, okay," I muttered and watched Georgie expertly weave her way through traffic.

I got on my own bike and pedaled hard up Damen. I didn't like being told what to do, as if I were not capable of weighing the pros and cons of my own decisions. I would hang out with Tutor Crush if I wanted to, and if she hurt my feelings I would deal with it. For just this reason, I supposed, I was not the kind of person who anybody worried about. General consensus among my friends, family and most strangers was that I was always fine. There wasn't any real discussion about what "fine" meant, but I too assumed that I could manage anything. I flew through a yellow light at the clusterfuck of Milwaukee, North and Damen, ruining the left turn for a green minivan. Its low horn blew at me.

Which, I reminded myself, slowing to a coast, made Georgie all the more valuable. I was lucky to have her worry about me. To remind us, my little bruised raisin heart and I, that we were as vulnerable as anyone, that somebody was scared for us.

⤙

At home, Whitney was on the couch with her iPad. "There you are," she said, without looking up.

"What're you looking at?" I threw my backpack on the floor and settled in next to her.

"I was thinking that I want a new necklace, but it can't be too girly. What do you think of this one?" She slid her finger across the screen and pulled up a photo of a yellow rhinoceros pendant. "Business casual or play clothes?"

"Well, normally, I would say play clothes, but since it's detailed in gold and on sale at J.Crew, I'd give you business casual if you were wearing a dress."

"What about a suit? With a nice blouse? What about a skirt suit?" Whitney sounded desperate, and I laughed. "This is serious," she warned me. "I need to know."

Both of our styles were heavily reliant on our casual "play" outfits, with a touch of preppy to convey elegance. The two of us trying to dress for work was always a shot in the dark.

"If you like it, get it. I think you can make it business casual. I mean, we are talking about a rhinoceros necklace. Like you're in kindergarten. But we've worked with bigger challenges."

Whitney placed the iPad between us so I could see better. "Why is it so hard to find gender-appropriate fashions? Why haven't people figured this out already?"

"I know," I said. "Everyone's so concerned about gay marriage, but what I really want is gay shopping opportunities."

"Like these suits!" Whitney tabbed over to a slideshow. "Tapered legs, textured fabrics. Why can't they do this for women? Why is Rachel Maddow the only one who gets to have one? I can't afford a Jil Sander suit!"

I shook my head. "I know what you mean. And then dykes get a bad fashion rep, which is totally unfair because unless you're that skinny dyke who looks awesome in men's clothing you have to be creative."

"And not everyone wants to look like Shane," Whitney added, and flipped back to her shopping tabs.

Logan popped his head out from the bedroom, and I realized he was home too. "I would just like to add to this conversation that I don't miss shopping in the women's section at all. It's always made better for men. Menswear is classic and women's is trendy."

"Exactly!" I exclaimed.

"Screw the patriarchy," Whitney grumbled. "I'm getting my necklace."

"Way to stick it to the man," I said. "On jcrew.com."

"Hey. Shut up." She added the rhino to her cart and continued shopping. "What'd you do today?"

"Well, I saw Tutor Crush at Metropolis this morning. She lives in the neighborhood now."

I met Tutor Crush, appropriately, at a tutoring center, where we had both gone on Wednesday afternoons to offer free homework help and general entertainment to kids. I was a big hit with a group of third grade girls who enjoyed asking me questions about my boyfriend-free life and offering me advice on hair styling. Tutor Crush joined us for a game of Outburst one afternoon, and she and I became pals after an unexpectedly good 30-second round, in which she and I named every John Grisham book on the list.

Whitney was less than enthused by Tutor Crush, which was confusing because she usually supported irrational crushes on girls too straight, too taken, too cool, or too young.

"And Tutor Crush is no longer with her boyfriend." I wiggled my eyebrow up and down.

Whitney laughed. "Look at you, you're glowing!"

"I'm not glowing, it's just a little bit exciting."

Logan popped his head out of the bedroom again. "Are you seriously trying to sleep with someone you used to tutor?" he asked me.

"Logan, can you either sit in here and join the conversation or just leave it alone?" Whitney shot back.

I dug in my backpack for my water bottle. I didn't know where this was going.

Logan seemed more surprised than offended. "Really? That's how you're choosing to talk to me?"

Whitney retreated to her iPad. "Sorry, it's just annoying and Aneesha can try to sleep with whoever she wants."

"What?" I turned toward the bedroom. "No, let me be very clear that I know her from when we used to tutor together. She is the same age as me. A fellow tutor. A peer."

"But you did have a crush on that high school girl," Whitney muttered. "The one who was smart with a bad attitude."

Logan made a point to come into the hallway to say, "You two are sick," and then went away again.

"I did not! She was half Black, half Japanese, and we bonded on mixed and the half Japanese front," I whisper yelled. "I only said that we had a good time taking her health survey together. Whit, we said we wouldn't talk about this with other people. Because it sounds pervy, like we mean it. Other people don't get that it's a joke."

"Good, whisper about me in the living room, that's respectful," Logan called.

"We're talking about Aneesha's underage crushes, not you," Whitney responded.

I hit her on the shoulder and she stopped. "Okay, okay, so you're gonna get with Tutor Crush. Finally. This has gone on way too long. Severine's not going to care?" Whitney delivered this like an insult, but now that she mentioned it, I wasn't sure what Severine would think.

I had put Severine out of my head since arriving in Chicago.

She was a girl I met in a fiction class that spring, and had fallen halfway in love with. Her voice was a low thrum, her tongue was sure and strong in my ear, and her dark hair looked elegant when it was a mess, which said a lot about the way she functioned. She smoked like an industrial-era oceanliner, and I could always dig up a half-full bottle of vodka in the nest of clothing in the backseat of her car. Unfortunately, Severine also embodied all of the irrational crush qualities, the most pressing being the fact that she seemed to consider herself straight. I was confused by this lack of openness from a girl who had given me a copy of Nabokov's *Pale Fire*, but maybe it was her way of warning me about the complex emotional landscape I had entered into.

"She's not even talking to me," I told Whitney. "I think she takes my being here as a personal affront, like I came to Chicago in order to fuck with her. I've tried all modes of communication and nothing. I assume she wants nothing to do with me." I was a little heartbroken over the matter, but everyone including me had known it was headed for a rocky decline.

Whitney put her iPad on the coffee table, and we stared at the wall for a moment. "Please don't look like that, it makes me depressed. It can't be that serious."

"Are you gonna?" I whispered and nodded towards her bedroom. "What's up with that?" He had only been home for a few days, and already I doubted my original notion that Logan had a secret magic I could learn.

"I don't know." Whitney rolled her eyes. "Yeah, you're right." She paused. "My relationship," she sang and slapped my thigh as she got up. I watched her familiar jaunty walk around the coffee table, the triangular motion of her hips.

"What?" she asked, her eyes meeting mine.

"Nothing."

"What?" she persisted, bending over to look into my face.

"Go talk it out," I said quietly. "Apparently you do that now."

Whitney smiled and shook her head. "Not fair."

I smiled and put my bag on. It was time for me to give them some space. "Probably not."

"We're going to Chances Dances this weekend. Come with us," she said, leaning through the hallway. "You know you like dancing."

"Believe me, I want to go dancing with you," I said. "I'm just not sure—"

"We said we'd go dancing. Summer bears," she reminded me.

I nodded and shut the door gently behind me.

The Heartland was bustling when I sat down at the bar. I looked over the guys in crisp button-down shirts and wondered who these people were.

"College kids come out on the weekend," Youngsu said, sliding a coaster in front of me. "It's good for us." He nodded toward Ben who was pouring blue shots for a group of young ladies in pastel cardigans. "You come by yourself?"

"Is that unheard of?" I asked.

Youngsu shrugged. "I don't know. You always have somebody around."

I knew what he meant, but I'd never considered it a fault. "Well, I want to chat with you. Though the Heartland isn't really a place for private conversation."

"Speaking of which…" He pulled out another coaster.

An arm fell lightly across my shoulders, and I knew it was Richard before his voice weaseled out. "Look who the cat dragged in."

"That's exactly what I was thinking of you."

"Knew you'd be here. I had a sense about it. I was lying on my couch listening to an etymology podcast, and I thought to myself, 'I wonder where Little A is hanging out right now.'" He pointed to his nose. "Do you think it could be a pheromones thing?"

"May I please have a whiskey neat?" I asked Youngsu.

He pulled a glass out from under the bar and looked at Richard, who went for one of the same.

"I'm going out for a quick cigarette in a few," Youngsu said, pouring our drinks. "Aneesha, I got one with your name on it." He took our money and was instantly swallowed by the crowd around the bar.

"What's that about?" Richard asked. "Everyone knows you don't smoke for real."

"I'm flexible," I said.

Richard set his glass down, suddenly very interested in me. "You wouldn't start something up with…?" He jutted his chin down the bar at Youngsu.

"Have you lost your mind?" I asked.

"You said you were flexible." When I didn't laugh, Richard tipped his drink up and continued. "Fine, play your hand close, that makes for great conversation." He drummed his fingers on the counter top. "Well, I got a haircut today from my second favorite lesbian. Her name's Ursula, she's a fabulous hairdresser. I'll introduce you if you want. Unless you have some secret romance you haven't told me about."

It was a reasonable offer, but the strict romantic in me bristled at the idea of meeting a woman because she was Richard's "second favorite lesbian" and not because I was struck dumb at the grocery store by the light touch of her fingers on a pear or her dark cackle on a stuffy bus. "That's okay," I said. "I'm not sure hairdresser is what I'm looking for."

"Oh, right, because you're Paris Hilton?" Richard asked.

I laughed, and thought this over. "You know if I were Paris Hilton, a hairdresser might be perfect."

"Who is this mysterious woman you're looking for?" Richard asked. "I have some interesting standards myself, but I swear nobody is good enough to get into your panties and be spoken of in public. You haven't said a word to me about a girl at school, and I know there is one. There's always someone just out of reach, propelling you messily into the night."

I hated when Richard's little daggers were this precise. "They're boybriefs, okay?" He was punishing me for not divulging the reason for my discussion with Youngsu, which was all about me minding my own business. I didn't even want to begin to explain Severine to Richard. He would think it was heroic that I'd managed to interest a smart young woman who was ostensibly unavailable. "I don't know who I'm looking for, hence my hesitance about it all, okay?"

I glanced across the bar, and saw Youngsu wiggling a cigarette at me from behind the screen door. I jumped up, relieved to be rescued for the moment, and went out to sit with him on the bleachers by the curb. Bar patrons were hollering loudly in the alley along the train tracks.

"I don't like to do this private talk drama stuff," Youngsu said, lighting both cigarettes and handing one to me.

"Neither do I," I said, wondering why he hadn't used a bit more discretion with Georgie. "I was honestly just trying to be helpful. I thought you might consider the whole college situation, and talk to Georgie, not get mad at her."

"What?" he asked. "So you're upset with me?" He threw his hands up in the air and opened his mouth—probably to tell me how unfair I was being—but gave up.

"It's not a big deal that she hadn't told you yet," I said. "I know it's terrible, it's very non-inclusive, but it's how some people figure out what they want: on their own, with a unique brand of personal logic. And then they slowly figure out how to share the results with the people who matter."

"It's a problem when Georgie can't tell me important things about our relationship and our future. Then I don't want to tell her things, and we don't trust each other, and then we're just avoiding each other, and what kind of partnership is that?"

I wanted to tell him that there would always be things about Georgie he wouldn't quite know, things I might not know, parts that nobody knew. You couldn't *have* a whole person, at least not the kind worth wanting. But he did have a point. Georgie had been talking about their future, and it also belonged to him. I admired his moral clarity and his willingness to confront what bothered him. "Like a contemporary Atticus Finch," Georgie had described him to me before.

"Georgie loves you, and she means well, and the things she doesn't tell you are not to keep you in the dark," I said. "If I thought these were damaging secrets, I wouldn't have shared them. But the big secret is that she wants to be with you, and isn't sure how to make it work best for both of you." I tapped off some ash and watched it tumble down the street. "I'm not mad, Youngsu. I'm asking you, on behalf of Georgie—without her permission, again—to cut her some slack."

He seemed to think about this. His plaid shirt was thin, and sweat had bloomed well beyond his armpit area. It reminded me of Georgie's reinforced armpits. "Is she upset with you?" he asked.

I nodded. "Yeah, I mean, obviously I shouldn't be going around telling people things I know about her. But you're not just people. You're important."

We shared the prolonged silence that smoking a cigarette allowed. I wanted to explain to Youngsu that we both loved Georgie in different ways, but for the same reasons, and that made him special not just to Georgie, but to me too. It was rare to find someone with whom you wanted to share your best friend. Then the train rattled above us, sending high-pitched shrieks out along the tracks, and I felt our moment had ended.

"I should go back in and keep an eye on Richard," I said, stamping out the cigarette.

Youngsu stood up and wiped his hands on his pants. "Well, thanks." He nodded his wobbly head and clapped me on the shoulder, which I took as a positive sign.

Back in the bar, Richard's mood had improved. He was gesticulating wildly at a pair of college girls, and I watched from across the room as he placed a hand on the shoulder of the blond one. He instructed her to hunch over a little so he could reenact his best story of the week. It was about his horror at being sent by a property management company to evict an elderly woman from the Howard Ave apartment she'd lived in half her life. When Richard arrived at her front door, the woman had been holding an array of medicine bottles in her cupped hands, unable to read the small print on the labels. Now Richard was pretending to read the labels aloud for the hunched-over blond girl.

The scene was at once genius and grotesque, and I didn't want to interrupt. I leaned back against the piano and waited for him to deliver his closing line: "So I bent down to that poor beautiful lady and I said, 'Ma'am, it seems to me that you need a lawyer, and lucky for you, the attorney standing in front of you would like to take your case.'" I was pretty sure this last part had not actually happened. Not that it mattered, Richard was a magician.

The girls laughed, and their body language softened. So charming, I imagined them thinking. What a gentleman, this lawyer with a slight southern accent, whose heart belonged to helpless elderly women. And that really was one side of Richard, I reminded myself. I forgot that sometimes he was a gentleman.

"Enjoy your cancer stick?" he asked as I approached.

The girls turned around to look at me, and their sweet open confusion stopped me from making pedophilia jokes.

"Everything is probably fine," I said.

Richard smiled and touched both girls' elbows. "Ladies, it was a pleasure, but my friend and I will have to take leave of you now. Enjoy your evening."

I raised my eyebrow at Richard.

He put some money on the bar, and led me out through the screen door, whispering in my ear, "They laughed too hard. They're either stupid or condescending."

꙳

We decided to go to Simon's, a small dive on Clark that often had a live band, and if not, a jukebox full of moody '80s rock. There was a popcorn machine on the back counter that glowed yellow, and a mirror behind the bar that featured photographs of youth soccer teams that Simon's sponsored. I wondered aloud once whether it was an issue that a bar was sponsoring 8-year-old kids, but this didn't raise any flags for anyone else. Richard and I picked out some swivel stools, and I kicked my bag into place under my feet.

"That's Mona," Richard said quietly as the bartender approached. She had severe black bangs that sliced across her forehead. "Another whiskey?" Richard asked me.

"Yep. That's exactly what I want."

"Hi Mona," Richard folded his hands politely and smiled. "My friend Aneesha and I would like a couple of whiskeys neat, please."

Mona eyed us and nodded. She walked back down to the well, and Richard leaned over the bar. "Actually, make mine on the rocks, will you?" he asked with a wink. "Thanks, doll."

On the whole, Mona seemed rather unmoved by the interaction. Her black bob continued to hang perfectly still. Richard leaned toward me and spoke out of the side of his mouth. "She doesn't remember me, but I know her."

"Really? Her?" I asked. I did not imagine Mona with Richard. I thought he was gay for three months after I met him, and this wasn't the sort of charm I took Mona and her severe bangs to fall for.

She placed my whiskey on a cardboard coaster. "Bushmills good?" Her voice was low and her consonants had soft edges.

"Perfect," I answered.

"If not, I'd just drink it myself." Mona let out a rumble of a laugh.

"Her?" I asked again, when she was down the bar.

"Well, no, actually it's not like that at all. I wish." He clinked his glass against mine.

"To things that aren't like that," I said.

Richard nodded and sipped his drink. "Speaking of which, where is Whitney tonight?"

"Movie night at home with Logan." She sent me a text reporting a truce, and had invited me to join her and Logan. I read the text again. "She can't even stay awake through a full movie."

"I see. So how is that whole," Richard whirled his hand in a circle, "that whole thing?"

"It's weird," I said, and shrugged. "Like always."

"But you and Whitney. There's still something there?"

I eyed him, trying to figure out where the grey area was. "She has a boyfriend and we're good friends. Also, currently roommates."

He looked at me. "But you're still in love with her."

I was surprised by Richard's confidence in this statement. I thought I'd effectively kept that to myself. I had spent the better part of the past year getting used to not sharing everything with Whitney, in creating some distance, and while it didn't make me feel great, I thought it had at least eased everyone else. "Richard, in the words of Ms. Tina Turner, what's love got to do with it? Anyway, Logan is perfectly nice."

Richard sipped his whiskey. "Well, I'll hate that. There's nothing right with nice people, they're all hiding something, restraining themselves." He set his glass down. "Karen always says that. It's what reminds me that I adore her."

"So you do adore her?" I asked.

Richard looked at me sideways and then swiveled in his stool. "Of course, I love her. But it doesn't mean I don't wonder."

"What kind of wondering?" I asked.

Richard had met Karen on the Red Line while she was on the way to the reading of her recently deceased boyfriend's will. There was conflict in the family about how much she was getting, and Richard had offered her his legal services, among others. They both knew perfectly well what they were getting into, and I greatly admired what seemed like the most mature relationship I knew: they maintained separate lives, but cultivated shared interests. I marveled at the beauty of a relationship that was in no part built on the dream of a romantic marriage, and the vanity of quaint beach houses or children. But it was clear that this was no longer the case, and now I needed to know where this was coming from. I didn't want to fully submit to Richard as the barometer for my future, but I couldn't ignore it either.

"Oh you know, the usual wondering," Richard said.

"Like what you thought was very important about a woman is actually not?" I asked him. "Like maybe you want some of the bullshit you used to scoff at?"

"We're all such clichés, aren't we?" He grinned. "Again, you're really not going to say anything to Whitney? Just to see? I mean, look at you two. You get along so well."

I appreciated Richard's confidence, but barging into rooms and declaring feelings had never worked out well for me. Then his eyes lit up and we were moving on. "Oh, so listen, I have a debate topic for us. There's been a lot of talk about education reform recently, and then this was brought up at a gathering last week with some old law school classmates, where it elicited some rather heated discussion."

I liked to imagine Richard in a room full of lawyers who didn't know that he generally met with clients in bars, that if he got an important case he rented an office downtown by the hour and wore a suit jacket over his pajamas.

"What?" he asked.

"Nothing," I said. "What was the heated debate over?"

Richard's questions seemed benign, but ultimately, narrowed down into divisive questions about worldview. He had pointed out to me that since Obama had taken office, there was actual reform to talk about, and heated debates over the details seemed less like an exercise in imagination.

"It was about cursive. How do you feel about cursive? Does it need to be taught in public school?"

"Cursive? No way," I answered.

"Of course. I disagree, but you were quick with that. Explain."

Richard knew how to bait me into taking the irreverent view so he could calmly defend "tradition." That was how our game worked. We presented arguments, switched sides, drank more, departed from the subject, and ended up somewhere unexpected. Everything melted together. It was like a sandwich, which began as a stack of distinct parts, but when grilled fused into an enhanced sort of whole. Simon's, a regular dive, was suddenly a chamber of my heart, and Richard's bunny head was pure and innocent, even while he creepily sniffed the poofy hair of the girl next to me. Our differences usually found some flexible point of agreement, and I was likely to spout half-truths such as "I'm not married to anything, not even being a writer," or "I feel limited by the glorification of low expectations in our zeitgeist," and Richard would egg me on until I had made a perfect argument against my actual beliefs. On this night, we end-ed with a question over whether technical skills or critical thinking skills were a more valuable part of an early public education.

"This all leads me to the one and only conclusion we can be sure of at this point in time," Richard said. His hair had gotten matted down a little, and his hands were doing a lot of the talking.

I grinned and sucked out the last of my watered down whiskey.

"Our friends have to form a commune," I said.

"One building. Different apartments for each of us. Shared courtyard, garden, wifi, HBO Go, and mutual funds. We'll raise the kids together so they can learn about both cursive and computers, regardless of what happens in school."

"It could happen," I said, as I always did. Because Richard was so certain, and when I lingered at the bar with him I saw the future as a bright and endless possibility.

"So come on, realistically, when can you commit to this?" he asked. "A career, the commune, a lady, our baby."

"Give me a few more years," I said, nodding. It seemed reasonable at this moment that in a few years I would have grown out of my impulsiveness, and the little twinge in my gut that was always telling me it was time to move on. It seemed reasonable that his overconfidence—a trait that was intrinsically male—would have had enough time to transfer to me.

"Right, we always think we've got a few more years of youth left in us." Richard had a smirk on his face. "A few more unknown paths to venture down."

"It's true," I argued, gesturing to the crowd at Simon's. A balding man in a Hawaiian shirt and black orthopedic sneakers was trying to chat up a pair of women behind us. "It's past midnight and we are not the most un-youthful people in this bar. Why the hurry? What do we have to lose?"

Richard didn't answer. He rubbed my hair and leaned over the bar in the annoying way he did to make sure Mona wouldn't miss him. "A few years," he said pointing to me, "I'm holding you to it."

⤙

In order to go alone, I insinuated to Richard that I needed to catch up with a girl. He accepted this with a series of knowing winks and tongue clicks but eventually rode away. I unlocked my bike and pushed off of the curb, cutting across Clark down Foster. Little Caliente felt steady beneath me: unhesitant, responsive, like an extension of my body. I always felt this way riding a bike after a few drinks. When I was first learning the art of city biking, Georgie had coached me by saying, "You spend too much time calculating. You just have to go and go hard." Now, I bent over my handlebars and went hard towards the beach. The breeze coming from the lake met me headlong, and I felt the stickiness of the day lifting off me.

I pulled away from the bike path to a little hill that overlooked the lake, and sat down in the grass. Cicadas screeched rhythmically above, and further down some teenagers drank beer and hooted on the jagged concrete wall. Here you are, I said to myself. This is your life.

It was beautiful. The lake was slick black, and above it handfuls of stars sparkled between patches of pinkish clouds. At the edge of a body of water like this, I could taste possibility like the slight tang of an aluminum can. The night was still open and alive. Anything could happen, and I held that feeling, let it flutter inside me. But what else could I possibly want? What did I keep hoping would come hurtling through my open window? I lay down, a starfish in the grass.

I remembered a night in Spain several years ago when I'd gone skinny-dipping in the ocean with a friend I was madly in love with. Elena had an extra-long torso and short wavy hair that bobbed up and down when we ran into the warm water. After our swim, she and I lay on a towel together, looking up at the sky. "Do you know any constellations?" she'd asked me and I'd said no—which wasn't true, but I wanted her to show me some. "Me neither," she admitted, her tiny nose scrunching as she laughed.

Instead she pointed out a group of stars, and made up a story about an ancient flying shark for which this constellation was named. Elena had a simmering laugh and a silver bar in her left nipple. I got the feeling everyone we knew was partially in love with her. That the two of us were alone and naked under the stars seemed to me like the most fortunate of coincidences. I'd felt so lucky to share the beauty of the evening with her, to know that it hadn't been wasted.

That's what I wanted, now. Somebody with whom to share this quiet moment, to enjoy its ephemeral beauty and let it go. Only everyone I knew seemed poised to set their feet and dig in. Richard was hounding me about commitments because he must have wanted some of his own. Youngsu and Georgie were evaluating their joint future and the rest of their lives. Whitney was a certified accountant, and with Logan, she would have a Subaru, a kayak, and a dog in no time. Meanwhile, I was lying alone on a hill in the middle of the night.

A week before I left Spain, Elena and I had coffee together and she teased me about letting her down easy. I had slowly stirred my coffee and asked her what she was talking about. "We were naked, lying in the sand and I was whispering stories into your ear," she said, exasperated. "What did you think I was doing?"

I sat up in the grass and adjusted my hair. I was stupid. I hadn't known—still found it unbelievable—that it was possible for such a charming woman to find me attractive. And not kissing Elena meant she would always be exciting in my mind. But I wasn't twenty anymore and I wasn't—as Richard had rightly pointed out—Paris Hilton either. It was probably time I started hoping for more than ripe potential and fleeting beauty. Not just hoping, actively trying. "Why the rush? What do we have to lose?" I heard myself annoyingly prodding Richard.

I saw the screen of my phone light up in my bag, and I pulled it out to see what I had missed. There were some texts from people who heard I was in town, a message from Georgie about a pimple she'd popped and a "night" from Whitney. This was everything I had.

I stood Caliente back on her feet, and rode her home over the gentle hills of the bike path, singing to myself about myself: "What have we got, what have we got to lose? Have we got, the losers have to choose, have we got, anything but boooooooze?"

Whitney and Logan's usual Saturday tradition was going down to Metropolis, and reading the *Savage Love* advice column out loud over coffee. I discovered this when I woke up after a restless sleep, and I also went down to Metropolis to get some writing done. I had brunch plans at the Heartland with "the ladies," as Amanda had put it in her text invite, and I knew I wouldn't work afterwards.

I locked up Caliente and walked toward the front door, but stopped when I saw Whitney and Logan through the window. They were in the back room, bent over a table. Whitney had a baffled look on her face, eyebrows at acute slants. It made her eyes look pretty. Logan was laughing with his mouth open, and he spun the paper on the slick tabletop to show her something. I was momentarily paralyzed by a sense of betrayal and insane curiosity. Despite the petty fights, they had their own little world together and that was a place I wanted to see. I watched the way Logan placed his hand gently on Whitney's shoulder. It was a soft, sassy "you won't even believe this" hand. He was like me, but without the over-thinking and the crises of being.

A couple on the street walked by, and their galumphing dog licked my leg. "Sorry about that," the man said, tugging the dog along. "Oh, it's fine," I waved them off. It wasn't the dog's fault that I was smelly and salty. When I looked back up, Whitney and Logan were waving and making faces at me.

My inner cynic reared up to sting them with something nasty, but I came up with nothing. Objectively, an adorable freckled couple in summery shirts were waving at me from inside my favorite coffee shop. They could have been related, and I wondered if there was some unconscious attraction in that. There was nothing to do except go in and join them.

"Listen to this," Logan said excitedly, when I sat down. "This guy got a hand job from a sex worker who had a hole in her check from a screwdriver fight."

"What?" I was definitely amused.

"What a unique circumstance," Whitney observed.

"Yeah, totally. So what's his question?" I asked Logan.

He sipped his coffee. "It was stupid. She rubbed her cheek on his dick when he was coming and he wants to know if he can get any diseases. Dan basically said unless his dick was torn up and raw, no."

"His dick was torn up and raw," I repeated slowly. "Wow. That's a way to start the day. What I'm going to take away from this story is screwdriver fights." I already had a picture in my head of

a girl gang in coveralls with bold eyebrows and wild hair, fencing
with screwdrivers.

"Ugh," Whitney gagged. "There was mention of a peeling skin
crust earlier that I can't get out of my head. It's not good."

Logan nodded his head emphatically, "Disgusting, yes. But this
is reality for some people."

"And that," I said, "is why you, Logan, will make a fabulous doctor."

He smiled uneasily at me, not sure if this was a real compliment.
But I meant it, and I thought it would sound more fake if I went on
to express my sincerity. I mentioned that I was going to the Heartland for brunch and that they were welcome to join if they wanted.
Then I excused myself to sit at my own table and write.

"Wait, really?" Whitney asked. "Sit here and read the paper
with us."

"You guys came here to do your thing and me to do mine." I
was making circles over the table with my palms, literally trying to
smooth it out. "Nothing personal."

Logan nodded. "Whitney has soccer so we can't do brunch, but
we're still going dancing tonight. You should come, it'll be fun."

I nodded my head. He was always so polite. It gave the impression of confidence, even if it was just habit. "Thank you. I'm having
dinner with the Summertowns, but I'll call you afterwards."

A few tables over, against the bakery window, I pulled out my
computer. Logan continued to read from the column while Whitney rolled her eyes at me. This was a normal kind of distance, I told
myself. I put in my earbuds so I couldn't be interested in their conversation, and soon I wasn't. Instead I was with Gloria, who today
was clad in a bright blue one-piece swimsuit, standing on the beach,
hands on hips, preparing to face the ocean for the second time. She
was only a little afraid. What could she expect? I set my fingers to
the keys and headed out to sea.

⤴

At the Heartland, I found Jurate flipping through the pages
of the *Tribune*. She was dressed in her usual outfit: earth-tone knit

shirt, chunky masculine watch, over-sized boot cut jeans, and her signature velvet scrunchie. I would have called it a lesbian look, but the closest I'd ever come to talking to Jurate about her sexuality was when she mentioned that The Rock was her type. Georgie, Whitney and I decided that was fine, and we'd be available if she ever wanted to say more.

"Guess who travelled on a hot air balloon?" Jurate asked me now.

I flattened the page of the newspaper to see the photos, which featured a patchwork of green farmland from high up in the air, and a shot of the operator looking up at the blue glow of the burner.

"Well, look at that, our Amanda keeps blowing up!"

"And ballooning up," Jurate added. "So who are these ladies joining us? I wasn't sure if this would be traditional brunch or something wild."

"Pretty sure it's just you, me, Amanda and Heather. Maybe Georgie?"

When Amanda and Heather walked in, they were in the midst of an argument over who was more girly. Jurate and I shook our heads, and headed into the back room to snag a booth.

"It's definitely Heather, right? Look at that skirt. It's purple."

Heather's face was smug. "You wear skirts too."

"Loose skirts," Amanda amended.

Heather opened her menu and sighed. "Okay, Amanda, maybe I'm more girly than you, but it doesn't even matter."

"What's wrong with girly?" I asked.

"Nothing. Feminine is not a euphemism for weak," Heather added.

"That's not what I meant," Amanda protested. "I just don't know how to use my femininity like Heather does."

"Is Georgie coming?" Jurate was playing with her utensils. "This is fascinating, but I rode my bike 30 miles this morning and I am a little bit hungry. You think we can order?"

Amanda looked at her phone. "Georgie said she was coming yesterday but now she says she's too busy."

"With what?" Heather asked.

"Probably practicing the tour she's giving later," I said. I imagined

Georgie pacing around her bedroom, cellphone in hand to record her voice as she expounded on the freshness of the Sultan Market's cucumber salad, which I knew she hated.

Sally wandered over to our table with a tray of waters and placed them on the table. She was a cute petite blond who wore a feather in her hair, and had once shared an apartment with Heather and Amanda. There had also been a time, before I moved to town, when Sally had considered Whitney her best friend. Since then, a number of petty fights had deteriorated those friendships, and I imagined she was not happy to see us.

"Well, look at you all together like the old days," she said. "What can I get you?"

"I will do the breakfast burrito with organic eggs, brown rice and avocado on the side," Jurate said.

Heather ordered a skillet with extra potatoes in place of toast, and Amanda went for fruit and oatmeal.

I scoffed. "Really? Oatmeal?"

"It's so good here. I'll give you a bite and you'll change your tune."

"Aneesha?" Sally tapped her pen on the order pad.

"The breakfast burrito, normal style."

"So how long are you in town?" she asked me.

I thought this might be a challenge and I tried to keep it vague. "For a few weeks, we'll see."

"Well, I'm bartending now, so come by when you want," Sally said with a smile. "I haven't forgotten that you used to shoot the shit with me while I was training. You always pretended to like my botched drinks."

It hadn't occurred to me that my freeloading might be considered a favor to anyone. "I wasn't pretending," I said with relief. "They were free, I definitely liked them."

When Sally turned back to the kitchen, Heather's death stare was on me. "Since when are you buddy-buddy with Sally? You know I don't like her, not since she ruined my frying pan—speaking of knives that used to be sharp."

I sipped my water. "I know, but she's always here and we're always here. Don't you think it makes sense to be friendly?"

Jurate shook her head. "No, it's just because you and Sally are flirts. She's always—" Jurate gathered her hair into a ponytail, flipped it over the top of her head, and batted her eyelashes dramatically. "Oh, thanks, sweetie," Jurate said in a high-pitched voice. "And you," Jurate said accusingly to me. She rested her face in her hands, giggled and waved a loose hand around. In what I assumed was a deeper, more dopey approximation of my voice she said, "Tell me more, you're sooooo funny and interesting." She adjusted her posture. "So of course you two get along."

Amanda, Heather, and I cackled, and then considered this with appreciative nods. "You are a very attentive listener, Aneesha," Heather said. "It's why I've told you my entire life history."

"Plus you have all these weird girl situations," Amanda added. "They have to start somewhere. It's probably because you're always flirting."

"That's not true," I said. Then I remembered my dancing plans. Was my main interest not to flirt as hard as possible with Tutor Crush to see what would happen? It was a game. It's why I thought of her as Tutor Crush. "Okay," I admitted. "I like a little attention, but that's totally normal." I told them about my plans that evening, and they collectively heckled me, tossing straw wrappers in my direction.

"And you wonder why you're always in trouble," Jurate said.

"So why her?" Amanda asked. "What are her highlights?"

Amanda could distill the most complex experiences into a top ten list, and it was a mode of thinking that I still hadn't learned to nimbly accommodate. I tried to single out Zoe's logical highlights. "She's really good with kids," I started. "Not in a gross mom way, but where they trust her. When we were tutoring together we both laughed and joked with the kids, but she knew how to set hard rules too. She inspires respect of yourself and her, if that makes sense." Heather, Amanda, and Jurate were looking at me with uncertainty, so I continued. "You know, and she reads a lot, listens to the same podcasts I do, likes to eat good food, has a great sense of humor. She's pretty?" They were still looking at me strangely. "You're just staring at me, so maybe I'm not explaining this well," I said.

"No, it's just that this sounds so reasonable," Heather said.

"Oh," I sat up. "Also, she's straight. Or not exactly queer. So there's that."

Jurate looked skeptical. "Has she told you that?"

"Well, no, but queer women usually tell you in one way or another. Especially when they have boyfriends, which," I put my hand up to emphasize, "she doesn't anymore, okay? I see you preparing an eye roll, Jurate."

"So she's funny, pretty, single and inspires respect," Amanda counted off on her fingers. "And you have common interests."

"This is the most promising crush you've ever talked about," Heather said.

"No, it's not real. You don't understand," I said. I didn't expect them to know the tenuous reality created by unexplored sexuality. "You can be proud, but it's only a hypothetical improvement."

In true Heartland fashion, our food arrived at different intervals and we encouraged Amanda to start before her oatmeal got cold. She prepared her bowl with honey and butter, and then made me try the first bite. "Tell me it's not way better than whatever you make at home."

I chewed and admitted that it was good, but anything would have been good smothered in honey and butter.

"Eat your burrito," Jurate said, pointing at the plate Sally had placed in front of me. "Real, hypothetical, who cares? You always enjoy yourself," Jurate reassured me.

I knew I was quickly approaching the point of diminishing return with Zoe, but it was summer and she was fun. I already knew what I would do.

"Well, what about you guys?" I asked. "I'm not the only one with a love interest."

Amanda had been dating Sam, another server at the Heartland, for over a year now. Sam was a thin red-haired guy who wore glasses and comic book t-shirts. He was a talented cartoonist and illustrator, and he and I had spent a number of evenings at the Buffalo Bar talking about art and storytelling, remarking on women we found attractive, and wallowing together in the seemingly endless struggle to live off of art. Sam was also a notorious flirt, with a reputation for crushing on women with queer styles and somber demeanors. Amanda and I had jokingly called them NPR girls, and so it was a surprise to me when she and Sam became a serious couple.

Amanda spooned a slice of banana out of her bowl. "Well, I have a boyfriend, as you know, and it seems to be going fine for now." She was always so guarded.

"Fine is good, right?" I asked Heather.

Amanda laughed. "He's not my usual type, but he makes me laugh. And he's learned that when we're out together I'd prefer if he didn't ask other girls to sit on his lap." She laughed. "I'm not sure where it's going, because I don't think I get this cartooning lifestyle, but he grew his beard out as you may have noticed, and I'm very into that."

Jurate smiled slyly over the top of her burrito. "So the physical element is working?"

"Yes." Amanda laughed. "The physical element is great."

Heather popped a potato in her mouth and chewed. "Can I ask you something? If I said that I thought I could marry Remi already, is that crazy?"

Amanda nodded. "Yes, Heather."

I took a break from my burrito. Heather's eggs were getting harvested in a few days, and this was the second time she'd done it, which meant there were already little half-Heathers crawling around in the world. "I don't know," I said. "What's marriage about for you?"

Heather crossed her arms and thought for a moment. "It's about committing to being a family. I already know he's all the things I want." Heather looked at Amanda, who was waiting for her to say more. "And yes, I do want to have my own kids. So that probably has something to do with the feeling."

Jurate carefully picked at the beans in her burrito with a fork. "When can we meet him? We'll tell you if you're crazy then." She wiggled her eyebrows and we all laughed.

Dinner at the Summertowns' always began fashionably late, but I wasn't sure they knew this, so I arrived on time. I rang the doorbell and examined the neon blue sign above the door that displayed their address. It was an unexpected touch on this historic brick home, and exactly her parents' style. I badly wanted to learn that skill—transforming tacky into sophisticated—but felt certain I was stuck for life with the casual kitsch I lent to anything in my presence. My younger sister and I wore similar clothes, but the effect was quite different on each of us, and she had affectionately asked me how I made Oxford shirts look like flannel.

Georgie answered the door and ushered me in. "We're having salmon. Mom isn't done with it yet, but of course the wine is flowing freely." Georgie held up her glass, and I followed her into the kitchen.

Her mom's long white hair was pulled into a ponytail, and her thin figure hovered, somewhat menacingly, over a salad bowl. She fluffed at the greens. "Oh I don't know what else to put in here," Laura said, and then looked up. "Oh hi, Aneesha. What else goes in this salad?" She poured me a glass of white wine, and I peered into the wooden bowl. It was just lettuce.

"Those tomatoes?" I asked. "Depends on what you've got."

"I told her you're the salad queen," Georgie reported.

"We've got avocado here too." Laura's grip on the knife was loose. She was raised in a proper, wealthy family, the kind with Help. Her knife skills made me nervous. "Do we need cheese too?" she asked.

"No, I think with avocado, we don't need cheese."

"How do you know these things?" she asked me, her eyes focusing sharply on me.

"Cheese and avocado are both fats, which cut acids well, but our only acid so far is tomato, which is pretty mild and sweet. You have to balance the flavors."

My own mom was the true salad queen, an artist really. Nobody could razor a thinner slice of fennel. Nobody used cauliflower in such a provocative manner. She was the kind of mom who picked us up from school hours late, and offered feminism as her excuse, but she loved to cook. If they had to spend more than thirty minutes together, my mom would be less than thrilled with Laura, but so far, they'd only shared friendly moments during mine and Georgie's college graduation. I kept a judicious distance from my own parents too, so that we might be able to imagine the best of each other. They were smart, successful, generous people with good taste, and they'd worked hard for their upper-middle class lifestyles. But they didn't know quite what to make of me, and were continually vexed by my lack of investment in long-term stability.

I took a sip of my wine. "All of this stuff is from my mom," I admitted.

"Well, that actually makes some sense, if I think about it terms of photography." Laura pointed the loosely gripped knife at me. "Aneesha, you know your way around a few things, you've got it together. Now, if only we can get Georgie on board." This was one of the reasons I enjoyed the company of the Summetowns. They were convinced that I was more successful than Georgie, though we were so similar I couldn't fathom why. If pressed to choose whose success was more imminent, my vote was Georgie because she worked harder.

"That's enough, Mom," Georgie said from the refrigerator. She was lining up small jars on the counter, with which I would be making a dressing.

"Why, what's Mom doing now?" Across from us in the TV room, Georgie's younger brother, Ryder, hung his long skinny legs from one end of the couch. He had just graduated from college and was working as a tennis instructor, which made him extremely tan. This was also the purported reason that he always wore bright white athletic socks, though I thought someone ought to try to push him on this.

"So what are your plans out here?" Laura asked me. She was delicately grinding pepper over a baking pan lined with salmon fillets.

"I'm writing a few more stories for my thesis, editing a few others. Catching up with friends, nothing gallant or glorious."

Laura grinned. "How nice that you can direct your own work." She refilled both of our wine glasses. "Very positive ways to occupy your time, aren't they Georgie?"

"I'm right over here, I heard." Georgie handed me an empty jar and motioned at the condiments on the counter. "Don't forget, Mom, that I have that tour guide job. I'm occupying my time positively too."

"Right, right, of course. We're very proud of you for that." The tone in Laura's voice seemed to imply that there was a 'but' that she would decline to speak aloud.

I, personally, was impressed that Georgie had already gotten what seemed like a fun job, one that required personality. It gave me a little hope for my own prospects. I poured olive oil and balsamic vinegar into the jar, and used a fork to plop in some Dijon mustard. "What did you do?" I asked Laura. "Before kids and all this?"

Laura leaned her head thoughtfully to the side, her long neck on display. "Oh, I worked for a little while, but it just never took." She smiled at me, a kind of lopsided secret smile, and Georgie glared at her back. It occurred to me that certain people never planned to work. "I prefer more social responsibilities," Laura added.

"That's just great, Mom," Georgie grumbled, getting plates to set the table. "You could help, you know," she called to the TV room.

Ryder took a gulp from a pint glass of milk on the floor. "Nah, I'd just be in the way. You've got Aneesha now."

"Are you hanging out on the couch drinking milk?" I asked him. "I haven't seen anyone over the age of eight do that."

Ryder sat up and laughed. "Hey, I'm reading *Harry Potter*, okay? Do you have any idea how addicting these things are?" Ryder's total lack of irony was one of his most positive qualities. "It's really action-packed. They even have their own made-up sport and everything. I think I'm gonna cry in this one. Nobody told me how good these were."

Georgie looked at him. "Ryder, you're the only person in the world who missed the Harry Potter memo."

"I have to say, Ry," Laura adjusted her red glasses frames. "I think Georgie's right about this one."

Ryder held up both hands in surrender. "Alright, okay. How many settings for dinner? I'll get out new napkins," he offered.

When we finally sat down at the long dining room table, there were ten of us.

Georgie's dad and Youngsu came up from the woodshop in the basement. Jean, an exiled Rwandan pop star, trotted down the stairs, and Ahmet, a visiting Turkish heart surgeon, marched morosely behind. Finally, Georgie's cousin Peg burst into the house with her partner, Marge, and announced, "We didn't bring the pugs, don't worry, but we did bring dessert."

Georgie's dad, Roger, eyed the spread from the head of table. "Well, let's get started, shall we?" He passed around a basket of rolls and reminded everyone that his famous coleslaw—which the Summertowns pronounced "co-slaw"—was at the other end of the table.

It was a lively dinner. Georgie's parents were experts at gently prodding all of us to disclose our plans for the future. They were never worried, they only ever encouraged and congratulated, offering to help out in any way they could. This unwaveringly positive attitude, I thought, this was true wealth.

Jean, Laura explained proudly, had decided to begin training as a truck driver so that he could start supporting himself. I looked across the table at the mild downturn of Jean's mouth, which led me to believe this was the kind of "social responsibility" that Laura preferred.

"What's really impressive about Jean," Ryder added, "is that he had to make a new Facebook page. A fan one. Because he already had the maximum number of friends on his personal page. I didn't know you could have too many friends for Facebook."

Now Jean laughed. "I didn't even know what a fan page was," he said. "Ryder had to show me."

"That video of you on the boat is fun," Marge added. "And those white pants look great, I'm sure the ladies are clamoring for you. I need to get some white pants myself."

Ahmet scoffed at this idea, which didn't escape anybody's notice. He apparently didn't know what he was dealing with yet.

"And this week," Laura continued, "Ahmet learned how to use the microwave. He microwaved a piece of lasagna from the fridge all by himself for the first time, didn't you?"

Peg and Marge directed applause in his direction, and we couldn't help but laugh. Ahmet sheepishly nodded and picked at his salmon.

Roger was an expert at diffusing tension. "For a guy who can put together and take apart a human heart, the microwave must have been a breeze, huh?"

"Aneesha got a steal on her little bike," Youngsu added and I, too, received over-enthusiastic congratulations. Georgie's dad offered to tune it up, which I readily accepted, though I worried Roger, an avid bike racer, would find Caliente too flawed for me to ride.

"Are you still dating the curly-haired girl you brought to our house on New Year's Eve?" Peg asked me.

"Yeah, she's pretty," Marge said, and received a sharp elbow from Peg. "What? She's pretty, you said so too."

"I asked the first question first for a reason."

They were talking about Whitney, of course. The past New Year's Eve, Marge and Peg had purchased several Costco-sized booze bottles for a big party, but had gotten into a fight with their friends a few days before the occasion. Georgie, Whitney, Amanda and I were the only ones who showed up, and all six of us had passed out on the thick carpet in the basement, with the gurgling pugs.

"Nah," I said, shaking my head. "We were never actually dating to begin with." I didn't know how much explaining my ambiguous relationships with women required, especially at this table of normal, attractive people, who seemed to do fine with traditional dating practices.

Peg gave Marge an I-told-you-so look, and I felt compelled to assure them I was okay, but Georgie beat me to it.

"Don't worry, they're still close friends somehow. And Aneesha already has somebody else in mind," Georgie pretended to rescue me. "A straight prospect."

"Straight girls? Aneesha!" Peg scolded.

Roger looked perplexed at his end of the table.

"It's just a flirtation," I said.

"It always seems normal at first, but straight girls are more trouble than they're worth," Marge said, taking a forkful of coleslaw.

"No offense," she put a hand out towards the group.

"It does seem normal at first," I said. "Deceivingly so."

"This all sounds really difficult to navigate," Roger politely chimed in.

"Girls will be girls," Laura replied. "I think we're all difficult. Though I have my own solutions for easing up." She winked and reached for her wine glass. "Well anyway, Rog just sold a table to Rahm Emanuel, so let's congratulate him for that, and I have a show opening in my gallery next week. You should come in and meet these rappers who keep me up well past my bedtime. There are photos of Jean in the show too," she added.

Georgie rolled her eyes. Laura had recently become the go-to photographer for the underground hip-hop scene in Chicago, and she got invited to all kinds of secret shows. She was definitely cooler than we were, and a more successful artist too, though she had always considered art a hobby. The irony of this was infuriating to Georgie, who liked to grumble, "There's nothing like a white lady with her camera to make hip-hop palatable to the masses."

After dessert, Youngsu, Georgie, and I remained in the kitchen to load the dishwasher and finish the wine. I was waiting for Georgie to come up with an excuse to cancel our evening plans. It was her style to bail at the last minute, to feel "overwhelmed" by the prospect of being among people she may or may not know and like. I understood the sentiment, but I hadn't forgotten the claim she made when she picked me up from the airport, that she might like fun now—and the fun of going out was the unexpected.

Youngsu closed the dishwasher door, and I warned them that I was going to rudely read my texts in front of them. I had a series from Tutor Crush, explaining the level of disappointment she would feel if I didn't show up. "Equal to taking in a dog who unbeknownst to you belongs to a distant neighbor, and after he's taken back, you still have to see them taking walks together," she had written.

"Are these texts to do with the straight prospect that was so casually mentioned at dinner?" Youngsu asked.

"Yes," I said. "And thank you, Georgie, for opening up my dating life to discuss with your family."

Georgie waved a hand at me. "Oh come on, Aneesha, this is real intrigue for them. Anyway, Peg and Marge love that shit. They're all boring, all married and everything. I bet they never hear good girl drama."

I shrugged this off. "So you're coming, right?" I raised an eyebrow at Georgie.

She withered into the marble top of the island, and covered her head with her arms. "When do we have to go?"

Whitney had just sent me a text about the dance party. She and Logan were drinking with friends, and would be heading to the Beauty Bar around eleven. "Come! I'll buy you tacos," she promised. Drunk tacos on the train home was a tradition of ours, and I understood that she was pleading with me.

"How long do we have to stay?" Georgie asked.

"Hold on, I need to pee," I said.

The downstairs bathroom was tiled in gentle white hexagons and featured washed-out princess drawings by five-year-old Georgie. I sat on the toilet and worked through my priorities. I couldn't ditch out on Tutor Crush. I wanted to see her, she wanted to see me, and that symmetry was not something I could afford to disregard. But I couldn't ignore Whitney either. This summer had been our plan, and I didn't want her to think that Georgie's "neutral" feelings or her relationship with Logan would invalidate our friendship. Though, they did a little. Georgie wouldn't want to go to see Whitney, and I really wanted Georgie to come out. I flushed the toilet, and washed my hands with the lemon-ginger scented bar of soap.

"Okay," I announced in the kitchen. "Let's go to Danny's and dance to some soul. You can leave when you want, and I will try to make it over to this dance party with Whitney and Logan later. Or if you guys are loving it, we can all go queer dancing together."

Youngsu tipped his wine glass up. "Alright, I'm ready." He pointed to his sneakers. "My dancing shoes are already on."

Georgie groaned. "Where do you guys get all this energy? Doesn't the basic maintenance of life wear you down?"

"Georgie, stop it," I said. "You have a new green belt you've been looking for a reason to wear, and your leopard-print shoes haven't been out in a while."

"How do you know all of this?" she asked me, interested now.

"Because you call me up to talk about it!"

Youngsu joined me. "I have heard some talk about the leopard-print shoes. This seems like a solid opportunity."

"You guys are relentless with your listening and remembering things," Georgie said in a huff. "I'm going, but I want you to know I'm grumpy about it."

"Fine," I said, and she went upstairs to get dressed.

＊

As the three of us rode down to Danny's Tavern, the wind blew hot and I felt electric. I anticipated the high-pitched floral scent of Zoe's hair, the way she'd flip it at me in a gesture that was somewhere between mocking and real. I intended to find out precisely where.

Youngsu and Georgie were lagging behind. "Hey Aneesha, cool those little wheels, the sweaty dance party isn't going anywhere," Georgie called.

This murky cloud of ennui that had gathered around her needed to be cleared. I slowed down so were riding in a pack. "I'm getting you drunk," I said, looking over my shoulder. "The complaints must end."

Youngsu laughed. "Look out."

"Okay," Georgie said, sounding rather optimistic. "I'm game."

The sweaty dance party was in full swing when we walked in. I left Georgie and Youngsu at the bar with my credit card, and instructions to open and abuse my tab. After hearing of my plans for the summer, my grandpa, a man of few words, had given me a check for what he called my "soda pop fund." It was all I really had until school started again, but if it shook Georgie up, it was money well spent.

Danny's wasn't a big place, and I spotted Zoe dancing in a circle in the corner of the stage. I'd never met her friends before, and I didn't expect them to be so tall, male and khaki-wearing, but they were all bouncing around with their drinks—rhythmically and without spilling—which I could appreciate. Zoe was in black shorts and a tank top, expertly swinging her hips in a slow circle. She looked up, caught me staring, and pointed at me. "Get over here," she yelled, and introduced me to her friends. It was far too loud to hear anything, but we moved our mouths, nodded, and patted each other like old chums.

Youngsu and Georgie were winding through the crowd, drinks held high over their heads, and I pointed at them, then at myself, back and forth. "No! You have friends?" Zoe asked into my ear. Her nose grazed the side of my face, and I was soaring again. I dance-shrugged in response, and our group became waving sea of shoulder shimmy.

Georgie, who was stepping loosely now, handed me a drink. "I got this move!" she shrieked, and put on the requisite frown for serious dancing.

It wasn't until I was swaying over to the bathroom, mine and Zoe's arms linked in an ambiguous girl fashion, that I remembered Whitney.

Zoe eyed me as I extracted my phone from my clammy shorts pocket. "Your phone is really hot, I can see the appeal."

I stopped walking. She was smiling, her head playfully tilted to the side. This was quickly sliding over to the real side of the spectrum, and I put my phone back in my pocket.

"I'm just messing with you, Aneesha," she said. "You should check your phone, I'm sure somebody is trying to talk to you." Her hand came up to give me a jovial shove, but rested on my shoulder instead. "Little Ms. Popular."

The curly wisps at her hairline stuck to her sweaty forehead. It was perfect. So I took a step closer, and put my booze-ballooned mouth on hers. Our lips rubbed together and then her warm soft tongue slipped against mine. A jolt ran through me, and I pressed my hips into hers, against the wall behind her. I wasn't sure how it was going until a sound slipped through her nose, and then she grabbed my hair to pull me in, and lodged her thigh between my legs. We paused to breathe, and I bit her bottom lip to tug her back in. I had forgotten how kissing the right person was like a good conversation. When we did part, there was a touch of surprise in her round eyes, a blank vulnerability. It quickly faded and her face resumed its usual poise. I was aware that I still badly needed to pee, and that I was making out in public outside of a bathroom like I was sixteen.

"Let's go in—," I started, and she shook her head before I could finish. "To pee," I said, taking her chin in my hand.

"Ahhh, okay." She chuckled, and pushed me through the swinging door. On the toilet I checked my phone, scrolling through the play-by-plays from Whitney of what she was drinking, how she was dancing. "Why?" I asked, as I considered the empty toilet paper roll, and that lusty kiss, and the series of texts glowing in my hand. "How else can I convince you?" Whitney had sent me last.

Zoe was washing her hands at the sink, and I did the same beside her. "No soap?" she teased.

"I don't know if you know this, but I'm pretty gross," I told her. "Though now that you mention it." I went for some soap. It dried out my skin, and I didn't like the scent of industrial cleaning products on my hands, but if I ever wanted to kiss her again, I thought soap might be a step in the right direction.

"What's wrong?" Zoe asked, handing me a scrap of paper towel.

"I just saw my reflection in the mirror," I lied, putting on a look of horror. "A little hard on yourself, don't you think?" She gave my head a messy rub.

"Look, your hair is perfect again. And soft," she added.

I was no longer sure what this was. It was too late or too soon for soft hair comments. I wanted to dance and play some more, and not worry about what I was doing with a lovely woman who had just split up with her boyfriend. "I think I have to go," I said, feeling my regret as I said it.

"Not because of…" She looked confused, and motioned to herself.

"No, I really liked that." I touched her arm. "But I told my friend I'm staying with that I'd come to a different dance party, and she's freaking out that I'm not there yet." I couldn't bear to leave Whitney hanging. Friendship with me involved unwavering reliability, and above all else Whitney was my friend.

Zoe leaned into me. "You're going right now?" I realized what I had started, and what I was leaving unresolved. A piece of hair fell across her face, prompting me to imagine her further undone, but I didn't want to navigate that tonight. There were certainly some hidden clauses, and I wasn't sure I could not take them personally. I wanted to get a glimpse of what was hiding out beneath the electric zeal of our attraction before we went there.

"Walk me out?" I asked, and she reluctantly agreed. I closed my tab, and then we stood facing each other on the pavement. It looked like it might rain soon.

"I'm glad you came," she said. "Thanks for blowing off somebody else to hang out with me."

Her cheeks were still pink from the heat inside, and it made her look sweet. I felt terrible. "It's not like that," I said. "I like hanging out with you, it's always a pleasure." I gave her a hug, and quickly kissed her neck as I pulled away.

She said something softly, and "tease" was the only word I caught. I knew it was a joke, but there was a streak of hurt in the lower notes of her voice.

I took her hand. "Hey, Zoe," I said, feeling honest. "You're awesome and I've had a massive crush on you since forever, which I'm sure you know." I raised my eyebrow. "But you had a boyfriend for a really long time, and I just don't..." I was losing steam. I didn't want to close anything off, but I couldn't begin to explain the implicit peril of a wonderful, straight-ish woman. The simultaneous allure. "I want you to be sure this is something you want." I dropped her hand. I'd already been all the places this could lead, and now I heard Georgie in my head, her clipped motherly warning: "Nothing is just for fun."

Zoe had an amused look on her face. "Do you think this hard before you sleep with everyone?"

I took a step back, looking up at the lowering grey clouds. It was my turn to be a little hurt and a little embarrassed, and it was time for me to go. "Yes, I do," I said.

Though this was the first time I'd turned down a woman I wanted to sleep with because it wasn't quite right. It didn't feel as

good as I'd hoped. "I realize that might not be very hot. I'm sorry."
I felt in my pocket for my keys, and began down the block where our
bikes were locked up.

"Aneesha." Zoe grabbed my arm, and I braced myself. "Don't be
like this," she said instead. "I'm only playing."

"I know," I said, probably too sharply. "I still need to go."

I shook my head and turned the corner. Youngsu and Georgie
were sitting on the curb, smoking together in the darkness. I worried
for a moment that I might be interrupting some romance between
them, but then I heard Georgie's voice. "Hey, I couldn't figure out
where you went. We came out here and your bike was still here, so I
figured something good?"

I replayed the thick scent of Zoe's hair and the flit of her tongue
in my mouth. "I don't know," I said. The item in my notebook
had not been fully considered. I still wasn't equipped to know the
difference between a good and bad decision. We pulled our bikes
and locks apart. "I'm going to Chances Dances, are you guys in?"
I asked.

"I gotta head home. School and work tomorrow," Youngsu said.
"But I'm glad you took us out, it was really fun."

"It was," Georgie confirmed. "I do, in fact, love soul. You were
right. And your crush is pretty cute. Very flirty, I might add."

"Very flirty," Youngsu said, pointing his cigarette at me. They
were both smiling, and it felt good to see them as a unit again.
Nobody else understood the value of tiny quiet triumphs like they did.

"Yeah, yeah, Flirttown, USA," I said, and swung my leg over
Caliente. "You guys are the best. Have a good night."

❧

I parked my bike near an alley, and then ducked in quickly to
change my shirt.

The theme of the night was Summer Camp, and my tank top
featured the peachy torso of a well-toned man wearing a blue thong
with a noticeable side bulge. A friend had gotten it for me on a trip
to Mexico, and I'd had more occasions to wear it than I'd imagined.

Just inside the door of the bar, I was met with a photo booth set-up. A group of young queers, in striped lifeguard swimsuits, were posing with their hands shading their eyes, searching the horizon. They all had an aqua stripe of zinc on their noses and neon whistles around their necks. I laughed with relief and recognition.

"That was a really good photo," I told them as they shuffled back into the dance party.

"Hey, thanks," said one girl. She was skinny, with striking blue eyes, and looked familiar. We stared at each other for an awkward moment.

"Spencer," the girl said, sticking out her hand. I knew then why Whitney wanted me here so badly. Spencer was the only ex who'd ever burned her.

"Aneesha," I said. "I think…"

"Are you?" she asked.

We'd only ever seen each other in pictures online.

"Whitney," we both agreed.

"I hear you're the coolest person ever or something," Spencer said. She spoke carefully and I could tell that her goal was to get along.

"And I have heard epic tales of your charm," I said.

"I'm not proud of them all," she replied.

Spencer had the delicate face of a deer. She spoke in a low composed tone that would have compelled someone who wasn't me to lean in closer to her. It had always eluded me what exactly Whitney found attractive, but this poised twenty-two-year-old with short blond hair, broad shoulders, and white suspenders made a whole lot of sense.

"Oh my god, you're actually here!" Whitney whisked across the room, and rested her elbow on my shoulder. "Spencer, this is Aneesha, my very good friend. Who is only here because I promised to buy her tacos afterwards."

"Tacos." Spencer smiled with familiarity.

"I'm a cheap bribe." An image of Zoe standing alone and pink-cheeked outside of Danny's echoed in my mind. I wanted to go back and explain my concerns, hash it out, and then kiss her everywhere. But when had that ever worked for me?

Spencer returned to her friends at the near end of the bar, and Whitney ushered me down to the other end. "Man, it's been a night!" She was using her high-pitched ironic tone. "Let's get martinis with a manicure. On my very large tab." Whitney was on the verge of breaking into a fit of laughter. I also felt that in moments of crisis it seemed most appropriate to stand back from yourself, and laugh at the exquisite makings of a disaster, the intricacy of your own complete failure.

The bartender took our order and called me 'baby,' for which I thanked her. Then we sat in a secluded couch area, waiting for our manicures. "So, what's Spencer doing here?" I asked. "Did she finish college or something?"

"Yeah, she's driving out west with her friends. Their graduation road trip." Whitney and I looked at each other. "Okay, it's true, I need move up an age bracket," she said. "I'm still mad at her for thinking she could break my heart."

"She didn't though," I reminded Whitney.

"Yeah, but she thought I loved her, so basically she did."

"But you didn't," I said. "When she broke up with you, you said, 'It's such a bummer, I almost loved her.'"

"Don't defend her," Whitney said. "She was probably cheating on me. And she lived in a dorm last week."

"You're right. Fuck Spencer," I said, and sipped my martini.

"That wasn't very convincing," Whitney replied. "It's because she's hot, isn't it? She does whatever she wants, and people let her. Ugh."

Out on the dance floor I noticed Logan dancing beneath a jeweled turquoise chandelier. His glasses were fogged at the edges, and he was shaking his butt at his friend Lana, an exaggerated wiggle. His was a guileless charm. "What does Logan think?" I asked.

"Of Spencer?" Whitney asked. She started to chuckle. "Well, he didn't exactly say because he was distracted by the fact that three of my ex-girlfriends and everyone I used to sleep with are here tonight and want to talk."

Everyone claimed to hate that queer dance parties were a scene rife with drama, but I figured that was part of the draw. If I didn't

think so hard about who to sleep with, I might have had something
to worry about too. I spotted Whitney's questionable decisions:
Lizzie with her baggy pants and drumsticks in her back pocket,
Quinn the obnoxious blogger with confrontational t-shirts, Rocky
the gawky vegan cook in the baseball cap, the Christian architect, the
waffle-making Republican. "Whit," I said, taking them in together,
as a group. "What a precious collection of women. Really the cream
of the crop. We just need Peach Tree to show up."

Whitney doubled over with laughter and spilled her martini on
my leg. "I'm sorry," she choked out, wiping at me with her shirt. "I
forgot about that one. I would have done it if you hadn't been there
to stop me."

I grimaced. "No."

Whitney shrugged. "You never know with me. Sometimes
I can't help myself. They're so wrong for me and they have
no idea."

"It did not occur to me until now," I said, "to be so fucking
grateful that it's Logan you're with instead of any one of these wild
cards."

"I'm glad you're here for this. I don't think anybody else would
understand. What's wrong with me?" she asked.

"I don't know." I had to pause because it really didn't make any
sense. "There are some hot, cute, fun, talented, cool people here.
People we see around. People we know. But that's not who you
generally go with."

Whitney had butted her head against my shoulder, and was
now threatening to spill my drink. I tipped the rest into my mouth
and set it on the table.

"I know," she said. "It got so much worse when you left, you
have no idea." She paused to finish her own drink and set the glass
next to mine. "Don't ever leave, Aneesha. You can't."

Whitney smelled too strongly of her essential oil, and her left
eyelid was at half-mast. I melted a little. "I won't," I said, because that
was how I felt right then. It was just a warm orange nightlight glow.
From the secluded beige couch, I watched everyone dance, and flirt,
and drink, and joke. These were the kinds of happy unlucky people

who Whitney let pursue her. All of them, with no idea of how far they'd have to go to actually find her, of how deeply hidden away she was. I wasn't exempt. Though I wasn't all that forthcoming with real feeling myself, and for a while I hadn't minded the slow exposure, like we were archaeologists dusting at each other with brushes.

I remembered the night when I'd finally snapped. We'd been drinking margaritas since happy hour, and after a sloppy bike ride home, I was debating whether or not to stay at Whitney's place. "Stay if you want to," she'd said.

"Do you want me to?" I'd asked. "How do you feel about me? You see me every fucking day, why can't you tell me what it means to you?"

"Make me," she'd fired back calmly. "If you want to know, make me tell you."

I hadn't wanted to make her do anything. It was enough to know there wasn't a feeling she cared to articulate on her own.

My meditation was interrupted when a woman with a platinum blond mullet called me up to her nail station. I stood up and patted Whitney on the head.

"I want the brightest red," I told Blond Mullet. She held up three colors, and I pointed to the bottle with a touch of orange.

"Do you like working these gigs?" I asked her.

"Honestly, it's a little late for me." She rubbed oil into my nail beds and trimmed my cuticles. "At least I'm in a bar, right? Do you mind if I?" She pointed to the PBR on the table.

"Go for it," I said.

"You have such nice big nails," Blond Mullet said. "Pretty."

I'd never known exactly how to take "pretty" compliments. It wasn't that I didn't think of myself as pretty—I did—it was the implication that I would want others to find me pretty, that pretty was my goal, which made me uncomfortable. But I was not quite femme enough to be beautiful, not butch enough to call handsome, not hard enough to be bad, too casual to be dandy. Not that there was anything wrong with pretty, I supposed. Whitney would say I was cute. I wondered what Zoe thought.

As if she'd been thinking the same thing, Blond Mullet cocked her head to evaluate my look. "Maybe I mean cool instead," she said, with a smile. "You have some stylishly tough nails."

"I'm not above pretty," I confessed. "I'll take what I can get."

When she was done, I had Blond Mullet tip herself from my wallet, and hovered over Whitney's table, flapping my hands around to dry. "Coral," I said, noticing her nail color. "A bold choice."

"Keep your judgments to yourself," Whitney instructed. "Unless you think it really looks bad." She craned her neck up at me, and the manicurist threw me a threatening glare.

"It's good bold," I said.

A group of women in satin dresses gathered around the table beside Whitney, and I had to wonder what they were doing here. One of them seemed to notice my less-than-friendly gaze.

"We came here with our bridal shower," she excused herself. "We didn't know it was a themed night."

I wasn't sure if she meant "themed" as in Summer Camp or as in queer. "Oh, fun," I said. "Bridal showers, pastel dresses, up-dos, gender roles."

Whitney knew where this was going, and kicked my leg before I could continue my list of wedding delights. "It's a really great deal," Whitney said in her accountant voice. "Drink and nails for $10? You can't beat that."

I couldn't listen to this. I had to remove myself to go dance—it was a dance party after all. Out under the chandeliers, I playfully bumped up against Logan and his friends. We were all drunk, and I moved with a tireless ease I'd forgotten. Logan introduced me to several people who had leather strings tied around their heads, and whose forearms were stacked with friendship bracelets. Some of them I knew from college and around town, which we acknowledged with loose hugs. It turned out Spencer's road trip friends were acquaintances of mine and we danced together, jumping up and down riotously.

At one point, I noticed the girl next to me, who was wearing tiny cutoffs over bright bike shorts. She bent down to pull her cellphone out of her hiking boot, and I saw that her shorts were printed with frames of superhero comics. It was a good look. "That's a very superhero place to hide your phone," I told her. She smiled, and pulled a little card out of her other boot. Screened in blue on the front, it said, "You should call me, my name is," and there was a blank where she had written "Alia" in tilted, skinny letters. On the back was her phone number. She could tell I was conflicted about the card gimmick. "My friends gave them to me for my birthday. They said I needed to be more outgoing." She shrugged and smiled. "Call me, if you want."

"Oh, okay, great," I said, and she wandered off to use her phone.

"What just happened?" Logan asked excitedly.

"I think somebody just hit on me," I said. "Maybe. She gave me this card." I wasn't sure why I seemed to be attractive all of a sudden.

Logan grabbed the card from me. "That's a yes. She did hit on you. Some things are not complicated, Aneesha, you just make them that way." He laughed, and I hugged him, and we danced around in a little sweaty circle, and it felt nice to be on the same team. Until I noticed Whitney standing across from us. She had a twinkling smirk on her face that I recognized. Logan ran over and did the same hug dance with her, holding her tightly around the waist. They spoke to each other for a while, and then Whitney grabbed my arm. "Come on, let's get out of here. Logan will get a ride home with his friends."

"My bike," I said, not sure I was ready to leave yet.

"It's tiny. We'll put it in the car," she said. "Aren't you ready for tacos yet? I've been ready. We don't want to overstay."

I imagined the harsh lights coming on soon, the sweet sickly odor of Spin or Berlin or whatever 4 a.m. bar we'd end up at, and the sour PBR that I'd guzzle in a poor attempt to hydrate. She was right. I thought of the movie *Clueless* for the millionth time, and heard Cher instructing her friends, "Just remember, 'Always keep them wanting more.'"

It was pouring rain when we stepped outside, but I didn't mind. The rain was refreshing after my sweaty dance interlude, and I decided to send Zoe a text to see if her night went okay. Maybe I'd made a mistake. I thought about asking Whitney her advice, but she was carefully packing Caliente into the trunk, and it was so sweet to have someone take care of my annoying business that I didn't want to interrupt. Whitney blasted Taylor Swift on the way to the all-night Mexican restaurant, and as we sang along, it struck me that these were the most emotionally open words we'd ever shared.

When we waltzed into the fluorescently lit restaurant, the young woman with bright pink lipstick already knew Whitney's order. "Six vegetarian tacos," she said solemnly, like we were being sentenced, and wrote it in her pad. I ordered a Dr. Pepper and sipped it empty before the tacos were up. I was fixated on the mural on the wall that depicted an adobe window looking out onto the beach. There were potted palms by the window frame, and the pristine blue water beyond. I was attracted to the wonderfully simple illusion of painting a window to the beach, if that's what you wanted to look at.

"You never told me about your night," Whitney said.

"Oh yeah." I smiled. "I made out with Tutor Crush."

Whitney's grin looked both sly and triumphant. I didn't know what to think. "So you got her after all. Do you feel like the king of the world? What's his name on that boat?"

She was going to make fun of me. "Leonardo DiCaprio? *Titanic*? No," I said. "I'm a little afraid she'll undo me without even trying."

"Yes, ruin things before they've gone bad," she said, and patted my arm.

I didn't know what to say. It was hard to listen to Whitney talk to me about ruining things when I tried so hard to be in the business of long-term preservation, but I didn't want to get into it now.

"How did you end up with Logan?" I asked her.

"I told you before. We're both volunteers at The Night Ministry, and we met at a fundraiser." Her mouth was loose, and the words seemed to slip out together.

"No, I mean, like how did you end up together? Him as your boyfriend, living with him."

Her bottom lip protruded as she thought. "I don't know. He knew what he wanted, so he told me so and did it."

"That works for you?" I asked.

She shrugged and narrowed her eyes. "Maybe?"

The young woman appeared at the counter with our box of tacos, and wished us a safe night. By now, the storm was letting up, and when we got in the car I rolled down the window to take in the earthy smell. I liked the crackle of tires as they rolled over the wet asphalt. Whitney was driving Logan's car, a new Golf that he'd bought with his ex-girlfriend and was still making payments on. The tacos were hot in my lap, but I held the box firmly, not wanting to leave grease on the upholstery he didn't even technically own yet. We maneuvered down an alley to get to Logan's parking spot, and there was a low "harrumph" as the car ran over something.

"Oh no," I said.

"It's just the stupid pot holes." Whitney waved me off. She had always been an extremely competent drunk driver—a paradox, I could admit, but one that I found endlessly appealing all the same.

We lingered for a moment while two men holding forties lumbered across the mouth of the alleyway. One man pointed us out to his friend, and they furrowed their brows, laughed, and walked on.

"We must look pretty bad," I said, turning to Whitney. "Or really gay?"

"They're just jealous of our tacos," she said, and pulled into the parking spot.

Once we got out, however, it became clear that we had run over a mattress, a flimsy twin with a floral pattern and two brown dried-up stains. It stuck out all lopsided behind the trunk, wedged up under one of the back tires. A gust of wind blew through the alley, and jiggled a few of the loose springs.

I started laughing and couldn't stop. Whitney stepped around to the back of the car and joined in.

"How did you not see this?" I asked.

"You didn't either," she said in her defense.

I wrestled Caliente out of the trunk, and we held on to each other, giggling as we crossed the alley to the back gate of her building.

"Imagine those guys," I said.

"We must look ridiculous. Do I even have keys?" Whitney

searched in her bag for what felt like an eternity, and then gave up
and threw the bag at me. The buckle of the strap nearly hit me in the
face, and I understood that everything was unravelling. "Where are
the keys?" she asked in an upward direction, to no one in particular.
"Do I even really live here? How did we get here? What is this?"
Whitney wobbled in zigzags toward and away from me, her knees
loose like they might give. Her brow was furrowed, and her head
drooped under her sweaty curls. She unexpectedly jilted to the right,
in order to avoid a dumpster, and then began running full speed
at the gate. With a whoosh she hurtled past me, and slammed her
shoulder into the bars. When it remained closed, she jumped up,
hooked her fingers in the grate, and hung for a moment, growling
fiercely.

This was the Whitney I loved.

"Look who's back." I rummaged in her bag and pulled out a
carabiner. "Were you looking for these keys?"

She grabbed them from me, and stabbed at the lock a few times
before it turned.

The gate screeched opened, and I let my bike drop just inside
it. I followed her up the stairs like so many nights before: the two
us bouncing off of railings, and falling into a safe, dreamy blackness.

When we stepped into the dark of the kitchen, Whitney grabbed
my arm to pull me in, and kissed me over her shoulder. Only half
of the kiss landed right, the other half draped over my chin, but I
dropped the tacos on the floor, and held on to her. She had a swirl
of fine hairs on her stomach that grew upwards, and when I swept
my hands down her body, they rasped against my palms. Her mouth
unleashed aggressive attacks. The phrase "tongue-lashing" came to
mind. So I matched her, both of us taut and tearing at one another
against the kitchen counter. I nipped at her neck, unzipped her
shorts, and pressed my palm up firmly between her legs. I let
her rock against me.

"Lace?" I asked, when I delicately lowered her underwear.
"You're such a lady."

Whitney pulled me in for what I thought would be something jokey or bitey, but instead was a soft, "I told you to keep your

judgments to yourself." She undid my shorts, and slipped her fingers into me one by one, so I was the one blathering breathy nonsense. We jumped into each other then, sucking, pinning, stroking, finding a quick rhythm, and leisurely separating when we had both finally caught the hazy, outer edge of a drunk orgasm.

.Afterward, we sat on the floor against the cabinets, eating tacos. The hot sauce burned on my tender lips until I smothered them in beans. I turned my bean-covered smile at Whitney, and she immediately did the same. It was just like any other night. I was relieved at first, but then felt the dawn of a terrible gnawing emptiness. Halfway through my second taco I dropped it on the floor, and went to my room. Courtney Love's face glowed softly above me, and I closed my eyes. I was so tired of perpetually stumbling toward each other in a dark alley, never getting closer or farther away.

"Why did you leave?" I heard Whitney ask quietly from the kitchen.

"Because you never let me stay."

"We're both here right now," she said.

But I wasn't sure what we were talking about anymore, and I didn't want to spend the energy to express a sentiment that she'd forget tomorrow. So I said nothing.

"Fine, this a You-leave-it-I-eat-it zone!" she declared.

"Okay," I said. I fell asleep with a picture in my head of Whitney curled up, tenderly eating her brood of tacos on the linoleum floor.

Part 2: Down Shift

It was silent the next morning. I gingerly creaked my way over to the bathroom, hoping not to wake anyone. There were still small piles of grease-splotched paper and shredded lettuce on the kitchen floor. A single taco lay on its side. I thought about cleaning it up, but that would have been hiding something, and neat appearances didn't seem right. The door to Whitney and Logan's room was closed, and their fan whirred softly. "All quiet on the western front," I thought to myself, and decided not to flush. Back in my room, I opened the window, and climbed back into my cot. It would have been a perfectly nice day.

I wanted to talk to Georgie, but I couldn't do that in this apartment. I leaned over the side of the cot to grab my water bottle, and I felt my body creak. I thought this was what it meant to be old, which I knew was absurd. But it was appropriate, I thought, to feel a little roughed up and run over. "So what now?" I asked Courtney Love, who offered the same gung-ho intensity as always. I knew I'd have to get out for a while and sort through my emotions. It wasn't my strong suit. I was always too concerned with how I wanted to feel, and not what was actually living inside me.

Georgie's phone rang twice before she answered it.

"Hi."

"How do you feel about Jesse's farm?" I asked.

"This is so spontaneous. I have to call you back." I pictured Georgie in her white linen nightgown, her skin puckered with dents from the eyelets. She'd be sitting upright in bed, counting the possible obstacles. "Okay," she called back two minutes later. "I'll try to borrow my parents' car. You tell him we're coming. Are we inviting other people?"

"No," I said. "Just you and me."

"Okay." She hung up.

I packed a backpack, grabbed a carrot from the refrigerator, and crept out the door. I called Jesse as soon as I was outside and he answered like Yosemite Sam. "Well, well, well, you two city kids wanna come play with the roughest, toughest gunslinger this side of the Mississippi, eh?"

"The Eastern side. That's what you mean, right?"

"Yeah, what's wrong with that?"

"Nothing. Are you sure it's okay if we visit? I could use a short getaway."

"On the lam, are we?" he asked. "You're lucky I just got some new interns. Otherwise I'd tell you to bring some boots and earn your time. You know how much I hate weeding."

"I'll do it," I offered. I pulled Caliente around the side of the apartment building, and noticed the mattress still caught under Logan's car. I deserved more than weeding. It wasn't like me to leave messes everywhere.

"Nah, I'm only joshing. Just call when you're close. And pick up some beer at the market in town, will you?"

"Done." I whipped down Kenmore and Bryn Mawr over to the Summertowns'. Georgie was already waiting outside in the Prius, her face still puffy with sleep.

"I'm up early on a non-tour day. We're stopping for coffee before you tell me what we're doing," she rasped.

We rode for a long while, drinking our coffees and listening to Radiohead. When we approached the Illinois border I began explaining the rest of the night's activities. George waved her cup at me when I was done. "Okay. And how was it?"

We were headed toward the smelly industrial stretch of Gary, Indiana. Tangles of pipes branched out in endless mazes along the highway.

"It was fine." It hadn't been romantic, really. "It was weird-good?"

Georgie pounced on my ambivalence. "Isn't that how it always is? She remains inaccessible. Nothing is ever settled, and the chase continues forever."

I stiffened. "I resent that oversimplification." I didn't like Whitney just because I couldn't have her. "It's not a game anymore, it's genuine."

Georgie turned down the stereo. "Okay, so let's just say for the hell of it that you and Whitney finally date. It's you instead of Logan. What would that be like? Because I still think, Aneesha, you hold on to this idea that deep inside of Whitney there are reasons for the way she behaves, and you like that open-ended mystery. You hang onto every single puzzle piece like they'll come together to mean something important, and I just don't think they will."

"Well I do," I insisted. "There's something about me and Whitney that's the same. Her 'mystery' is linked to my own—which I know sounds like bullshit—but if we're talking about what's important, it's not just about finding someone to be with. I'm looking for someone to enhance my whole life." Outside the window everything blurred by. "When we're together, the world is an enormous gift we can't possibly ruin. We used to do the most inane things, and the whole time it would feel like I was running through the streets with streams of rainbow light shooting out of my mouth, and my eyes, and my heart."

Georgie kept on driving. I was as surprised as she was to discover such a specific sentiment. "Well," she said eventually. "That's disturbing, but really something."

Off-kilter drumbeats throbbed low on the stereo, and it sounded like rain. I watched as Georgie breezed past the I-94 branch to Michigan. She was not a great navigator, which on a figurative level, made me feel bad about her directing me to this insight.

"We just missed our exit," I said. "You should get off and turn around when you get a chance."

"Maybe you should do the same," she replied, and then broke into laughter. "Get it? That was pretty good, right?"

I was not in the mood. I pointed at the exit coming up ahead.

"Okay, seriously," Georgie said, as she pulled to an eerily silent Prius stop. She made a wide, swooping left to get back on the highway. "What do you want to do with a feeling like that?"

"I wish..." I stopped. I wished I were unafraid of the deep swaths of need and desire running through me. Ignoring my vulnerability clearly didn't make it disappear. I had to imagine myself as a person who expected to receive what she wanted, so I could begin to ask for it.

"Well?" Georgie had her aggressive mom voice on. I pulled a piece of thread from my cutoffs.

"It doesn't have to be so hard, Aneesha. Do the easy thing for yourself."

I was so intertwined with other people that often it felt impossible to separate our fortunes and identify the easy thing for just me. Right here, rolling down the road with Georgie, I had nothing to fear or lament. "That's what we're doing on the farm today. The easy thing." I said. "So I don't have to stand around with Whitney and Logan, and drink coffee, and pretend that everything is normal and regular."

"How telling," Georgie murmured, and rubbed her chin like a detective. We both heard my phone vibrate in my backpack, and she eyed me sharply. "Don't answer that. We're having a nice, easy farm getaway here." Her frown faded and we both laughed.

I knew I had allowed Whitney to linger for too long. For my birthday the past March, she had sent me a cootie-catcher. It was a toy that kids folded out of paper, and wrote improbably good or bad fortunes under each flap. The one Whitney made me was covered in striking close-ups of colorful make-up on models from an art magazine, and under each flap she had written a secret about herself. They ranged from mundane to unexpected, and were told plainly without editorializing. It was a series of rich portraits: that she had once stored her pee in a jar for a week intending to throw it on her friend's ex-boyfriend's car, that she smoked crack for a month, that she watched a *20/20* special on hermaphrodites as a kid, and figured she must have been one.

It broke my heart that Whitney kept this precious collection of stories hidden away as secrets. Together they showed me somebody so vulnerable and impressionable, the side of her I had always been seeking. This was her "gift" to me and it left me torn. "My days are better when you're around, even if I don't know exactly why," read the secret in tiny cramped handwriting that haunted me the most. I didn't know what to do with these pieces of her. She wasn't a manipulator in the traditional sense, and I knew they hadn't been imparted with a direct intention. The cootie-catcher was a masterpiece, and it was hard to resist the belief it inspired—however misguided—that this was Whitney's way of finally, belatedly delivering me her love. The nature of that love was yet to be determined, but it was there all the same.

"I'm assuming we need to stop for beer." Georgie interrupted my thoughts as we entered the town of Three Oaks.

"Oh. Of course." I let the matter rest for now. It was farm time, and I always came to more insightful conclusions after I had escaped my own mind.

The market closest to Jesse's farm was run by a pair of older country folks. They looked hard at me and Georgie as we pushed through the doors, and asked what we were doing in town. Most of the time I feared the baggy-faced white people who blatantly stared at me, but I enjoyed the open address now.

"We're visiting from Chicago," Georgie responded and handed me a few six-packs from the refrigerator.

"I'm sure you know Jesse," I said. "Bearded burly man on Flinner Farms. Drinks a lot of whiskey and Miller."

"Oh, we know him." The man smiled, and bagged our beer.

"Great head of hair," the woman whispered, and winked. She rang us up and suggested we try the round 7-Up cake on the counter.

"Did you make it?" Georgie asked, as she closely examined the spongy confection in its plastic container.

"Don't be silly," the woman chuckled.

But we bought it anyway. It didn't seem like we could go wrong showing up with beer and cake.

The fields were cast in a perfectly golden light as we pulled up beside the barn. Flinner Farms was owned by Jesse's cousin, a successful real estate man who had designed the farm as an aesthetically pleasing place to host fashionable getaways and dinners prepared by guest chefs. It had been featured in *Architectural Digest*.

All the buildings featured galvanized corrugated walls, red trim, and wide glass panels that slid open and shut. But it was also a functioning farm, so within the finely designed walls of the farmhouse, Jesse, an earthy man, to say the least, lived among clods of dirt, piles of greasy dishes, layers of dog hair, and sweat-stiffened clothing. It was all a beautiful illusion.

"Our esteemed guests!" Jesse hollered from the doorway. He and his dog, Gargoyle, came charging at us.

"Oh no, not this, I forgot about this part." Georgie tucked her arms into themselves, and turned sideways.

I ran to meet Jesse halfway up the path, and jumped into his hug. "Man, I was looking forward to that," I told him, when he cracked my back, and set me down again.

"Don't be bashful, Georgie. Get over here." Jesse motioned his hand forward, and she went limp as he gave her a tight hug. "Okay, well, it's less fun when you play dead. But come on in."

We presented Jesse with the cake, and he ate half of it immediately. Then we cracked open beers and took a tour of the fields. They were more bountiful than I remembered. Tomatoes hung like misshapen breasts in fiery colors, crook-necked squash were strewn everywhere like abandoned caveman clubs, beets and kohlrabi burst from the ground, the greens like stiff webbed fingers and their roots the purple red of newborn babies. I had forgotten how much nature had to offer. I kicked off my shoes and felt the grit of dirt on the bottoms of my feet.

"So what do you think?" he asked, throwing his arms open at the land.

As Jesse proudly flashed his dusty-faced grin, it became clear that he and his work were one. He'd invested his life in this place and they were thriving together. I admired him. "Very impressive. You're not a half-bad farmer for a drunk."

Jesse just laughed. "They never tell you that the two go hand in hand. Trade secret."

"Sometimes I can't believe you're in charge of this," Georgie said. She bent down to throw a tennis ball to Gargoyle. "All these plants, and the interns, and the tractor, and the greenhouse, and the chickens."

Jesse waved his arm at her. "Don't talk like that, please, it reminds me of all the worrying I have to do. I've become a dad. I go to bed at night and hope to god that nothing terrible happens to my precious babies while I sleep." He brushed an ant off his hand, and instructed us to pick some vegetables for lunch while he checked in with his interns. I thought of Richard then, of our baby. He wanted what Jesse had: an absolute function, a role determined at the most basic level by necessity. I understood that Richard was restless and impatient because he wanted give all of himself to something.

Georgie rocketed the tennis ball to the other end of the field and turned to me. "Don't you think it's weird that not long ago Jesse was the guy punching holes in walls at rugby parties and hanging out with people who called themselves Meat Stick?"

"The amazing thing," I said, wrestling a beet out of the ground, "is it's still the same guy. I don't think Jesse has time to punch holes in walls right now, but if given the chance, I'm sure he'd like to. And he can also, apparently, teach himself to manage a farm. Same guy."

"That's a pretty big deal. I don't think I could do this." Georgie squinted at me and shook off an onion. "It's like suddenly finding out that your friends are superheroes."

"If your grandparents needed you to manage their farm, you'd do the same," I said to her. "I think we're capable of much more than we attempt." I lifted the beets up and felt their heft. "We're all just a bunch of beets." I smiled cheesily. "Our greatest, meatiest parts, concealed in the ground."

Georgie nodded. "The true beet generation." She laughed, and then stopped and smiled.

"What?" I asked.

"This is fun, and me saying so isn't going to ruin it." She pointed at the green beans and I followed her over to the lattice.

"I know I'd be bored in a week, but it's so alluring to live like this. I'm kind of jealous of Jesse," I said. I took off my outer denim shirt, and laid it on the ground to collect the green beans.

"Aneesha, you'd be out of here in an instant. You'd be the only non-white person around, nobody would care about your outfits, and you'd have to explain to the people at the country store why you're still not married. Plus, nobody would want to discuss Internet matters with you."

"I'd have to Facetime every day, and write a blog about my Internet isolation." I laughed. "But maybe I wouldn't." I started to imagine the jeans I'd wear on a daily farming basis. They'd stretch just enough, but not so much as to expose my butt-crack, and wear out well, so as to properly linger sweat-stiffened in my image on the floor.

Georgie threw a handful of beans down and put her hand on her hip. "Aneesha, what is your deal?"

"What?" I asked.

"How can you not know the baseline of things you need? At this age, your persistent wondering is hard not to take as either reckless or stupid." She bent down and tied my shirt into a knotted bundle.

I stared at her. I wasn't shocked, exactly, but this was what we did: try on scenarios together and imagine our way through them. "Georgie, I'm not going to go live on a farm. I was just remarking on some of the positive qualities in Jesse's life. They need not be obtained solely in a pastoral setting. But can't you imagine a situation in which you'd be perfectly happy on a farm? You'd be a hip mom who is overly involved at community events, where nobody trusts you because of your city roots, and you'd write a lot of famous poetry like your mentor, the hermitess, Louise Glück."

Georgie turned and we started back to the farmhouse. "Okay. All true. But not you." She paused to look at me. "You could be a real writer, you know. If you really tried. Everyone relates to you. You're this chubby, ethnically ambiguous dyke with a mean diva streak, and somehow you share a common thread with everyone." She shifted the shirt knot of beans in her hands, and watched her feet. "You know, I used to be jealous of that. The way you swoop in, and everyone—including friends I've known my whole life—are instantly connected to you. People like you, they root for you, they trust you to understand them, and you do."

This part surprised me, and I suddenly wanted to cry. I looked at the sky, hoping any loose tears might fall back into my nasal passage.

"It's terrifying."

"Well, it's true. So, no, you can't go hide away on a farm. You have to put the kibosh on the bullshit—the wide array of bullshit that colors your life—and focus on the good stuff."

Of course I knew she was right, and it felt good to hear it, but putting the kibosh on anything was not my specialty. I nodded. "How come you and Louise get to run away?"

"Because people like the idea of me much better than the real thing. I'm only good in short spurts. It's true. I'm usually uncomfortable and generally not fun." Georgie held up her hand to stop me before I could tell her she was wrong. "It works for my poetry."

We stepped through the sliding glass door to the spacious kitchen. Jesse had popped open new beers for us, and was sliding a pudgy loaf of dough into the oven. "You guys are going to love this sourdough," he said. "I got the starter from my neighbor by trading him some weed plants—shhh, don't tell. Then we can put together a salad and make some grilled cheeses, that sound okay?"

In his element there was no evidence of the crazed imbalance, the nearness to the edge I was so used to associating with Jesse. It was soothing to watch his routine around the messy kitchen. I had to assume that some of the wildness was an act he put on for his visits, so we could all laugh and feel familiar. Or maybe that's how he really did feel when he was back in town. It was becoming clear that's how Chicago was for me. When confronted with all of people I had been and could still be, it was hard to deny any of them, to let any of them go. I thought about what Georgie had just said and, as we sat down to enjoy our lunch, I knew that I would have to.

⌇

Back in town I tried to make a lot of noise coming up the steps. I was struck with a tense fear that Whitney and Logan wouldn't be home, and then that they would. The light was on in the kitchen, and the floor shone brilliantly. The taco mess had been erased. In the living room Whitney and Logan were sitting close on the couch, finishing up their sushi takeout. They looked like they had been kissing, and I was definitely intruding.

Logan noticed me hovering in the kitchen door. "Where have you been all day?" he asked. "I thought maybe you'd never made it home, but Whit said you did."

"Yeah. We both passed out," she confirmed.

Whitney wasn't wearing any make-up, and the skin around her eyes reminded me of worms, so soft, pale, and vulnerable. Despite my tender thoughts earlier that day, I felt a loathing for her. She was perfectly content with the two of us pretending that we had not done anything out of the ordinary. I knew we would not talk about it, and if we did, it would be evasive and easy, nothing truthful. Whitney was the one with something to lose, yet she could sit so smugly with Logan's arm around her and blithely eat sushi, no blip, no tension, nothing. In college, Georgie and I had seen a documentary about young girls born into prostitution in India, and the madam, explaining that there were no circumstances in which the girls could skip out of work, had used the phrase, "no grandmas, no dead bodies, nothing." It was so heartless and extreme. That was how Whitney looked to me now. I knew the madam parallel was extreme in its own right, but it felt good to allow myself that disgust.

"I'm half the party responsible for the mattress under your car and the taco disaster in the kitchen," I reported. "I'm really, very sorry."

Whitney chuckled. "But it was pretty funny."

"It was definitely a surprise," Logan said. The way he spoke— the breathy exasperation—I could tell he'd been angry earlier. I recognized the resignation with which one accepted a Whitney non-apology. "And the tacos, whatever, that happens around here all the time."

"Just let me know if I can do anything." I took off my backpack, and headed toward the door to my room.

"Don't worry about it, Aneesha," Logan protested. "You're our guest, and if Whitney decides to run over a mattress, I'm sorry you have to witness that."

"Yep, you're blame-free, Neesh. It's all on this horrible night-ruiner."

I stopped to revaluate the scene. Whitney was pointing at herself, eyes wide, head wagging. I recognized that she was pissed off and annoyed.

Logan shook his head. "No, babe, you were just excited because Aneesha's here and the two of you are having a lot of fun." He turned to me. "I'm the one who's sorry I didn't drive you two home. I'm really glad nothing worse happened."

So this was his tactic, I thought. He was going to trivialize me by invoking my status as a guest. I wasn't jealous of Logan. Whatever made him more attractive to Whitney wasn't something that I wanted. His current position with Whitney was one I had intentionally avoided all along. Now Logan was going on about how he had failed me as a friend, with his arm around Whitney like it was an agreement they'd made. As if that's what it meant to be in a relationship: to tell the other person how they felt and why.

But then, I thought, so much of dating was a mutually agreed upon delusion that you fed to each other. I reached for my door. If that's what Whitney wanted it was hers.

"Wait, but where did you go?" she asked.

I turned around. "Jesse's farm. To refresh."

"Oh, that must have been pretty. And very relaxing." She pointed to the chair adjacent to the coffee table. "There's more sushi than we can eat. Help us out."

I didn't move.

"Did you text that girl from yesterday?" Logan asked me. "You should."

Whitney's eyes narrowed for a moment. "Aneesha has her own weird way with girls, she's fine."

I was covered in a thin film of sweat and dust, with my backpack dangling from the crook of my arm. The day had given me a lot to consider, and my weird way with girls wasn't one that seemed important right now. I watched Logan's delicate fingers as he lifted a piece of salmon nigiri and held it in front of Whitney's mouth. Her lips and the fish displayed the same limp apathy. She opened her mouth and slowly chewed.

The Whitney I knew did not want sushi hand-fed to her. She

didn't get corralled into making half-assed apologies or living with
bookshelves made from half a canoe, and on Sunday evenings she
was passed out in bed or still drinking. I missed her spunk, her fight,
the way she did what she wanted because she didn't know or care to
do otherwise. When I first met her, Whitney had a habit of slicing
avocados in half the short way around, and even though Whitney
had been working in restaurants for years, she was shocked and
confused when I came over to make guacamole, and cut an avocado
the long way. Whitney's method was always good enough for
Whitney, and that was my favorite quality of hers. This Whitney
sitting in front of me, however, had given up on herself and I didn't
know why. Though Georgie had now put in my head that this was
all just my own idea of Whitney, one that didn't really exist. It was
all too much to sift through.

Logan was still going. "So did you text her or what? She's hot,
and clearly into you."

"Not yet." I put my backpack over one shoulder. "Hey Whit,
we should go check out that new pizza place over by the train
this week."

She knew what I wanted from her. "I thought you might want
to. I'm not sure it'll be any good."

"You know I want to try it."

"Of course you do," she sighed.

"You want to do it all together?" Logan asked.

I stared at him hard. "Not really, no." He couldn't tell whether I
was being serious or not, but he pulled away from Whitney a little.

She shifted out from under his arm, and got up from the couch.
"I'll figure out my work schedule and let you know."

"Well, I'll clean up. You can look right now. I'll be back on
Friday." Logan began stacking plates. His controlling behavior was
quickly eroding my empathy for him.

I looked past him at Whitney standing in the doorway of the
bathroom with a piece of floss dangling in her hand. It was caught
on the hem of her soccer shorts and she struggled to pull it free. The
day had reached a point when she needed someone to excuse her
from regular bedtime routines, to toss off her shorts and roll her into

bed. I disliked myself for being this attentive to her.

Logan passed between us carrying a ridiculously high stack of plates, cups and containers. "Look, I'm all out of your way," he announced.

But whoever this Whitney was, I didn't know how to abandon her entirely. "I'm headed straight to bed," I said loudly. "Plaque-filled, greasy and dusty, just like this." Though of course I never did that.

Whitney's face lit up, and she tossed the floss on the floor. "Me too." She shrugged like a self-important celebrity. "That's my style."

We shared a smile, and Whitney strutted off to her room.

"And now begins the plot to reinvent the heroine," I said to Courtney Love, as I waited in my cot for a good time to use the bathroom. "May she be bold and fearless, may she have zero traces of her previous flaws, and may she emerge from her cocoon with confident wings."

Heading Out To Space

After the Halloween party, I didn't have to wait long to see Whitney again. I had started doing work at a coffee shop down the street from me, a place called Stella. It was by no means hip. The awkward baristas had several Incubus playlists on repeat and the older crowd seemed to prefer the saggy couches in the back that were loaded with chenille blankets. This meant I didn't have to fight to get a table, and I never bothered to check my appearance before I left my building.

It was with some surprise that I sat down one day and noticed, that to my right, Whitney was also sitting at a table, staring blankly into her computer screen.

"Hey, don't I know you from somewhere?" I asked her. "From on top of a cheeseburger maybe?"

"Oh hello, Beef Stew. You're a Stella worker too."

We decided to share a table and instead of doing work, we talked about how Whitney had just started watching *The L Word* for the first time and google-image searched the new backpacks that we wanted. I realized I was already in over my head when Whitney lifted part of her sailboat-printed shirt to show me her tattoo. It seemed like the most natural thing in the world. It was on her right side, just below her ribcage. The tattoo was a kid-like drawing of a flying saucer with stick figure versions of her and her best friend waving from inside the little bulb on top. I knew which one was Whitney because of the corkscrew curls of her hair.

"Do you often vacation in space?" I asked her.

"Oh yes," she replied. "On long weekends. You should check it out, it's really dark. I'm studying to become a CPA, so I can live there."

"In the darkness?" I laughed. I had never known anyone who wanted to be an accountant before. Not anyone I wanted to know anyway. I had certainly not expected that person to have a cool tattoo.

"Yes," she said solemnly.

"I hear CPAs have enough money for things like that," I said.

"Don't they say that about computer people too?" she asked, and motioned to the CMS form that was open on my screen.

"They say that about the people who make computers do things. I just fill the boxes with inane strings of words that might make someone buy something. I'm a writer. I will never be going to space."

"You never know. But I doubt you'll be missing anything," she said. Our eyes met briefly over the tops of our laptops, and I needed to excuse myself to go to the bathroom.

Inside the tiny room I stared hard at myself in the mirror. My eyes were a little baggy, and some eyeliner was gobbed in the corners. I pulled at the stick-up hair on the side of my head, evaluating how long I had before another cut. When I peed it smelled like caffeine.

"This is really nice," I said aloud. It echoed off the porcelain of the sink, and the tiles on the floor. Until quite recently, I'd had a girlfriend who loved me. That was what I left behind when I said yes to Georgie and moving to Chicago. It wasn't without certain sharp regrets that occupied many pre-dawn hours, but I had read a line in a Wells Tower story that resonated heavily with me. It was about a teenage girl who was getting dropped off at home by a skeezy older boy, and the feeling she had when they pulled up to her house to find her dad, in his saggy socks and ugly t-shirt, watering the lawn, and waving idiotically at her. "The wordless, exposed sensation over-whelming her was that her father wasn't quite a person, not really, but a private part of her, a curse of pinkness and squatness and cure-less vulnerability that was Jaycee's right alone to keep hidden from the world." Which was not to say my ex-girlfriend wasn't capable of handling herself. I was the one who didn't know how to stop going out and watering the lawn in my saggy socks, and I didn't want to be responsible for that being a private part of anyone. What I wanted was for someone to join me out there—heedless and silly, flawed and exposed. Whitney seemed like the right candidate for that.

"I'm going to give you my phone number," Whitney said, as we were leaving Stella. "I don't really have friends, but I was planning to go see that monster puppet movie, the one with a Karen O soundtrack. If you want to go."

I was sure she had friends, and I wondered what kind they were.

"The monster puppets, I know what you mean." I had been meaning
to see the movie too, even if I was tired of the particular brand of
hipster culture behind it. "Definitely let me know if you go," I said,
and I gave her my number too.

A few days later I went to the grocery store to buy ingredients
for chicken soup.

In the produce section there were only plastic bagged bundles
of celery. I wanted the ones with leaves that came in small bunches
so I wouldn't have to buy an entire pound. I was hunched glumly,
looking at the brightly lit displays when Whitney touched me gently
on the arm.

"Hey, it's you."

"And it's you," I said. Her flouncy head was right in front of me.
"What are you doing here?" It was a stupid question I always asked
whenever the answer was obvious.

"Good question," she replied, to my relief. "I'm here to buy flowers.
I don't know if you know Sally, she's this girl with a million
boy problems, but they seem bad this time. Like she might need
some flowers."

"That's extraordinarily friendly of you."

"I make an effort once in a while. What's in your basket?"

"Can't find the right kind of celery," I reported. "I'll just have
to ruin this nice plastic bundle." I removed a few stalks from a sleek
pack and placed them in the bottom of my basket.

"They look lonely," she said, and tossed in a couple of carrots.
"There." I chuckled.

"So I haven't seen that movie yet, but I'm hoping this week,
maybe tonight. You free?" she shifted her basket over to one arm.

"Oh no, very busy making chicken soup. Just kidding, text me
or something."

Her eyes were bright and pinched in the right places when she
smiled and waved goodbye. Digging through the mountain of red
potatoes, I had the sense that each one was the perfect size.

⤴

After the excitement of the weekend, I decided to keep my head down and stick to my writing. I was determined to sit by the kitchen window at Metropolis everyday until I had a new draft of Gloria's ocean encounter. I was getting closer. There were ghosts circling Gloria's ankles, ghosts from the past that wouldn't let her go. When I arrived at the ending, I changed it so that the man, who avoided the ocean for the whole story, finally went in after her.

"Don't let them!" cried the familiar voice of the man. *"You don't belong to them!"* But Gloria was slipping. I wrote slowly, calibrating each word, and then rereading it with skepticism. This was my incredibly slow process. *As she hung beneath the surface, she noticed a churning tornado of ghostly bodies at his ankles too. She knew now they would sink together.*

I looked out the coffee shop window at the moms with strollers, and the men in sweatpants who looked to be on the way to the liquor store. "She knew now, they would sink together," I said to myself. It was a condemnation, simple and true, but it pulled the heart in only one direction. There was something hopeful and neutralizing in their togetherness that I needed to coax out. I tried again: *They would sink together into the belly of the ocean. She knew now there was nowhere else for them to go.*

I let the bright sparkle of the of save button wash over me and closed my computer. It was fine for now. My stories were frequently about doom and different ways to approach one's darkly tinted fate. So the art of each individual story was striking the right combination of notes when the doom hit. I spent hours this way, on doom orchestration. It couldn't have been a coincidence that I saw myself in the same light, always expecting to be struck down.

"You've been working hard," Georgie said proudly when she met me for beer at the Heartland.

"How do you know?" I asked.

"Because you're all quiet and serious, and you have bags," she said. "Your glasses hide them well, but when you're working hard, you're like...a depleted teat." Her eyes narrowed, analyzing the effectiveness of this comparison.

"Thank you, I'm a depleted teat. Floppy, pitiful, not even

aesthetically pleasing. My brain's been milked." I had a tendency to become numb to the world if left alone too long, and Georgie was the perfect antidote.

"Do you remember that time in India?" Georgie asked.

She was talking about the time we'd stayed at a girls' college dormitory in Delhi for a few weeks, and every morning, when we sat outside with our tea and plates of lentils, an old, scrawny cat would wander over and nurse several other scrawny cats of its same size. It was like the last scene in *The Grapes of Wrath*, except in India with cats. "I guess it's breakfast time for everyone," Georgie had said, which threw the desperate nature of the scene into a slightly less depressing light.

"Isn't it cool that famous writers are like that cat to the rest of society?" she asked.

"Robert Pinksy getting milked," I said.

"Robert Pinksy's depleated teat," she said, and we broke into laughter. Youngsu was behind the bar, and he brought me a Honkers. "I heard you had a weekend." He waved his eyebrows up and down.

I looked at Georgie. "Did he?"

"He's talking about you and the girl at Danny's," she clarified. "Your tutor friend."

"Tutor Crush," I corrected her. I had been trying to figure out what I should say to Zoe. Despite my rude exit at Danny's, I had promised myself not to repeat the Elena and The Ancient Shark mistake.

"So have you seen her or are you not into it?" Youngsu asked.

"I haven't seen her," I said. But every time I sat down in Metropolis, I was tickled by the possibility that she might happen in. "I hope I see her again."

Georgie looked at me with wide eyes and then back at Youngsu. "What?" I asked.

"I owe Youngsu a dollar," Georgie reported.

"You were testing the waters," he said. "It's a sly move."

"Yep," I said playing along with him. "First you flirt with girls senselessly, then you make out with them to see if they like you, and then you turn them down for sex. It's very straightforward, and makes them feel great about themselves."

Youngsu had turned his eyes to the ceiling to thoughtfully consider this strategy. "I'm being sarcastic," I told him. "I have no idea what I'm doing."

"Huh, okay. Well, you owe me two dollars," he said, slapping the bar.

"What for?" I asked. "What did Georgie bet you anyway?"

"For the Honkers. Have you not heard that the Heartland is in decline?" He shook his head. "You're a paying customer, aren't you, Aneesha?"

There was a group of customers, primarily middle-aged men and women with off personalities, who were not paying customers, and who were at risk of being banned from the bar at any time, though this didn't usually happen unless they acted up. I was a little irked. In the past, my actual tab rarely added up to more than $7. I paid the rest of what I owed directly to my bartender as tip, and I thought we'd all benefited nicely from this exchange.

"Thomas is all over us," Youngsu whispered. "If we get caught giving away free drinks, we'll probably get fired."

"Well, there goes the allure of this bar," Georgie murmured.

"Maybe it's a sign, huh?"

"Hey," Youngsu warned her.

"Tell me the bet," I cut in.

"Oh," Georgie paused. "I just thought you might be off the girl train for a bit. In light of what I thought was an insightful and productive day at the farm."

"I'm not looking for trouble," I said. I wasn't sure where Zoe stood on the trouble scale or what stood opposite of trouble on said scale. Goldenness? Promise? I told them we had exchanged some boring texts about the errands we were running and the stupid things we'd seen people do in public, but nothing all that personal.

"You're still in," Ben swooped over to add. "You're in touch with her daily habits."

Sam came over to pick up drinks for his table and joined in too. "If you know she's into you, Aneesha, you need to do something kind of embarrassing. Let her think your guard is down, so that you're both on the same level."

"Thanks, you guys, but I can handle this. I'll just hang out with her and see what's up," I said.

"I'm feeling generous," said Georgie. "I'll allow you to invite Tutor Crush to Iowa even if it's all part of some elaborate tease of hers."

"Well thanks, Georgie," I said. "I'm glad to know that your generosity extends all the way to my stupid mistakes."

She lifted an eyebrow, and finished her beer. "You know I love being on the cutting edge of gossip. By the way," she added to the boys at the bar, "second week in August is our date for the farm. So let me know soon if you can come. We need to figure out our sleeping configuration."

"Can't we figure that out there?" Sam asked.

Youngsu just looked at Sam, and continued to place beers on his tray.

"To quote our very own Georgina Summertown, 'a good host leaves nothing to chance,'" I said, and folded my hands.

"And a good guest knows the tenets of good hosting," Georgie said, patting me on the shoulder.

We grudgingly paid our tab with a big show and went out for our bikes. Georgie and I were meeting people at our friend Arthur's for pizza and drinking.

I snapped on my helmet. "Georgie, I hope you know that the farm day was enlightening. I am putting the kibosh on things, I'm just also trying to take advantage of an opportunity with a smart, fun girl. Do you think that's stupid?" I asked.

"Honestly, if you're intent on giving Whitney the heave-ho, it's probably not bad to focus on somebody else. I just can't shake the feeling that we've been through this before. Didn't you leave this exact situation at school with Severine?" We got on our bikes, and I rode ahead of Georgie while she continued. "It ends with you being her friend, having many repressed feelings about it, and becoming essentially unavailable to anybody else because you're so sad."

"Well, yeah, but it's me." I slowed so she was right beside me. "My life is a set series of loops that repeat over and over, sometimes in new locations, sometimes in the exact same place. I'm trying to at least bend them a little, you know?"

"So where are you on the Whitney loop?" she asked.

"Kibosh on it," I said. "I can't do that again, and neither of us has any reason to tell Logan."

"Okay." She nodded. Georgie didn't need details and I liked that. "I guess that's a decent place to be."

Our friend Arthur lived at the top of a stately apartment building on Kenmore. Everything in his life was classic and stylish, from the knit ties he wore when he played in his swing jazz band, to the cream-colored Volvo station wagon that he spun around town in. I thought of him like a character in a book, a man Gatsby would have wished to be, whose story, though not without twists, reliably ended well. I liked Arthur because he was always having a good time. I also appreciated that his idea of a good time included lots of ambitious projects, like teaching himself to build motorcycles.

"It's because he has ADD," Georgie's older brother—who was friends with Arthur in high school—had dismissively reasoned. "Arthur wasn't always the belle of the ball, you know. He was a huge spaz for years." But that only made me like Arthur better.

"We anxiously await your arrival on the 4th floor," his voice buzzed at us through the intercom. "The pizzas are hot, the drinks are cold, the company is fine."

"I'll bet it is." Georgie elbowed me and chuckled.

Arthur had been living with his extremely elegant roommate, Frederica, for about six months, and was crazy about her. She had finally broken up with her serious banker boyfriend in New York, and there was now a good chance that something would develop between them.

"You have to buddy up with Freddie and get the dirt from her," I said. "Do that thing where you say nothing and then people reveal their secrets."

"That's your thing," Georgie said. "I'm the one who asks invasive questions."

"Okay fine, we'll have to work in tandem."

Georgie and I were intrigued by the recklessness and inherent ruin of dating a roommate, but if anybody could pull it off, it was

Arthur, and I was rooting for him.

Upstairs we were met with a funky soul record and a group of Arthur's friends: tall bearded men and bespectacled women, who drank brown liquors neat, and had last names for first names, like Egan, and Ward, and Lynch.

Upon our arrival Arthur danced a little jig with his wiry legs, then ushered us over to the bar in the corner of the living room. "Tequila to get us started."

"Oh, no," Georgie refused. "I don't do shots."

"It's good stuff," Arthur said, perching a lime on our glasses.

"It's for enjoying, not shooting," I added.

Arthur put his arm around my shoulders. "Aneesha knows."

Georgie poured hers into mine. "Can I begin with a High Life and work up to this?"

Arthur laughed, and returned with a beer from the fridge. "Can we toast to how maniacally gleeful I feel all the time?" He shot a careful look around the room to locate Freddie. "We kissed," he hissed at us. "It was," he leaned against the wall with his legs crossed, and adjusted his rolled-up shirt-sleeves, "a conservative, measured affair. We have no room for mistakes. But," he leaned in close again, "she slept in my bed!"

I held my glass up. "To Freddie in your bed," I whispered. "Way to move in quick," Georgie seconded.

We clinked glasses, and then whisked around the apartment to chat with everyone. I got Miles, the bass player in Arthur's band, to let me try on his special heeled sneaker. His right leg was two inches shorter than his left, and I'd always wanted to wear the extra padded shoe. When I hobbled past the kitchen, Freddie was pulling her homemade pizzas out of the oven. "Oh, you'll like this one, Aneesha," she said, tugging me into the kitchen by my elbow. "Lemon and smoked mozzarella. I just made it up."

Freddie's perfect face was ever-so lightly freckled, and I was surprised by the open grin she wore. Normally, she was a reserved mysterious woman who wore scarves like she was French, and rarely expressed her opinions with words, but tonight she was glowing. "Come on, try it," she said, handing me a sliver.

I did as I was told, and was delighted by the sweet and bitter tang of burnt lemon against the richness of smoked cheese. "Freddie. That's fucking delicious. How are you so good at everything?"

"Trader Joe's. Plus I've been in a good mood. He told you, right?" she smiled. "Of course he did. If I didn't know better I'd think he has a crush on you."

"It's of a brotherly nature," I assured her.

"He is such a gentleman. It makes me feel like a teenager again, it's so stupid." Freddie tucked her hair behind her ear, and looked bashfully away. I was warmed by the tequila, and the infectious excitement that was swirling around their apartment. If Arthur could manage a woman like Freddie, I thought there might be hope for me yet. I was aware that I wasn't an Arthur, that I'd have to work up to it. In the way of Georgie and the tequila, I thought, as I watched her tip up the bottle and declare herself ready for another.

"Stupid is the best," I said, taking Freddie's arm. "Come on, we have to share this pizza masterpiece so you can contaminate every-one with the beautiful taste of your love disease."

"Well, thanks, Aneesha, but nobody is saying love," she cautioned me.

"I'm just being figurative," I said. "It's new, it's fun, along the lines of springtime, and balloons, and fresh battery packs."

"Sure," Freddie hesitantly agreed, "all of those things."

After pizza, we went out to drink on the roof of the apartment building. "Isn't it so wonderful to stand above everything else, and feel close to the stars, and so far from reality?" was what Georgie was saying.

I was thinking it was sort of sad to have this sentiment at the top of an apartment building instead of say, a mountain. My thoughts drifted to Zoe and I wondered what she was doing. I imagined her in a pair of little shorts, her hair in a messy bun, drinking a beer and doing a crossword puzzle. That sounded really attractive right then. I pulled out my phone to tell her that I was at the top of an apartment building not far from where she lived, and that maybe if she stuck her head out the window and I yelled, she would hear it.

As I sent the text, I heard a cluster of voices from below, and

I looked down to see my friends trailing toward our party, like little ants. This was the benefit of the building over the mountain, I thought, that your friends could still happen by.

"Oh look, all your other halves are here," Arthur said, turning to me and Georgie. "And I bet they've brought beverages."

It was exactly how I thought of our friends. He and I exchanged glances then raced inside to harass them through the intercom.

"I don't recognize those names," Arthur said, after they'd identified themselves. "You may have the wrong building. Do you know these people?" he asked me.

"They'll need to present us with the password, don't you think?" I asked.

"It's Insane Clown Posse, your favorite band," Heather answered tartly.

"Ouch," I said.

"Just let us in!" I heard Amanda yell.

"The pleasure of your company is requested on the fourth floor, please." Heather had brought Remi, Whitney and Logan sashayed in next, and Amanda, Sam and Youngsu followed behind with a case of beer each. "We wanted to show that we're good guests who know the tenets of good hosting," Youngsu responded when Georgie asked what they were thinking.

"I was asking for it," she said.

"Don't underestimate the power of a beer surplus," Arthur said, as he rearranged things in the refrigerator. "It offers a sense of security, which in turn inspires dance."

By then, most of Arthur's original friends had started to thin out. I assumed they had real jobs that required sharpness of mind or at least adherence to previously laid plans. Arthur convinced some of them to stay, and for a while we slid across the apartment as he and Freddie selected records. I was known for my "fancy footwork," which was just a series of tiny hops back and forth, front and back, heel to toe. I thought of it as rhythmic running in place. All the same, it impressed my friends and it led to group dancing impressions of each other. Remi was particularly good at Amanda's show-tune-style hand gestures paired with little kicks, and it made me love him. He already had an elegant face, and a manner of speaking which assumed nothing yet implied complicity all the same.

"He's perfect," I said to Heather in what was surely a non-private volume of voice. She could finally drink again and we were in the kitchen refreshing her gin and tonic. I took a moment to rest my head on her shoulder. "He's just big enough, but still so perfectly small."

"Right? Check out my hot boyfriend," Heather said proudly. "I don't usually get to say that and mean it."

"He's so sweet and has such good style," Whitney joined in. "Look at those pocket flaps." She elbowed me and smiled. "Don't you want those shorts, Neesh?"

"I think I might have some like those," Logan said, gliding in beside us.

"I think I'll borrow them," said Whitney.

"Excuse me, ahem!" Georgie had quit dancing, and now stepped into the middle of the room. She motioned for the music to be turned down, and we all stood around waiting to see what was coming. "Earlier this evening I was in opposition to this tequila that Arthur was proffering, but now that I've had some—" she nodded her head "—I have to recommend it." Georgie took a long sip and tilted her head to the side, trying to remember the reason for this speech. "You are so beautiful, such beautiful people," she mused. Then, as if it had come back to her, Georgie adjusted her skirt, and stood up taller. "I'm really glad to have all of you as friends. You all mean so much to me. So I want to share with you my most favorite place on earth, the Summertown Farm, for a summer getaway you won't soon forget. Cheers!"

With that Georgie raised her glass again, and slowly made her way over to where I stood in the doorway. I was a little surprised she'd decided to make the trip happen, and I figured she had to be wasted to want to announce it so publically. This was confirmed when she petted my head and looked at Whitney. "Let's forget the past. I hope you come up. And Heather, bring your boyfriend. He's adorable." She spoke in her formal host voice and flounced away.

"What was that about?" Logan asked me.

"Georgie's been 'neutral' about me forever," Whitney answered. "She didn't invite me to Iowa last year."

"Maybe less neutral now," I said. "I think she wants to be friends."

"Now?" Whitney eyed me skeptically. "Well, I guess she is drunk."

Whitney set her drink down, and a flash of self-doubt crossed her face, as she watched Georgie weave her way through the room. It had never occurred to me that Georgie could be an intimidating character, but she was tall, and sure of herself, and there was a sharp hawk-like quality to her face. Even though I was exasperated with Whitney, it didn't seem fair that she should be left out because she didn't like me enough. That was absurd.

"Hey," I said to her and Logan. "It'll be fun if you come. I can even bargain with the hostess to make sure you get a good bedroom." I turned sorrowfully to Heather. "I'm guessing we won't be sharing a tent this year."

"Remi could always sleep on a couch," Heather said. "Our tent is such a party tent, we wouldn't want to give that up."

"Party tent does sound fun," Whitney agreed. "Tell me the dates when I'm at my computer, and we'll come up for a weekend," she said. Whatever passed between us, Whitney never held grudges or gave me the cold shoulder. She was always incredibly generous. Suddenly, in the glow of this party, the fear I'd felt upon my arrival began to lift. We were all so close already, so intertwined, and used to giving our best to each other. I felt flexible, like I could still manage to hold us together. I was thinking that I was becoming as sentimental as Richard, when he made his entrance.

"Is this where you hooligans have been hiding out the whole night?" I heard a door close loudly, and Richard appeared in the hallway walking loosely, and wearing a short-brimmed hat. "I've been calling you like crazy. I had to follow some people in like a vagrant." He came over to the doorway and inched between me and Heather. "Give me some time with the ladies," he said, gesturing at Logan to leave us.

"What the hell, Richard?" I admonished him.

"I don't want to be here anyway." Logan put his hand on my shoulder, and ducked back into the living room.

Richard was swaying side to side, which wasn't characteristic of him. Certainly he had some lush habits, but he never acted like a drunk in the stereotypical manner. He was generally more unwavering and fluid while brimming with booze, even if he was walking steadily into a glass door.

"What happened to you?" I asked, primarily out of disgust for his tactless behavior.

"What happened to me is." He paused and glanced around the counters, looking for a drink.

Whitney swiftly removed a beer from the refrigerator. "Not that you especially need it," she said under her breath, which I found poignant coming from her.

He opened the beer and took a sip that left a shiny stripe on his upper lip. "I am officially free of Karen," he said. "She and I are no longer. Yours truly will no longer be required to sneak away from wholesome friend gatherings like these to cab over to a white shag-carpeted condo with a beautiful view of the lake, that we will never ever share with anyone else. The future is all mine now. How fortunate that we're already celebrating," he said, and grabbed Heather's hand. "Come on, H, let's dance."

"This seems like a big deal," Heather was saying as she was dragged away. "Well, that's a disaster," Whitney said to me. Richard had a sharp intensity in his eyes, and was shaking his hips back and forth like Shakira. "Look, oh look, at Heather's face," Whitney said, and we broke out into hysterical giggles.

"I don't know how you're friends with that asshole," Logan came back to remark.

"Friends is a loose term," I said. "He's more like a third arm."

"You should be ashamed to spend time with him."

"I am," I said, which made Whitney smile.

"And yet..." Logan pushed.

Logan was so straightforward that it shouldn't have surprised me he had little tolerance for what I knew to be the inherent good and bad in everyone. I figured all queers could understand duality, and the vacillation between spaces that seemed in opposition but were actually part of the same whole. Logan's eyebrows, however, remained knit in an indignant V over his glasses.

"You're right, Richard is an asshole. I'm sorry he was a dick to you. But my own personal friendship is in not reserved for the morally immaculate," I said to Logan.

"You would find a way to say something defensive and self-important about a drunk man behaving badly."

I laughed because it was true. "That is very me," I said. I found it refreshing that he was being honest with me, and I was starting to get the warm fuzzies again.

"Oh, but now it's getting creepy," Whitney said.

I looked over, and Richard was shimmying low to the floor with his face far too near the vicinity of Heather's crotch. She pushed his shoulder, tipping him backwards, and walked away.

"Come on, Heather," Richard was calling from his prone position on the floor. "You know I was joking!"

Remi walked over to give Richard a hand up. "The choreography wasn't bad, but maybe the style can be improved," he said with a wink.

Richard was laughing. "We have learned a hard lesson here today." He clapped Remi on the back and introduced himself.

"Oh, Richard," Remi said, delighted. "I've heard so much about you. I'm Remi, Heather's boyfriend."

I watched the cheer drain from Richard's face. Even he had been a huge fan of Remi for a short while. There was a tough lull before his drunk self was able to recover, and I was afraid that he was going to say something that I'd regret on his behalf—which I supposed was exactly what Logan meant. I could feel a breeze coming in from the roof so I left Logan to make whatever judgments he wanted.

Outside, Georgie was smoking a cigarette with her arms crossed while Youngsu gesticulated wildly to her and Heather. Amanda had her camera out, and I walked over to the far corner where she was taking long exposures. The entire length of the roof was wide open, and covered in a sun-warmed layer of black tar that muted conversation.

"Do you think my photography is journalism or art?" she asked.

"Both," I said. "Isn't that the point?"

"Sam doesn't think it's art," she huffed. The shutter closed and she changed a few settings.

"Well, that's certainly debatable." My first job out of college had been taking school photos for a portrait studio. The task was to homogenize every single person with the same hot lights and gendered poses to insinuate whiteness and prosperity. It was the opposite of anything Amanda did. I'd noticed the way she unassumingly entered spaces, and there was a surprising intimacy to her shots. "I don't think you're an avant-garde photographer, but I think your photos have a lot to say."

"Thanks." Amanda leaned back, and tossed her long hair to the side. It was a running joke that in real life Amanda aggressively tackled all manner of challenges, but in photographs she transformed into a delicate supermodel. For a moment, that's how she looked now. "Whatever. I don't need to be an artist. I just want to see if I can cut it as another kind of photographer. All of the people in higher positions at the newspaper are men, and they're not giving up their positions to me anytime soon." She shrugged. "I'm applying to some things, we'll see what I get."

"You're bound to get something," I said. "You've shot a Bears game with John Cusack."

"And he even held my hand," she said. "Don't forget that part."

We laughed and sauntered over to the group, where Georgie offered me some of her cigarette. "Youngsu is telling his tequila Alaska story to make Heather laugh," she explained. I took a drag, and leaned up against the wall beside Heather. I loved this story. It was about how Youngsu, though manly enough to fish for salmon on a commercial boat, was not able to hold his tequila as well as his fellow fishermen. At the end of fishing season, he got kicked off his flight home, and spent his first night off the boat on the floor of a Juneau jail cell. It started so high and fell so low—a trajectory that I really loved.

"So imagine that I'm on the plane, my head wobbling all over the place. I really can't control myself at all," Youngsu explained. "The next thing I hear over the PA system is that there is some passenger on the plane who is 'unfit' to fly."

I saw a figure at the door to the roof, and then Arthur was leaning against the wall next to me. He listened to Youngsu for a moment then whispered into the top of my head. "We've got a little situation. With our own unfit passenger." He raised his eyebrows and smiled. "Can I?" he asked, and I gave him the rest of Georgie's cigarette. "I've had some bad nights myself, and this is mostly entertaining, but it's starting to grate on Freddie," he whispered.

Youngsu was at the part of his story where the police escorted him off the plane, and he immediately ran to a trashcan at the gate, and puked his brains out in front of a crowd. Georgie and Heather were laughing riotously, and I couldn't help joining in. We always enjoyed a vigorous vomiting story.

"But wait," Georgie said, and I already knew what she was going to ask. "Why would you ever think that you could drink as much as those big, hard fisherman? You're beautiful, and not like them."

"I was just on a boat with them, doing the exact same work, eating the exact same food, taking turns sleeping in the same bunks!" came Youngsu's reply.

"I can't believe this," Arthur said. "You, this Youngsu, was escorted off a plane by police?"

"Sometimes I can get out of control," he said with a wicked smile.

"Speaking of which," I said, taking my leave. I wasn't responsible for Richard, but I also was. I never wanted to be someone whose friend ruined a good party. "I'm gonna take Richard out of here."

"Good idea," Heather said. "I think he needs some personal attention. Just not from me."

"Me neither," Georgie said.

Inside, I found Richard deeply entangled in an argument with Logan about the merits of being good at charades. Whitney was watching silently, and I could tell she was enjoying how much they both seemed to have invested in the debate.

"Charades, the ultimate human question," I interrupted them, and put my hands on Richard's shoulders. "Get your hat, Mr. Barben, you and I are going out on the town."

I knocked into Whitney a little as I maneuvered Richard towards the door, and I put my hand on her knee to steady myself.

"You're good," she said, and briefly laid her hand on top of mine. There was something sweet and apologetic in the gesture that caught me off guard.

"You're good too," I said, and patted her hand.

"And you're not ashamed now?" Logan asked, nodding towards Richard.

"Shame is a social construction created by sad people stuck indoors in cold weather who wanted to deny their humanity. Now, if you'll excuse me." I collected my bag, gave my best to Freddie, and skidded out onto the sidewalk with Richard in tow.

"The night is ours, we can go anywhere in the world!" he announced, and adjusted his hat. "So Simon's?" he asked, much to my relief.

There was a healthy crowd around the bar at Simon's, and a wave of trepidation washed over me when I saw that Mona was working again. Then I remembered my recent lecture on shame, and I really couldn't have cared less what Mona thought of me and Richard.

"What am I pouring you two tonight?" she asked. "Whiskeys?"

"Actually, let's make the first one a scotch," I said. Mona raised her eyebrow. "Celebrating?"

"My much older, much more attractive girlfriend dumped me," Richard said flatly, and crossed his arms on the top of the bar.

I watched Mona put together that Richard wasn't gay, that he wasn't dating me, and that his bluntness was defeat, not self-deprecating humor. This was expressed through a series of head nods and glances back and forth between Richard and myself. "So, okay. Rocks or neat?"

"Whatever you feel like, doll." "Make mine neat," I said.

"My condolences," Mona said when she returned. "Holler when you're ready for more."

Richard was limply slumped on the bar. "So listen," I said. "I realize it's much too soon to say this, but you know it's for the best, don't you? You knew you didn't have a serious future with Karen." I had never been good at break-up debriefings. To me, it seemed best to confront things in their full awfulness all at once and move on, rather than slide slowly into their blackness.

"Jesus, Aneesha," Richard said, and reached for his drink. "And I thought you might cheer me up."

"Fine," I said, raising my glass. "To sniffing all the hair you'd like, openly and unabashedly."

He laughed, and hooked his hand around my shoulder so he could sniff my hair. "You always have such nice-smelling hair product. It's spicy, earthy."

"It's for men," I said.

Richard laughed again. "It would be, and I would find that appealing. Do you think a lesbian would have sex with me now that I'm available?"

I beamed. Richard was back. "Let's think about this. Because I don't think it's totally implausible, but what kind of lesbian would be into you, do you think?"

We drank our scotch, and brainstormed, and switched back to whiskey, because I wanted the beer back and couldn't figure out why they didn't offer them with scotch. "Tradition's a bitch," Mona answered when I asked. The Cure was playing in the background, and there was a group of girls by the popcorn machine, one of whom in a tan leather jacket looked particularly adorable, and I had a lovely view of them. Richard was explaining to me how much he liked penetrating versus penetration when I felt a buzz in my pocket.

"Well, what about Mona, for example?" he asked.

"Mona's not gay," I said, and saw that I had a text from Zoe.

"What, because she doesn't have a pink triangle tattooed on her face or because she didn't hit on you?"

"Obviously neither," I said, and watched Mona bring beers to the cute girls at the end of the bar. "She's into dudes. The skinny kind with deep voices who look good in diagonal-zip punk leather jackets, which make them look scary, but they're actually very sensitive, thoughtful guys with neat apartments."

Richard looked at me skeptically, and then back at Mona again. "Really? How can you know that?"

"I just do. I'm not saying she would absolutely not sleep with you, she just doesn't count."

Zoe had texted me to say she was sorry she had missed my top of the apartment building scream. She wanted to know what I was doing now, and my life suddenly felt so bustling and complete. Richard was sitting at a jaunty angle, ready to flirt. He was almost normal and I wasn't going to leave him alone, not right now. Situations like these were the greatest impediment to me chancing upon meaningful romantic encounters. And yet, this was exactly how I wanted to spend my time: at Simon's with Richard pinpointing the hypothetical type of lesbian who would or would not sleep with him. I texted this to Zoe and asked if she wanted to hang out the following day.

Mona smiled at us when she passed by. "You doing okay?" She had a great smile, and her teeth looked particularly white in the dusky bar lighting.

"So Mona," Richard put his elbows on the bar, and was leaning way over it again. "Aneesha and I are having a discussion and I have a bit of a personal question for you.

Have you ever dated a woman?" he asked.

Mona smiled and put a hand on her hip.

"Or," I said, "do you prefer a sensitive, androgynous man in a motorcycle jacket, which means occasionally you've liked the girl who pulls that off, but you'd rather have the dude?"

Mona did her deep, rolling laugh and her slick curtain of hair shimmered. "You," she pointed at me, "are dangerous." She started to walk away and then stopped. "Am I that transparent? I thought I might be kind of mysterious." She shook her head until her hair had fallen into a mussed tangle in front of her face. "No?".

My crush on her jumped up a few notches. "Well, maybe now," I said.

She pushed her hair back and removed my empty whiskey glass from the bar. "And what about you?" she asked me. "Which ones do you like?"

Richard was jealous of the attention I was getting. "The straight girls," he answered for me. "The heartless kind."

"The ones who like sensitive, androgynous types in punky leather jackets." I maintained eye contact with her while I finished my beer and placed the empty can on the bar. I like to think that I made Mona blush, but it was rather dark, and I was drunk so it was hard to tell.

"Like I said. Dangerous." Her smile was guarded, and she disposed of the can with a quick toss. In a slick movement, she plucked the whiskey from the well and poured me glass. "On me," she said, and disappeared to the other end of the bar.

"Oh my god," Richard whispered excitedly in my ear. "You're gonna bag Mona."

"We're just flirting," I said. "It's a game. Nothing's going to happen."

Richard leaned back in an exasperated fashion. "This is why we're never going to have our baby. Because you never close the deal."

"This isn't a deal."

"Our baby is withering and drying up. He's turning into an aged salami because you won't go after a woman with the full force of your own womanly powers. You had her pegged from the start and you didn't even use it to your advantage. You showed your cards right off!"

He was reminding me of his lesser qualities, and I wanted him to stop talking. I had a long speech lining up about the misogynist nature of his logic, but I opted for the dagger to the heart instead. "How old are you again?" I asked.

"Older than you."

"I know, but how old exactly?"

"Why is that even an issue? I'll be able to produce babies for a long time. You're the one—"

"Exactly how old are you, Richard?" I asked again calmly.

"I'm thirty fucking four, okay?" he yelled.

His voice rang across the bar and there seemed to be a pronounced silence. He was smiling, but I could still hear the pitch of his hysteria piercing the walls of our little bubble. I saw him for a moment as another person might. His blue eyes were a touch watered-down, his pink neck was like chicken skin, and his hands moved in helpless flourishes around his empty beer. The white lengths of Richard's socks were too close to the bottoms of his shorts. This was my adult friend, a father-to-be, I thought to myself.

Mona was slyly holding up another beer in front of Richard. It was both a question and an answer, and I was moved by her skillful nuance. I cleared my throat.

"Why not." Richard reached for the beer, and set it down on his coaster.

"That's what I thought." I put my hand on his shoulder and looked into his face. "Richard, have your own fucking baby."

He looked at me with genuine shock. His shoulders began to shake, and then he was doubled over with laugher, a galloping bellow coming from his chest.

I started laughing too, to keep him company, but then I stopped because I meant it, and I said so. "You can have your own baby, Richard. You do know that, right? That's why you and Karen were moot from the start. That's what you want."

He was looking at me strangely. It was strange because he'd never been entirely serious with me before. His eyes were so slack. "The kind of woman who wants to have a child is not the kind who wants to be with me. Or the kind I want to be with. Same goes for you. What did you think the baby joke was about?"

"Isn't it just that the women we would consider having babies with are our friends? Because that's who we trust?"

"That's why I said I'd give you my sperm, you're my friend!"

"So then it's serious and not a joke?"

"Are you lonely, doll? Is that where this is coming from?"

I was infuriated by his condescending tone, and his less than adept attempt at turning this around on me. "Aren't you lonely? Isn't that what the joke is about? I've never wanted kids!"

"Why would that be funny?" He looked at me harshly, humorlessly.

"Maybe it's not." I started calmly, but this time I couldn't avoid the wound-up speech. "Maybe that's why we should stop joking about it. Maybe that's why I asked you to leave that party, so we can discuss not joking about things that aren't funny, like you breaking up with Karen, and then being weird with Heather and her boyfriend. Like me trying to live with Whitney and Logan, and

pretending it's totally normal. Maybe these things indicate something seriously wrong going on in our lives, which—by the way—I
don't understand how the two of us, who are very different, even
have a semblance of the same thing going on in our lives."

Richard was suddenly intellectually intrigued. "Do you really
think we're that different?"

"Well," I said, because I didn't want to say that I did or didn't.
Aside from obvious matters, the real issue was that I didn't want to
be Richard when I was thirty-four. I didn't want to be linked to him
and this future, where we had all of the pieces, but they didn't fit
together. There was no way to point that out politely. "I keep hearing
you in my head. The commune, our baby, our shared future, it's time
to commit. It's driving me crazy!"

"So that's the ugly heart of the matter then? My greatest life
concerns annoy you?" He sounded exasperated, but it could have
been pain. It had never occurred to me that I had the power to hurt
Richard. "You were a part of this too," he continued. "The commune
was our joint fantasy."

"I'm not annoyed by your concerns," I said. "I'm deeply invested
in your happiness, but maybe we're selling ourselves short with the
commune. Maybe," I ventured, trying to decide how blunt I should
be, "it's a compromise we've made so that we don't have to create
something better. Maybe the commune is a crutch."

"You're the one who doesn't want the commune, it's your crutch."
Richard turned to me, and his face was hard, like he was preparing to
berate a stranger. "I figured, hey, we both love our friends, we cherish
and invest in our relationships with them, and our romances are fun
but real shit. At least we have each other. I thought this was special
and something to bank on. However, it seems that you, Aneesha,
don't even really care about that. You just pretend to so that you're
not totally alone! Who means enough for you to commit to them,
huh? For you to say, yes, this," he was now animatedly smacking
the top of the bar. "I will dedicate myself to this for the foreseeable
future? Because it's clearly not me. And not anybody else I know
of either." He turned away from me so we were sitting shoulder to
shoulder, staring down the blue-lit mirror in the back of the bar.

I didn't know how to respond. In the reflection we looked like an old married couple, both insulted and hurting, but without any inclination to part ways. I remembered a night in the Buffalo Bar when only a blue Molson's light was on, and Richard had said to the woman he was talking up, "This light is terrible. It makes everyone look like they have AIDS." The woman had immediately gotten up and left, but I thought it was an apt description of the clammy, pale sheen on everyone's faces. The graveness it lent us all. That's how we looked now.

I rested my chin in my hand, and sipped from my whiskey. "Richard, in all honesty, would you like to father a child?"

He was silent. His gaze wandered over to the jukebox, toward the cute girl in the tan jacket, and eventually back down to me. "You know," he said with chagrin. "I think I do."

"So stop joking about it."

Richard's stare bored into me. "Because you've lost your sense of humor?"

"No," I said, facing him. "Because the joke is what's keeping you from being with—" I was still feeling vicious and paused to use air quotes "—the kind of woman who wants to have babies."

Richard shook his head. "Jesus, doll. You're such a downer tonight. You're such a great fucking friend."

"I just wanted us to have a moment of reality together."

"Certainly, sure." Richard threw his hands in the air. "Reality is messy and unanswerable. That's far less depressing than a dumb joke." His eyes were fixed on his drink and I avoided them. I thought I might cry if I saw that he was on the verge.

We had another drink to let things settle into a kind of truce. Then we called it quits. There was nothing left to talk about. In silence, we put on our helmets and rode up Clark. Our paths diverged at Bryn Mawr, and we hollered goodbyes to each other as we peeled off towards home, but I could tell that the foundation of our friendship had suffered some serious blows. I looked over my shoulder and caught his blinking red light fading into the distance. "Be safe!" I yelled in Richard's direction, even though I knew he couldn't hear me anymore.

I awoke in the morning with an ache in my jaw from having clenched it in my sleep. The previous night still lay heavy on my mind, and, recalling the conversation, I winced at my unfriendly timing. Poor Richard. I had kicked him while he was down, but I had meant everything I said, and I doubted he would have taken me seriously otherwise. I went into the kitchen, and was pleased to find that Whitney had left me coffee in the pot. I poured some over ice and added a splash of milk.

In what I considered the natural balance to my awful Richard situation, Zoe and I had agreed to meet up at Foster Beach to spend the afternoon together. I took a shower, and spent an unreasonably long time matching my purple shorts, then my fuchsia cutoffs, with a variety of t-shirts, plaid shirts, and tank tops.

Georgie called me as I was packing my backpack. "What are you doing right now? Want to go to the beach and thrift with me and Amanda and Heather?"

"I'm meeting Tutor Crush." I dug around in Whitney and Logan's utility closet until I found a Frisbee.

"Oh, boo," Georgie said, but she was in a chipper mood. "Well, I'm sure you'll delight her pants off."

"I'm hoping," I said, and stuffed my handkerchief in my pocket. "Hey, I got into a thing with Richard last night. I hope he's okay. Maybe ask him to join you."

"I'll schedule a Two Person Book Club meeting."

"Perfect," I said. "And Heather's birthday is coming up too, so keep an eye out for anything she's into and doesn't buy."

"I don't know how you do this."

"What?" I asked.

"You carry around so many people in your head at once, and not just superficially."

I was confused. "Doesn't everyone?"

"I just keep Youngsu, and my brother, and you in my head. Everyone else enters and exits by accident. Often, but by accident."

"That's the difference between you and me, Summertown: accidents."

"Thanks, that's nice of you. Don't forget to be yourself," she said.

My first stop was Gaztrowagon. It was a little storefront on Clark and Elmwood that served saucy, tender flatbread sandwiches with homemade pickles. When I'd lived in Chicago, the Wagon was located evenly between mine and Whitney's apartments, which made it a fitting beginning to our neighborhood drinking sprees. Matt, the owner, didn't mind when we brought in a six-pack, ate, and chatted with him while he cooked.

My grand idea today was that I'd bring these delectable sandwiches to Zoe and casually impress her. I'd never actually been on a date with a girl I knew and hadn't already slept with, so I didn't know how to tell whether I was over- or under-doing the impressiveness. I had thought to ask if there was anything she didn't eat—as any good queer did, I congratulated myself—and much to my relief she'd replied, "Buttons, pencils, wool, tennis balls."

As I left the shop, hot sandwiches tucked securely into my backpack, I did suddenly feel guilty. I was extending a Whitney tradition to Zoe, which seemed an affront to the both of them, but as I rode down Ardmore to pick up the bike path, I told myself that this was crazy. It was my little piece of Chicago to share with anyone I wanted, and right now, I wanted to share it with Zoe.

I rode along the lakeside path, and was hopping off my bike when I saw Zoe crossing the street with hers. She was wearing a purple and blue dress that looked to be made out of t-shirt material. It fluttered gently above her knees. I had always taken issue with her sunglasses, which implied the possibility of an impromptu extreme sports outing, but I forgave her the moment she took them off. Hers was an unfairly illuminating smile. Her whole face sparkled. She handed me her bike helmet, and shook out her hair in a fashion that was equally beach babe and biker hunk.

"I am super sweaty," she said. "You still want a hug?"

I absolutely did. "Do you not recall that part where I told you I was gross?" I asked.

"Yeah, about that." She eyed me skeptically even as she slipped an arm over my shoulder for a hug. "You have to use industrial soap, even if it dries out your hands. You do know about Hepatitis A? Or the Plague?"

"I just know that vaccinating babies makes them autistic, raw milk gives children superpowers, and you catch diseases from penises. That's all there is to public health, right?"

She laughed. "This is pertinent because of the whole thing with Julian."

I pointed to a shady spot under a tree, and we walked over. "Oh, Julian." I wanted to know how her ex-boyfriend had fucked it up. "Tell me what happened with that."

"I realized he was cheating on me because he gave me crabs."

"Crabs? That's gross."

She punched my shoulder so quickly I nearly caught my foot in my front spokes. "That's not nice," Zoe said. Her glare was real, and I detected our nearness to her inner cliff, the one that certain women liked to laugh about and dance around, but which everyone else was meant to take seriously. I had to admit that I liked this kind of jumpy, mercurial behavior. It was something that I admired and found fascinating, because the world rarely felt that close and immediate to me.

"I meant him, of course, not you. So what'd you do?"

"Got rid of them, obviously!" she scoffed.

I chuckled. "No, not with the crabs, Zoe, I mean with Julian."

It was a gorgeous summer day, overly saturated with color, and there were even tiny waves cresting on the lake. It was safe weather for a story with an unfortunate ending. I laid my bike down and spread out a blanket for us. Zoe sat down without any skirt holding, and still managed not to show anything she didn't mean to. I was amazed by this elegant feminine gesture, and she acknowledged this with a sly smile.

"How thoughtful of you to bring a blanket," she said.

"Might you even call it impressive?" I asked.

"Might you call this impressive?" She lifted a large bottle of Fin du Monde from her backpack, and I clapped. When I unveiled the sandwiches, she stuck a victory fist into the air.

"Our picnic ideas mesh very well," I said.

We ate messily while Zoe told her breakup story. Julian, who was an immaculately dressed design student at the Art Institute, had been sleeping with Zoe's friend Hannah. Hannah had come to Zoe for advice on what to do when the guy you're sleeping with has given you crabs. Zoe, who had recently suffered the same fate and who knew Hannah was married, suddenly became suspicious.

"Wasn't that an outrageously stupid thing for her to bring up?" Zoe asked me. "To someone whose boyfriend you're fucking?" She threw her hands in the air.

When Zoe confronted Julian, he admitted that he and Hannah were secretly arranging her divorce so the two of them could run away together.

"I thought you and Julian were moving to Portland," I said.

"Yeah, me too. I was getting a new teaching certificate and everything. All so we could be near his family."

"Wow," I said. "Julian. Far more surprising than I imagined."

Her face was scrunched up. "I have never felt like such an idiot."

"I know this is going to sound terrible," I heard myself saying, and then stopped. I recalled from the previous night that what people in post-breakup mode needed from me was to be heard and acknowledged, not to be reminded of our collective doom. "Oh, never mind," I said as Zoe put down her sandwich.

"Come on." She shook her head. "Now you have to say it. I'm too curious." I winced and took a sip of my beer.

"Aneesha, share your thoughts with me. Otherwise there's no point in me telling this whole thing to you." She ate a pickle off of the butcher paper in front of me, and I liked how easy it was with her.

"I was thinking," I said, "isn't it kind of a relief to know that even people like Julian, who are so regimented and together, even they have an insatiable desire to suddenly drive off in a car headed whoknowswhere, windows down, hair blowing in the wind? I mean—and this is what might sound terrible—but aren't you sort of impressed with him for being so moved and ballsy to follow through on a plan so immensely ill-fated?"

Zoe was staring me. She was deciding whether or not she hated me for offering this challenge instead of my sympathy.

"Which is not an excuse for his hurtful, deceitful behavior," I added. "There's just something hopeful about people you know well still being able to surprise you. It's a reminder that we're all still alive, and festering, and capable of anything. Even if..." I paused and put my hand out.

Zoe grabbed it and squeezed my fingers together in her fist. "He doesn't deserve to have you on his side."

"I'm not on his side," I assured her. My fingers were turning white in her hand. "I'm just trying to find something else for you to feel besides stupid. Something positive and resonant with a brassy splash of absurdity. For humor's sake?"

Her smile made an appearance again, and she scooted over so we were shoulder to shoulder, staring out at the lake. "You're very mean-sweet. It's strangely personal."

"I'm sorry." I started to crush our sandwich papers into balls. "What I intended to say was, 'That Julian, what a crummy bastard! Musta been a real knucklehead to lose a precious broad such as yourself, doll.' How about that?"

"Now listen here," she continued in the 1940s Hollywood-speak I had apparently been using. "That bum was a lying, cheating bastard, and I deserve better, someone who knows how to treat a lady."

"This would be the part of the movie," I said, returning to my own voice, "where the golden gentleman, who apparently has very high morals, still finds it totally fine to mack on a woman because she's having a moment of crisis, which is his main opportunity to give her a stiff and forceful kiss."

Zoe was laughing. "Speaking of which, I thought about what you said last time when you ran off in a huff."

I looked away, feeling sheepish about what should not have been such a dramatic moment.

"I'm no longer in a moment of crisis. You're just going to have to trust me on that," she said. Her perfect chestnut hair waved in a lively arc across her forehead and instead of the riot of excitement I expected, there was a calm opening up in me. "Anyway, I think you should come over later," she said.

"Are you inviting me over for sex?" I asked, in what I hoped came off as teasing question and not the clarification it was.

Her eyebrows shot up at a sharp angle. "I'm sorry, were you hoping for more, like, sex and popcorn maybe?"

I laughed then, at myself mostly, but also at her for liking me and my mixed signals and my overinflated heart, which at times hung so close to my face it blocked my vision.

"You know what, you're pretty awesome," I said. I turned my head to the side so I could smell her hair, a cinnamon apricotish waft, for Richard and me, because that's what always got us.

She turned her head and rested her chin on my shoulder. "Thanks. Ditto. Now, tell me something about you that is not about other people, just you."

"What are you curious about?" I asked her.

"When'd you do this?" she asked, running her hand along the side of my head.

"That is going to take a while because when you ask about my hair, you're asking for the overwrought story of my queer coming-of-age," I warned Zoe.

She laughed and lay down on her stomach. "Which is all I wanted to hear anyway."

"It all began on a warm day in San Diego," I began, "when I was visiting my friend Darin. He'd just finished his finals, I'd just finished a two-day marathon of *Firefly* in his living room—as well as the last of his macaroni and cheese. We challenged each other to go to the barber shop, right then, to kick off the summer with mohawks."

To my great relief, Zoe didn't make me tell the complete, linear story, which would have ended—as all of my most honest attempts did—in overcompensating lies. Zoe chimed in, and told me that she had shaved her head once, right before a big marching band performance, much to the shock and horror of her family and her school.

"It was a little extreme, a little too obviously a call for attention," she said, bashfully. "But I was serious about it, and when people asked me why I'd done it, I'd shrug and go, 'Why not?' or—this is so embarrassing." She squeezed my arm and winced. "I'd just say, 'feminism.'"

She gave me with a cold hard stare, and I fell over laughing.

"I know."

"It's hard to argue against feminism," I said.

"Well, that's what I was banking on."

We took our time getting home, and when we arrived at Zoe's building the sun had begun to set. I followed her into the echoey apartment, and once I closed the door, it was nearly dark inside. I reached out to find my way in this unfamiliar space and found her back. She turned swiftly into me, and we unleashed the sort of greedy kissing that revealed how much we'd been pretending not to think about each other.

"So," she paused. "Before I get ahead of myself, you're not just going to run out in the middle of this, are you?" She threw a smirk at me.

"Hey, I'm sorry about that," I said. "I have this terrible affliction where I live most vividly in my head. I honestly just needed a little time to fantasize about you in a realistic way."

Zoe considered this for a second. "Okay, so…?" She ran her fingers over her lips. "What happens first?"

"Well, this," I said. "And then—" I motioned to her couch "—you're sitting over there at your computer and you're having trouble with your Internet connection."

"That is your fantasy?" she asked. "Internet trouble?"

"Yes, well that's the beginning anyway. I told you, I like to keep it reality-based and in the realm of my abilities. What?" I asked.

"Nothing." Zoe smiled and went over to the couch. She picked up her laptop and banged around on the keys. "Whew, I am having a really hard time downloading these important security documents?" She paused and looked at me. "Wait, are we reenacting a Mariah Carey video?"

"Do you have water guns?" I asked excitedly.

It was a treat to spend the night with her. She was confident and silly, and there was no hesitancy. I had forgotten how the small things could floor me: the luxury of her hair sweeping against my body, the slightly bitter taste of her ear, or that serious shift when we were suddenly hurtling toward an orgasm and I knew I better not stop exactly what I was doing.

She kneed me awake the next morning, saying, "Surprise! I wake up early." So I got up and we went for coffee at M. Henry. I knew the guy at the counter, who threw in some pastries for free, and we sat outside and made up dumb names for the baby strollers that went by.

"If you find any crabs, you know who to blame," she said when I gathered my things to leave.

Her lightness relieved me, and I bounded down the steps, waving at her as I went. I had been renewed. On my ride home, I sucked the air of a new day up through my nose. There was some music blowing out of an open car window at a stop sign, and I gave the guys inside an open-mouthed thumbs up as I flew by. I was comforted to know that I could be moved like this. In a moderate way that was all zings and citrus bursts, and not something dark and horrible, like the Great Molasses Flood of 1919. I didn't know why it was my point of comparison, but it seemed to embody the sense of imminent doom I usually felt at the possibility of genuine romance: that I was standing in a cobbled street, living my life, when a molasses tank burst, and all I could do was stand there watching the sticky black waves of death come oozing slowly at me. But this wasn't that, not even close. "Not even a little, not even at all," I sang cheerily. Which did, then, seem like I was taunting death, and while on a bicycle, so I decided to whistle instead.

July arrived with thunderstorms that exploded on me every night. I loved when the humidity suddenly dropped and cold winds came whipping up around every corner. It all enhanced my new favorite bike ride fantasy: that I was a hardy sea captain and Caliente was my ship. "Time to let our sails drop," I'd call out when the fat drops started to fall. I knew I only had a few minutes to find a suitable bar to wait it out.

That's how I ended up at Moody's one night, on the way home from Zoe's. I'd gotten to Bryn Mawr and Broadway and could have easily booked it home, but I wanted an excuse to prolong the evening. I entered through the heavy wooden door and waited for my eyes to adjust to the dim cavernous interior. Moody's was located in what had once been a chapel, and since I hadn't grown up religious in any way, my strongest associations with church were the sinister rooms of the California missions that I visited in elementary school. I was prepared to include this in my sea captain fantasy, and chat up some colonialists at the bar, until I was jarred back to reality by the sight of Whitney and Logan picking out a table in the back.

"Is that Aneesha?" Whitney asked, walking towards me.

"Hey, what are you doing here?" I asked.

"We were outside, but the rain is back." The pounding of a steady downpour had begun to drown out the low chatter in the bar. "I haven't seen you in a while," she said. "Never tried out that pizza place."

I nodded. "I figured you were right. It's not like we haven't tried before. Did you have anything new to say?" I asked.

Whitney shrugged. "I don't know, but I miss you."

I had been spending more time with Zoe and helping her unpack the wall of boxes in her second bedroom. For reasons that Zoe couldn't quite explain, every single box she used to move had the word "EGGS" printed in huge block letters on each side. I found this endlessly hilarious because it gave the impression that all of her possessions—the knotted hair ties, the discolored mug collection, the tangles of electronics cords—were precious bundles of potential life. I wanted to share this irony with Whitney, but I wasn't sure if it was too cute and private to be universally amusing.

"Aneesha, come sit with us," I heard Logan call from their table. He held up an extra glass and poured me a beer from their pitcher. I couldn't figure out how he mustered so much niceness for me, the only precarious piece of his stable life.

"Do you mind if I join?"

"Of course not." Whitney looked at me like I had offended her. "Unless, were you planning to meet someone?"

I dried my glasses on the bandana I kept in my pocket. "No, I was just biking home and the storm seemed like a good excuse to come in." If I had been meeting someone, I wondered, would I have been less welcome to sit with her?

"Where have you been?" was the first thing Logan asked. "You're like a cat who only shows up in the afternoon to eat and sleep."

I liked his good humor. "I am so rarely compared to a cat," I mused.

"People said you've met a girl," he continued.

"You look so happy," Whitney remarked. "Is it? No. Is it Tutor Crush?"

"Yeah," I said, "it is." Only it sounded weird to hear Whitney call her Tutor Crush, as if that were a different person, because Tutor Crush was a different person, a not-real person.

"That's all you have to say?" she asked. "Hm. Okay." Whitney rearranged her legs and watched me.

It all felt too fragile to talk about, but I knew I had to share something. I was about to say that we got along well, but that had always been Whitney's explanation of her and me, which would have been confusing. "I like her. It's both intriguing and relaxing. We read together and walk around, drink beer and shoot the shit. Also she's very pretty, which I don't mind."

"Of course you wouldn't," Whitney said. She was smiling at me, acknowledging the whole other conversation that we would normally have, regarding the ex-boyfriend, the sex, how much time we spent together, and what Zoe had told me about herself that might be suspect. Since Whitney and I met, I'd never been involved with anyone she might potentially meet, nobody I took seriously anyway, and I wondered if that kind of discussion might be impertinent now.

"I think this is great." Logan congratulated me and it felt validating. He was, if nothing else, a man who appreciated wholesome companionship, and that's what it appeared I had accomplished.

"Well, it's not like I'm expecting the world from it, guys, but thanks," I said.

"Don't think like that," Logan reproached me. "I don't know where this negativity comes from. It seems to me like you've got everything you could want."

He was right that I had more than I required, but this was also coming from someone who clearly did not wrestle on a daily basis with how and who to be in the world. "It's just that my romances tend to unfold in a asymmetrical fashion."

Whitney nodded. "That's a good way of putting it."

"What are you saying?" Logan asked.

It had never happened that I loved a woman who loved me too, and then we just went on loving each other. There was always a skewed time frame, extenuating circumstances, or insurmountable obstacles that we pretended not to see for a while.

There had been short periods of time with several incredible women when we had both thought it was possible to love each other. Then the moment had unceremoniously passed. Generally, after some avoidance and petty bickering, my pride reconstituted and we became close friends.

"I'm just saying, these things always get unbalanced, and I won't be surprised whichever way it falls. Look, I like it, and not any less because I don't think it'll last," I said.

I knew this thinking was antithetical to Logan's way of life. He made plans that worked out better than he hoped, and went places that didn't disappoint him. I was a little jealous of him for that. "Well, anyway," he said, "Whitney and I are going up to my parents' lake house for the 4th of July, and you're welcome to join us."

"Unless you have plans, because you always have plans." Whitney waved her hands all around to illustrate the plethora of plans I supposedly had.

"I don't have plans, actually," I reported. Heather and Amanda were going up to a lake with their boyfriends, and I knew I was invited wherever Georgie went but nothing had been discussed. This was my chance, I thought, to cash in on the bankable guaranteed positivity of Logan Ash. I was beginning to see that if I intended to maintain a place with Whitney for the long term, I would need to find a reasonable place to stand. Being against Logan was not sustainable and it wasn't much fun either.

"If you really don't mind, I'd love to join you," I said.

Logan clapped his hands together. "Okay, great."

"Anything in particular I should plan to bring?" I asked.

"A swimsuit," he said. "We usually take my parents' boat out and drink beer, make dinner, watch the fireworks. It's pretty chill."

"You can bring your crush if you want," Whitney said, but there was a tone in her voice that sounded hostile.

"Yeah, she's welcome," Logan added. "I'm going to bring a friend so we could fit one more."

"I'm sure Zoe has her own plans." I stared Whitney down. I didn't know what she was thinking, but if it was related to jealousy—running in some underground sewer of her heart—I had no intention of setting her off.

❧

Word around the neighborhood was that the Heartland was in dire straits again. This meant that Lucy and Tom, the owners, would go on TV and remind the city of the cultural importance of the Heartland Café. They would point out some of the run-of-the-mill efforts they made—the sale of bracelets made by a women's collective in Guatemala or organic tampons—and imply that it was still a place of change and activism. Generally these calls were heeded, favors called in, loans forgiven or extended, and everyone went on as usual. At least that was the impression I got from the blasé reaction everyone seemed to exhibit.

Whitney and I had gone to the Buffalo Bar to have a drink and find out what the fundraiser would be this time. "I've seriously recommended that they stop calling themselves a business and find some other category for filing taxes," Whitney said.

"Like a non-profit?" I asked.

"Except that won't ever happen."

I thought of the Heartland like a stubborn old aunt, but it wasn't all that funny to think she was on her last legs. It occurred to me that because I'd never worked there and hadn't personally suffered from the disordered business end, I had never seen the Heartland as doomed. For me it had been a reliable standby, consistent in its mediocrity, if nothing else. We had always joked about its instability, but I never thought it was that serious.

"You're worried," Whitney said. "But this has been happening for years. Why do you think we all cashed our checks as soon as we got them?"

Sally was working the register when we came through the door. I gave her a wave, but she saw Whitney and went to reorganize the t-shirts at the back of the store.

"Still?" I asked Whitney.

She shrugged and we went around to the bar. "She was a shitty friend anyway."

"It doesn't bother you that Sally feels the need to literally run away from you?" I asked.

"She doesn't even really know me," Whitney answered. "I don't care."

Underneath the buffalo head, Heather and Richard were rolling dice on the bar and drinking mojitos. Someone had put Bob Marley on the jukebox and it was like I'd walked into a tropical-themed retirement home. I hadn't seen Richard since our explosive night at Simon's, but he looked good, relaxed.

"Hey, you two," Richard welcomed us warmly. "Come join us."

"There's some project going on." Heather motioned towards the back.

"We've heard it's bad," Whitney reported. "So what's the solution?"

Ben placed a couple of beers on coasters in front of Whitney and me. "The plan is to build a garden on the roof."

Whitney smiled. "I guess that would eliminate a few expenses."

"That will change everything," Richard said wryly.

A line of cooks came through the store carrying potted plants and I had to laugh. Tom looked harried as he followed behind. His shirt had a round oval stain on the front, as if something had recently spilled on him, and he was getting repeatedly cut off by whomever he was on the phone with. As Tom passed the bar, he pointed emphatically at us and winked. He had once referred to me as Whitney's "hard woman," a description that was so terribly off I hoped to use it in a bio one day.

"There will be a news crew here next week," Ben said. "So put on your best outfits, kids, and bring your friends." He patted the bar and went back to work.

Heather raised her drink in the air. "To the Heartland. She'll never go quietly."

We clinked our glasses and chuckled. In the silence that followed, I studied my companions. Richard wouldn't look me in the eye, Whitney was hunched up tightly over her beer, and Heather's leg was swinging quickly, as if she were waiting impatiently.

Throughout my schooling as a writer, people had critiqued my stories for their lighthearted humor, the way darkness never lingered long. Nothing ever fully exploded and broke your heart—people just kept on joking. As I sat here with my friends, at the same musty bar where we had met and gotten our lives all knotted up, I knew that was how life went. It was much more heartbreaking that there was no finalizing explosion. There was always more that followed, and the farther you went, the more the lightness became the darkness and the dark, the light until it was all fairly murky.

That afternoon, even though Richard and I had offended each other, though he and Heather had offended each other, though Whitney and I still had something brewing, we all wanted to be here together. It should have been a relief because it had been my greatest concern that we might simply drift apart, and here was our loyalty, in full color. But maybe, I thought now, I should have been concerned that we weren't pushing onward. We had all loved the Heartland because of the flexible rules and heedless approach to the future—it matched our lifestyles. But there were certainly other bars to frequent, ones whose clientele was closer to our age and paid money for their drinks, who were not suffering from acid flashbacks, or trying to seduce teenage boys, or fleeing to Canada because the police found their weed stash. We could all do much better. There were other lives for us to live. The beer had caught up with me, and I felt my thoughts swirling, the shades of light and dark washing over me.

"What are you guys thinking about?" I asked, and Whitney smiled because that was her question.

Both Heather and Richard started speaking at once, and he leaned back, deferring to her.

"I'm moving back to Milwaukee in the fall," Heather

announced. She was rattling the dice in her hand. "Actually, something terrible happened yesterday." Heather was a master of conveying gravity without melodrama, and that was how she revealed that her best friend since childhood, a girl named Vera, who I'd met on a few occasions, had lost her husband, Zach, in a strange boating accident. "She's a wreck. Zach is her best friend. Was her best friend. Oh, that's weird," Heather said.

"Isn't that just wicked?" Richard asked. "You commit your entire life to somebody and two years in, it's all gone."

"Fuck," Whitney said.

I suddenly understood the tense, dour mood. I felt foolish to have attributed it to petty friendship matters, but it affirmed my suspicion that there were worthier causes for our loyalties. "Heather, wow," I said. "I'm so sorry. For you and Vera and Zach and everyone. That's awful. So you're going to live with Vera then?"

"If she has to sit around and cry all day at least she won't be alone. I can make her food and do her laundry or whatever. You know," she added, "it's Amanda who introduced Vera and Zach. She and Zach were best friends in college, so Amanda's not doing well either. We're supposed to go up there tomorrow for the funeral and she hasn't returned any of my phone calls."

I sighed. "How tragic. And with all the fireworks and fanfare tomorrow. It really puts a morbid spin on the idea of independence day."

Whitney swatted my shoulder. "Jesus, Aneesha, somebody's dead." I grimaced. I was so clearly inexperienced with tragedy.

"I'm sorry."

But Heather was smiling. "I think Zach is still around. I don't know in what form, but I don't think his spirit will just leave us. I think he'd appreciate the irony, Aneesha. He would pretend all of the fireworks are for him. Richard has some better news though," Heather said, nudging him. She looked so proud, and I wondered if he'd landed a big case.

"It's nothing in comparison, I just met a woman. I'm not trying to get too excited, but I think she's special."

He was looking sheepishly at me, and I wondered if he had, in fact, taken our discussion at Simon's to heart. It was just as likely chance, but I wanted to be important to him. It felt wrong that Heather knew more about this lady than I did, but then I hadn't told him anything about Zoe, and I had refused to have a real discussion about Whitney, so it was only fair.

"Where'd you meet this woman?" asked Whitney, trying not to laugh. She always had a hard time saying the word woman.

Richard had an excited twinkle in his eye and it made me excited too. "Now, everyone here has heard my endless diatribes on the inherent pitfalls of looking for love on the Internet, but Sherry—that's her name—and I did start talking through an online medium. I'd like to emphasize, however, that we were initially introduced through mutual acquaintances, and that the Internet merely played a role in our method of communication."

"They met playing *Words With Friends*," Heather said flatly.

"What is that?" Whitney asked.

"It's online *Scrabble*," I answered.

"Oh," Whitney said. "You can do that? Did you play words that said you liked her? Wow, there are so many ways to meet people online."

"It's not just *Scrabble*," Richard interjected. "It has a chat function, which is very important here."

"But you've never met this woman?" I asked. "In person?"

Richard crossed his arms. "She's coming to visit next week. From Los Angeles."

I was shocked. "That's soon."

"We like each other," he said. "We're both adults. There's no reason to play games, we're going to try it out, and I get the feeling," he leaned in closer to us, "she's got the bank roll to support that kind of thing."

"Hmm," Whitney said. "I need to get a situation like that."

Heather laughed. "It seems like you have a situation like that in the works." "Yeah," Richard added, "you're the accountant with an overachieving doctor-to-be."

"Oh. Well, yeah," Whitney answered and finished her beer. She didn't elaborate and her dismissal of the subject made me think I'd been too quick to assess her future with Logan. "Aneesha's got a girl too," she deflected. "Tutor Crush."

"She has a name, it's Zoe," I said. "And I wouldn't say I 'got her,' exactly. There's no ownership involved."

Whitney rolled her eyes at me. "Fine, okay. You spend all of your time with her. You're at least dating."

"We do seem to be dating," I conceded.

"You know, Aneesha, you can be incredibly wishy-washy about these things and I don't know why," Richard said. "Put yourself out there, live a little."

I glared at him. One *Words With Friends* girl and now he was an expert at taking serious life risks.

Heather caught my look. I'd told her all about me and Zoe, and she'd agreed with me with that sometimes it was worth going out on a limb. She cleared her throat. "I'd just like to add that Aneesha is dating a girl who has never dated women before, and this girl just moved out of an apartment she shared with her boyfriend," Heather said. "All while Aneesha's here just for the summer and living with—" she quit talking and gestured broadly towards Whitney. "I think Aneesha's living plenty."

"Thanks, H," I said. Whitney said nothing.

"Alright, fine. What do I know anyway?" Richard held his hands up innocently.

He left with Heather not long afterwards—they were going to check on Amanda. He pushed the screen door open from behind Heather, and I was reminded of what good friends they were long before I'd come around, and regardless of whatever feelings had or had not passed between them.

"What about our dear Remi?" Whitney asked. "In his adorable shorts?"

"I think Heather knows her priorities. She always has."

"God, Heather is just the best person."

We had a few more beers and chatted for a bit with Ben about the kinds of v-neck t-shirts we all preferred. Eventually he went back to get the kegs all setup for the night and Whitney fell silent again.

"Hey, what's up with you?" I asked, kicking gently at her foot.

She frowned at me. "You're going to laugh because I'm sure it's been obvious to you since you arrived."

"I won't," I promised.

"I think I have to break up with Logan."

"What? No, we're going up to his lake house tomorrow," I said.

"I don't mean right now. Not even soon, necessarily, but eventually." She said this with great annoyance, like somebody who realized that the Drano wasn't working and they were going to have to call a plumber.

"Oh, Whit." I felt terrible for Logan, going around, working, studying, making plans, and not knowing that his heartbreak had already been decided. It wasn't the same thing, but I thought of Heather's friend Vera casually bidding her husband goodbye before he went out on the boat: the shock, the empty space that followed.

"Am I a bad a person?" Her face, usually so radiant, looked like an old newspaper.

"Of course not. Just don't wait too long to do it."

I had no idea what it took to hook Whitney, to really move her. I wanted to see that. The only reason I even toyed with the idea that Whitney might secretly love me was that so few people managed to express feelings for her, receive her rejection, and still be allowed in her life. I understood too, that this was because she didn't pity me. I knew her better than she did, and I had an optimistically high opinion of my own intellect.

"You can tell me I'm a bad person, it's probably true. Robot Whitney, plodding along."

I put my hand on her shoulder. "Whit, you'll fall in love with somebody one day and you won't even have to try."

"Is that how you feel about Tutor Crush?"

I laughed. "Not quite."

"But you've had some serious, stormy involvement with women," she said. "Really deep emotional stuff."

She was right, I had. But before her, I had never loved anyone I could realistically spend all my time with. It was, in fact, our ease and our friendship that had pulled the rug out from under me. I wanted to mention this to her, but it seemed like that would only be more confusing. "I think maybe the best part about being queer is that recognition of yourself in someone else," I said. "And not a mirror image, not the idea of your other half, but the exact sameness, like a duplicate. Because then you know you won't have to leave your true self that far behind in order to meet them halfway. When I was younger I used to think there had to be this emotional volcanic eruption in order to achieve that. But I don't think it has to be that way. You know?"

"Huh," came Whitney's reply. "I can see that. Though you're the only person I know who openly wants to date yourself."

"Not entirely myself, just part myself."

"You spend a lot of time thinking about this."

"It's why you find me so depressing and still so indispensable."

She nodded. "So you don't love Tutor Crush?"

"So you don't love Logan?"

Whitney reached in her bag, the one she called her Army bag, brought out some cash, and put it on the bar. "We should go home. We're leaving early for the lake tomorrow."

꙳

We arrived at the lake house around noon, all of us stretching and making a big scene of kicking out our legs, even though it had only been a few hours. The majority of the drive had been spent listening to Katy Perry so loudly that I hadn't spoken a word to Raleigh, Logan's friend, who had shared the back seat with me.

"Hi," I said sticking out my hand, and introduced myself.

Raleigh smiled. She had a striking, platinum blond pompadour and was wearing a bright cut-off t-shirt, similar to my own. "I've heard about you. These guys say you're a writer."

I hadn't written in a few weeks, and it felt embarrassing to define myself as such. "Something like that," I said. "These days I'm a summering freeloader, but I am working on some stories."

"Don't you and Whit call it something with bears?" Logan asked. "Your whole thing with the cutoff shirts and shorts?"

"The lifestyle is called Summer Bears," Whitney explained. "A mix between gay man bear and real bear interests." I liked how seriously she took this and how thoughtfully she presented it. I didn't dare reveal that Bear Life was something I had invented in college with my old friend Lynd. Whitney had taken it on as her own and found an identifying depth I couldn't have imagined.

Raleigh and I went around to the back of the car to help carry in supplies. "Hey, nice shirt, by the way," we turned to say at the same time.

"I got Two Hearted, just for you, bud," Whitney said, and handed me a case of beer to carry in.

"Hey, thanks," I said and put the case up on my shoulder.

We had parked under the deck of the grey wood-sided house, and as I walked up the steps, a breeze ruffled the loose strings on my cutoffs. I turned around to appreciate the view. The lake sloshed against a dock, where a butter yellow speedboat was gleaming in the sun, just waiting to zip off. There couldn't be a more beautiful way out, I thought. Looking at perfection made me brace myself against its inevitable undoing. In light of Heather's friend, it seemed that I had experienced too many of these luxurious moments to be allowed to stalk around for much longer. But life was unfair, I thought, and often to my advantage. Even if I died here, at age twenty-five, I'd already had a disproportionately amazing life compared to the rest of the world.

"I know I already said this, but thanks for the invite," I called down to Logan. "This is going to be a great day."

He looked up at me, perplexed by what had brought on this particular revelation. "Well, yeah. Good," he said and placed the last of the bags on the ground so he could close the hatchback on his car.

Logan was not concerned with nuanced turns of feeling, but the big picture. That, I supposed, made him a very good match for the emotional plateau that was Whitney.

The both of them were so good at picking a point in the distance and marching, purposefully ahead. As they heaved the bags on their shoulders, and charged up the stairs, I was reminded of how efficient and capable they were. I suddenly understood the mechanism of their coupling, the synchronization and power. The previous night, when I had spoken about love appearing around unassuming corners, I hadn't meant with her and Logan, but here was her same self, the both of them robotic in their own ways. Even if she and Logan didn't last, he was dating a different Whitney than the one I knew, not the Summer Bear or the curly-haired Gumby, but somebody else whose best qualities were ones that I overlooked or maybe even disliked. I wondered how I could have been so stupid for this long. She had always been so much more than mine.

"You just going to stand there all day?" Whitney asked good-naturedly, as she made her way into the kitchen.

"I think I'd better not," I said, shaking my head.

The four of us took the boat out that afternoon and the hum of the engine sent me into a trance. I had always loved the sensation of skidding across water—the quick lifts, dull thuds, and the rush of air. Logan navigated to a spot where we could float idly amongst the tufts of cattails and reeds. We each claimed a flat section of bench to lie on and nurse a beer. Despite the buzz and shrieks of our fellow lake-goers, we'd fallen into a peaceful silence. The combination of the sun and the slow rocking of the water got me thinking of Gloria. Her demons lived in the ocean because it was so vast, and there was a way that time could blur and lost memories could come tumbling back to you. I was feeling on the brink of some revelation when my phone vibrated loudly. Nobody said anything, but I knew it had interrupted all of our delicate daydreams.

"Alright, so let's make a plan," Georgie was saying into my ear. "We have two options and a possible third, but I know you won't want to do the third. It involves a certain house of a certain high school friend of mine."

I felt good to be so far away from these kinds of considerations. "I'm already on a boat at Logan's lake house," I reported drowsily. "With him and Whitney and their friend Raleigh."

"Well, fine. You could have just told me."

"I did, Summertown. I sent you a text this morning."

"Oh." She sounded dejected. "I guess I forgot. I'll just have to go to a certain pool party by myself and wait until you quit getting special girl invitations."

"That's not even what happened. Go with Youngsu and Jurate

or your brother. I'll definitely see you tomorrow," I said. In fact Zoe had also invited me to a party at her parents' lake house, and I knew it was casual, but it seemed like an awkward scenario that I could easily sidestep.

"Oh hey," Georgie added. "Did you hear the thing with Heather and Amanda and their friend?"

"Yeah," I said. "Really bad news."

"Yeah. Be careful on that boat," she said. "You have to come back tomorrow. There's Iowa to plan. And you know, the rest of our life."

"Okay." It was appealing to think of our lives as one life. Though I wasn't thrilled about Iowa, not like I had been originally. The summer had lost some of its luster. I could feel that things were quietly rearranging, and our insistence on tradition was starting to seem more desperate than genuine. Or was the insistence my doing and therefore my desperation? This lake was an entirely new place, without expectations, and for the first time since I arrived, I felt the sense of freedom I'd come looking for.

"I guess we should have invited Georgie, that seems rude now," Logan said as I put my back phone in my pocket.

"She wouldn't have wanted to come," I said. "But it's thoughtful of you."

"Yeah, what's with that?" Logan asked. "She so rarely accepts invitations."

"Neutral," Whitney roused from her nap to say.

"You have to explain this to me," Logan demanded.

It meant Georgie took it personally that Whitney didn't want to be with me. That's what it was. Georgie was begrudging and sensitive for us, and I was open and forgiving. It was our dynamic. But I was never going to explain this to Logan, Whitney, or anyone. It was impossible to describe Georgie's and my consolidated sense of self without sounding like we were in love or religious or nuts.

"She's a host person," I replied. "She's bossy and likes to be in control."

"Some people are like that," Raleigh added. "I think it must be the way that some people have a hard time receiving presents. Or compliments."

"I have a pretty rough time with compliments," Whitney agreed.

"Me too. Instead of thanking people, I just agree with them. Like of course whatever I made or wore was great, I'm such an asshole."

"Yep," Whitney and Logan agreed.

I tossed my empty beer can so it let loose a light spray of foam on them.

Whitney had a shirt across her face and was resting her head on Logan's thigh.

"Nice aim," she said without moving.

"Thank you very much for that compliment," I replied.

Raleigh propped herself up on one elbow. "You don't seem so bad, Aneesha," she said, in a tone of voice that made me suddenly self-conscious, as if she had been examining me for visual signs of assholeishness—or worse, open niceness—of which I wasn't even aware.

Whitney chuckled. "Yeah, Aneesha, you're not such a bad asshole."

I rolled my eyes. "Said the pot, calling the kettle black. And thank you, Raleigh." Raleigh shrugged it off with a smile, and I thought that this was the kind of person I should have liked. I winked at her and then laughed at myself. It was a shame I didn't.

By the time evening fell, we'd all had our share of beer and I was bouncing around the kitchen. We dipped into a bowl of guacamole and prepared goodies for the grill. I'd put some chicken in a bag to marinate the previous day and, my contribution completed, I opened drawers and cabinets, marveling at the items inside. There were contraptions like garlic presses and egg slicers, tools I'd never buy because a good knife could do it all better. But I liked all the options available in this kitchen, the homeliness of mismatched bowl sets and painted wooden flowers hanging from ropes. From my visits to various friend's second homes, I gathered that this is where people kept the less-than-glamorous items they still loved, and that was my favorite side of everyone.

"Are you looking for something?" Logan asked. He was slicing onions and struggling against the sulfuric acids. "I might be able to tell you where it is if I can stop crying for a second."

"You're such an emotional wreck," Raleigh chided him. "Hey," I said, "I can do those onions, if you want."

He willingly handed over his knife and went out to start the grill.

"Team work!" Raleigh sang. She and I held up our knives and Logan and Whitney held up a BBQ lighter and corncob, so we could clang them together.

Out on the deck, fireworks went off, the cracks and booms so loud that the four of us ate mostly in silence. We motioned at each other to pass certain dishes and put on clownish expressions to compliment the cooking, which had turned out pretty well. Our beer supply was running low, and there was a brief charades exhibition about going out to get more, but then it occurred to us that nobody was exactly sober enough to drive.

"Well, let's go out on the lake then!" Logan said excitedly.

"Yeah!" I wanted an adventure.

Whitney patted her stomach. "I'm feeling pretty content right here."

"Too bad you can't drive that speed boat around," Raleigh lamented. "I'd be lulled to sleep like a baby."

"That's what's happening to me right now," Whitney said. "Consider me lulled."

Logan turned to me and I nodded. That was how the two of us ended up in a double kayak together, quietly skulking around the edges of the lake, while the sky exploded above us. How strange, I thought, that fireworks—a universal form of celebration and cheer—were the cousins of a bomb. Maybe that was part of their beauty, the inversion of their destructive roots. I remembered the first time Logan and I had cooked together and the high hopes it inspired for our compatibility. Mostly because I'd wanted to see myself in him—a form of generous selfishness, particular to me— and I had since been disappointed. But out there on the water, our strokes fell into sync, and I was pretty sure that if Whitney had never been involved, he and I could have built a meaningful friendship. He just wanted to be treated like a leader, and I was nothing if not an enthusiastic sidekick.

"So what's it like where you are in Southern California?" Logan asked. "You know, my brother moved to LA recently." We were gliding along, and I didn't care that the backstroke of his paddle was splashing me.

"It's not LA," I said. "It's strange and unreal."

"That does sound a little like LA. Not that I really know."

I kept forgetting about Riverside, that it was my present and my foreseeable future. "I'm not sure what it's like where you are in southern Illinois, but I'm thinking they might share some of the same culture."

Logan laughed. "You mean buckets of domestic beers consumed in bars, where you'd be afraid to go in if it weren't the only real bar in town, and the mix of people was already weird before you arrived?"

"That's it," I said. "Exactly that. When I go run errands, everything about me is so out of context that I can't fathom all of the reasons people are staring."

"Sounds like fun. Is that what you were expecting?"

"The thing is," I said, "nothing is ever what I expect, and so I expected that. But do you ever find yourself slogging through some metaphorical bog, of your own choosing, and you know the pros and cons of continuing to slog come out to be perfectly even?"

"Really? To slog?" he asked.

"It's a word. Difficult work. So you're slogging in the bog, and you decide that since you're already here, you have to get all the way in, over your head, mud in your ears, because if you try hard enough you can make it worth something. Even if it's not necessarily good, you can at least join the bog, and gain some perspective."

"I think I know what you're saying," Logan said. We had paddled into an open channel and there was an island with a neon-lit bar straight ahead. I wondered if that was the destination our leader had in mind. I liked finding out what secret plans people had been hatching all along. "You're saying that you just have to commit to something to make it worthwhile, right?" he asked.

I grinned. "You don't like working in bog and slog metaphors?"

"Alright, fine." He sighed and I was excited that he was going to humor me. "The more you slog, the better the bog?"

I burst out laughing. "Yeah, that's it. I think you have to slog without knowing what you'll get out of the bog. I think that's what I need to do with Riverside."

"Can I ask you something?"

"Yeah, sure," I said. And I was overcome with the sudden panic that he had figured out that night with Whitney.

Instead he asked, "When do you just leave the bog?"

"I don't know yet. Maybe when you've grown to love it? Or hate it? Hey, are we headed towards that bar?"

"Yes. I figured if you can be counted on for something, it's wanting another drink."

"Oh, right. Sure." I was insulted for a moment, but then, it wasn't untrue. I liked to think that the drinking I did was a shortcut to the heart of matters, to open up all the doors and windows, and consider all possible options.

"I'm sure you know that Whitney and I have been fighting a bunch," he ventured. "Is Whitney the bog you're talking about?" I asked. I was still trying to figure out if he was testing me or if we were really having an honest conversation. "Aneesha," Logan said, "we're moving on from bogs."

We approached a low edge of the island and each grabbed a handful of reeds to pull the kayak in. He hopped out first and then held the boat as I hoisted myself onto the beach. I followed his lead and we let the boat rest, face down, near a large tuft of stiff grass.

"They say that fighting is a natural part of relationships," I said and wiped my hands on my shorts. I was more inclined toward the Vichy France approach myself— surrender quickly, save what you can—but Logan had integrity.

"We get along great, and then out of nowhere we get in fights about the most trivial things. Like I shouldn't have asked if she wants to wear sunscreen or something, like my caring is an insult. I just want the best for us." He looked so earnest, so young, and I felt pathetic for having assumed some kind of manipulation from him. "You know her. What am I doing wrong?" he pleaded.

The barn-like structure of the island swamp bar was looming just ahead, and I thought if only we could get in there I could avoid the entire wrongness of this conversation. Surely it would be loud and lewd, and Logan and I would be thrust onto the same team again, so I could conveniently forget that I had actively participated in damaging the relationship he was seeking my advice to save.

"I'm not sure," I said at first, because I had only earlier that day noticed their potential as a couple. But I did know Whitney, he was right about that, and the least I could do was tell him how I would handle the situation.

"I think you just need to leave a little more room for her to figure out stuff for herself. You're really lucky because you seem to know exactly what you want all the time. Whitney doesn't like making decisions," I said. "Especially after work or exercise, when she's hungover or hungry, before coffee or if somebody has recently annoyed her—so, any time."

Logan and I exchanged a chuckle. "There are still things she does and doesn't want. So give her a beer and pizza before you talk about something important, and don't expect an answer immediately. Also, you probably know that she hates debating."

His eyes were fixed at some distant point on the river, and in his silence I heard the gruff roar of Bruce Springsteen coming through the walls of the barn. I was ready to move forward into this palace before us. I wanted the half-hearted relief of a leaky air-conditioning unit.

The moment was lost on Logan, however. "So you're saying that I'm just being too direct?" he wanted to clarify. "Too confrontational? Don't address things head-on?"

"Well," I said. "It's not like I can give you a map to a successful future with Whitney. There isn't a single plan. Just don't assume because she hasn't come out and told you how she feels, that she has no thoughts on the matter. She'll go along with anything for a while, until she knows for certain that she doesn't want it, and then everything is fucked. But if you can pretend you're her, and imagine what she would want, I think you can go for a very long time." I said this and suddenly understood that this was my own personal plan.

"But that seems ridiculous," Logan said. Not dismissively, more with something akin to awe. "When you can just ask her? Why? How?"

Because that's what it was to love another person, I thought. To incorporate them into you. I didn't want to own Whitney. There wasn't anything I had to have from her, I just wanted permission to carry her wherever I went, and for her to do the same with me. I also understood that Whitney had no idea what she wanted. Everything was just a trial for her. But I had already shared more with Logan than I expected to. "Do you always push so hard all the time?" I smiled and grabbed him by the shoulder. "Come on, your pet lush wants a drink."

We walked into the bar and were the only ones not wearing bathing suits. There were thin, long-haired dudes, and chunky men in baseball caps, and leathery bikini-clad women, and girls with belly-button rings—all of them vigorously flailing to "Dancing in the Dark".

"Gotta love America," I said. We ordered ourselves some tall boys and joined in.

The bittersweet power-chords pumped through me, and I knew it was just like Bruce said: there was no way I was going to start a fire crying over my broken heart or worrying that my world was falling apart. I jumped up and down with this throng of hopeful, restless beating hearts, trying to work up the courage to become some better version of me.

When we got home that night, Logan and I shared a brief hug and then went our separate ways. I unfurled my sleeping bag on the short couch in the basement. Raleigh was asleep on the long one, her arm hanging like a pendulum, exposing the pretty floral tattoo that began at her elbow. All the beer had numbed me and all I wanted was sleep. I took off my soggy shorts and tank top, and though I was trying desperately to be quiet, I still knocked my leg into the side of the coffee table.

Whitney came down the stairs as I was bent over my shin, silently exclaiming in pain. I heard her soft giggle before I saw her, and in the dark she put her hand on my back.

"Aneesha, what are you doing?" she whispered.

"I'm drunk and ran into a table. I'm being normal. What are you doing?" I asked. "I just wanted to say goodnight. Thanks for playing with Logan, he had a good time." She was wearing an undershirt and no pants. Part of me wanted to kiss her, but the other part was annoyed that she hadn't just come along in the first place, if she was bothering to get up now.

"You don't have to thank me," I said. "There were no favors being exchanged."

"I was just thinking about what I said before, on the boat, and I wanted to make sure you know that I don't actually think you're an asshole."

"Are you serious?" I asked. We were standing around in a shadowy basement in our underwear in front of Logan's best friend. I couldn't stand Whitney for putting me in this position, but I couldn't deny that I enjoyed these moments, in which she insisted on odd and inappropriate ways to express care, without consideration of how they might seem to other people.

"Yes, I'm serious. You're a good one, okay?"

"Well, thanks, Whit." I put my hand on her shoulder. "I assumed us being such pals and all, that you did in fact like me, but it's nice to have confirmation."

"You know what I'm talking about." she said, stepping close to me and glancing over at Raleigh. "I'm sorry, and I don't know what to do."

Her hand was on my waist and she smelled so familiar, but she could not have picked a worse time or place to repeat or discuss our kitchen interlude. "Not now. Maybe not ever. But not now. Go to bed," I said. I gently pushed at her elbow, and she started back up the stairs.

I wondered if I had been too harsh, and as she walked slowly up the stairs, I was reminded of our favorite Ke$ha song. "You wanna dance with no pants on?" I whispered.

She looked over her shoulder. "Holler," she whispered, and threw her hands in the air.

✦

Back in Chicago, Georgie made me meet her at the Coffee Studio for a writing session. I hated that place. It was all matte plastic curves and tightly packed, low-to-the-ground seating. But what I really couldn't get over was how—in the midst of this heavy-handed minimalism—fancy moms with strollers packed for the Iditarod felt comfortable coming in and filling the place with excess.

"Stop glaring at the babies," Georgie said to me. "It's not their fault." She picked up her latte bowl and took a sip. "You better not look at me that way when I'm a mother."

The truth was that Georgie was going to be a fantastic mom. She only concerned herself with the essentials. We had discussed how damaging it seemed for girls whose moms wanted to be their friends and confidants, as well as mothers. She would never be that way. "I'm sure I'll like your stupid baby," I said.

"You better. It's going to be a girl and she'll need to have strong Asian women role models in her life." Georgie was tapping her pencil against the journal that she'd brought along, and I motioned to it to let her know we could get down to business.

"Right," she said. "But first, Richard and I had a Two Person Book Club meeting, and it went very well. We discussed Tom Sawyer."

"Why?" I asked. "There can't possibly be anything new to say about that book."

"That always makes it a safe choice. Listen, he's clearly doing fine, and now he wants to invite the *Words with Friends* woman to Iowa." She looked at me with wide eyes.

I smiled. "Of course he does. Better give them a bedroom."

"Do we have to? I mean, really?"

At the Hill House, where we stayed on the farm, there were three bedrooms upstairs and one downstairs that could be given to couples. Georgie relished the act of graciously bestowing them on her favorite pairs.

"Yes. Otherwise they'll just have sex in front of everyone."

"You think?" Georgie asked. She drew her chin in so she looked like a disgusted toad.

"You know Richard, he's always talking about—"

Georgie put her hand in front of my face. "You know better than I do, and let's keep it that way."

"You know about his term 'rub one out,' I'm sure you can extrapolate."

"He treats you like a man, but you're not."

"He treats me like he'd treat himself, and I don't mind that." Saying this aloud made me realize how much I actually missed Richard. I wanted to apologize, but that would also require him admitting that I'd hurt him, and I didn't want to put him in that position. "Is Youngsu coming?" I asked.

"Maybe. He said he wasn't sure if he could take work off because he offered to cover for other people. Who are coming." She paused. "Because he didn't realize that's why they needed a sub. Did I tell you he bought a scooter?" she added. "That guy is full of surprises. It's broken, but he's going to fix it." She looked at me like this was routine and for a moment I thought we'd turned a corner, one in which we trusted Youngsu to complete an involved project like this. But then she smiled her fake smile, the one that belonged to Georgie, the untrustworthy mom with city roots.

"Well, it's not technically your problem," I said to reassure her. Georgie expected Youngsu to fail miserably, but I thought it was a decent gamble on his part. If he ever got it fixed, he'd be a hero.

We wrote in silence for a while. Georgie scrawled things in her journal with the Montblanc that she liked to subtly flash around. It was the only object she was very proud of. I didn't make snide remarks since we were writers, and there wasn't anything else to show off.

I had finished with Gloria, and needed to work on a host of other stories, but I was writing something new. I had recently read an article about chimp retirement homes. Many of the resident chimps were washed-up Hollywood actors, who were used to being the center of attention, and were accustomed to human living standards. However, like so many young stars, they had lost their youth, their innocence, and their allure. Full-grown chimps were immensely powerful creatures, and it wasn't safe for them to live with people, but they weren't capable of surviving in the wild. Some of them had been sent to Florida to live in a special home, meant to reintroduce them to wild behaviors.

It was so absurd that it broke my heart. Aside from my general shame about the way humans treated nature, I considered the humiliation of recognizing your own decline in value, of having

to relearn habits that were supposed to be inherent. I supposed
time would do that to all of us. I thought of my younger sister, a
calculating introvert who was often described as my personality
opposite. We did, however, share a sense of humor that favored
the simultaneously sorry and absurd. In the evenings, my sister
volunteered at a retirement home, teaching computer skills to senior
citizens. So many of her students wanted help sending emails to
their family members, asking for tragically simple things, like a trip
to In-N-Out or KFC. "Sometimes they get mad because they don't
remember that their son or daughter just took them the day before,"
she once reported to me, and it was so depressing that we couldn't
stop laughing. The chimp scenario was the same, I thought, and
grinned to myself.

"What?" Georgie asked.

I shared my train of thought. "Don't you think it's kind of a
unfair that some people die before they lose their dignity, potential
and beauty?" I asked. "Like they never know what they are without
youth?"

"Yes. Like how some people leave at the best part of the party,
before it deteriorates into madness and crying, and they don't have to
live with bad decisions or a hangover the next day. They don't really
know who they are."

"Yes, exactly that! I don't like those people," I said.

Georgie smiled. "Why would you want to skip out on the ugly
part? It's the best part. I've never understood this preoccupation with
beauty. It's entirely overrated and boring compared to terribleness.
That's why you're writing about those limbo chimps," she said, gesturing at my computer. "Because the beauty is much sharper when
something falls apart or was never meant to be in the first place." She
said this off-handedly and went back to her journal.

"If I ever have a book, you're writing an introduction," I said.

"When," she said, and eyed me. "We're working in whens now."

"Absolutely."

Her writing frown deepened and I was convinced that it was
true. For all my frivolity and electric-colored brouhahas, I was
serious and morbid enough for Georgie. She was my reminder of my

own subtext, and I needed to be reminded.

Near the end of our writing session, Georgie and I were inter-rupted by a high school friend of hers. Gillian was wearing a lacy French maid bonnet and metal earrings that stretched the hole in her earlobes. "I just wanted to say hi," she said breezily.

Her bangs were intentionally far too short and stuck up a little. "I have some important computer work to take care of, but it's always good to see you guys around. Keep the art coming, it's the only thing, really." Gillian patted our low table, and then sauntered over to a corner in the back and pulled out her computer. Georgie watched her for longer than I did.

"It's the only thing, really," I repeated in Gillian's voice, breathy and confident, like she'd just had multiple orgasms.

"Should have known," Georgie said, turning back to her note-book. "Look." She nodded to the back and I saw that Gillian's "important computer work" was editing and posting photos to Facebook.

"Importance is relative, I suppose."

"I can't believe how cool she thinks she is," Georgie marveled.

"What she said about art though. I mean, that's basically what we were just saying, but more direct."

"Fine." Georgie let out a hollow sigh. She squinted through the window, just like Youngsu. "I've never felt this way before, but I think I can do better than this."

"Than what?" I asked, alarmed.

"This. Anything I'm doing here. I'm feeling down, Aneesha. I should just go back to China where I don't belong. I'm never going to be a famous poet, or a hip mom, or part of a subtle power couple."

"Because of Gillian?" I asked, shooting my thumb at the Facebooking.

"No, because of me. But Gillian will. She's crazy and her earlobes are going to split in half, but that will somehow be cool, and that's what people care about."

I thought we were "working in whens," and this sudden down-turn was disturbing.

I didn't know Georgie was so fragile. "Hey, come on, let's get out of this ridiculous coffee shop, it's killing your soul."

"I'm sorry?" Georgie surprised me with her breathy Gillian lilt. "It's a studio, not a shop?" Her mood had lifted for the moment, but I needed to return to the original sentiment. I didn't want her to do better than 'this.' This was our joint life. She could go to China for a while, but one day she would have to come back again.

We walked up Clark and into a small dollar store, hoping to find some birthday supplies. Later in the week, our friends were throwing a surprise party for Heather, and Amanda had put me and Georgie in charge of festive décor. I flipped through a t-shirt rack and found a neon Power Rangers shirt that Heather might like. A pack of bright pink wrist sweatbands had fallen to the floor and I picked it up. "In case she works up a sweat," I said to Georgie.

She had found the piñata corner. They were twirling slowly from their hooks in the ceiling. Georgie was tall enough that she seemed to be looking them right in their big, innocent eyes, and suddenly the idea of striking a little Dora the Explorer or a happy dinosaur seems cruel.

"This guy," Georgie was saying to the woman brandishing a pole. "You like him, Aneesha?"

The "him" in question was an adorable round bird with a red body and blue belly. "Yep," I said, "let's take him home and fill him with goodies. And then bash his head in."

"You're not supposed to fall in love with the piñata. Jesus, Aneesha." Georgie hugged him and he filled her arms. "Let's put some slap bracelets in him too."

I was always in love with the piñata, as it were. "You can't just say you think you can do better than this and not specify what 'this' is."

"One minute," Georgie said as she dug through her wallet and pulled out some cash. "It looks like we were throwing a party for a kid."

"Here, streamers too," I said. "And glitter, why not?" The finality of this place and time was creeping in on me, and I wasn't going to cut any corners.

"Okay," Georgie said as we headed toward her parents' house. "What I mean by 'I can do better than this' is it's time for me to leave again."

"You're going to China," I said.

Her face was smushed up. She was trying to find a way to say that I was wrong, but I wasn't. "Don't tell Youngsu yet," was what she said instead.

We were standing outside of the McDonald's that advertised 30-cent cones, which did throw the priorities of this country into question. "But you just got back."

"I got that travel fellowship from my MFA program."

"So you'll go be the tall white foreigner again, and spend all your time figuring out the basics, and not have time to consider anything else? So you can come back and wonder what to do with your life all over again?"

Georgie did not glare at me like I would have glared at me. She looked calmly over the head of the chubby bird in her arms and rested her chin on top. "Yes. What if that's what I would like to do? What if I would like to find a different way to be in the world? Foreign and isolated, bumbling and frustrated. Don't you think there would be some kind of poetic merit in that? It's not any different than here really, there's just a good reason for feeling that way."

I kicked a bottle cap on the ground. It was actually a great point. Georgie's poetry was all about the unexpected moments of sync and synthesis in an otherwise disconnected world. "Fine," I said. "But you have to come back. You can't be one of those pathetic white people who floats around Asia because you're boring at home. You have to come home, and be interesting and special."

I expected her to laugh at this demand or at least roll her eyes, but Georgie nodded thoughtfully. She was wearing an ugly blue cap from her friend's Beijing tour company, and only the top gem button on her leopard-print cardigan was done. She would never not be someone special.

"I'm going to come back," she said. "And I will wonder what to do with my life."

"Well, good."

"And you? Where are you going?"

"What do you mean?" I asked. I saw my future as currently on hold while I was in grad school, like I was being stored in a refrigerator for the next few years, and I had no idea who I would be when

I emerged. I anticipated getting a little bendy and sour.

"I mean I'm not the only one who has to go home and be special," Georgie said. I swung the plastic bag filled with streamers. It was hard to admit that this city—where I could gather a group of people at the drop of a hat, where my friends exchanged personal surprises routinely, where I could sit down at a number of bars and drink for free—that this was not, in fact, my home. It belonged to Georgie, really, and Whitney and everyone else who had been accommodating enough to let me borrow it for a while. "Alright, true," I said. There was some delightful mystery in not knowing where home would be for me, but I was suddenly confronted with the terrible, awful reality that Georgie's and my joint life would not be shared like this forever.

She saw me understand the implication of her question. "I think it might be okay eventually," she said. "Not great, but okay."

I sighed. "If not, there will always be the poetic merit." "And a book of our collected letters."

"It would make sense that our shared life takes place primarily on paper."

We stopped at a crosswalk, and a leathery man in a wheel chair knocked his fist on the bird. "Hey, are you on TV?" he asked.

"No, but that would be cool." Georgie said. "Okay," he muttered and went about his business.

"Wouldn't it be great if some screwball wanted to put us on TV?" Georgie asked me.

"*The Real Unwed Women of Chicago?*" I asked.

She laughed. "It would have to be as good as that bad lesbian show you and Whitney watch."

"*The Real L Word*, no way!" I said. "Don't underestimate the entertainment value of people behaving in ways that demonstrate they don't actually care about each other, but then spend all their time claiming that they do. I think that's how lots of peoples' lives are."

Georgie thought about this. "Yeah, wow. To think that some people are even more lost than we are." We chuckled loudly to ourselves, the arrogant fools we were, and continued on past the giant clock face on Devon Hardware, past the Jackhammer leather dungeon, past the convenience store/taco counter where they showed soap operas all day long, past the naval academy where kids in peaked caps were always kicking a soccer ball on the astroturf. There wasn't another city I could navigate so well, that lived so vividly in my mind. I hoped the even grid of Chicago would be easy to fold up and carry with me.

There were other pieces that would not be so easy, however. Most often my romantic interests began as playful, and when I realized they had no practical staying power, became an all-consuming mournful swoon. With Zoe, my plan was not to get consumed. I had finally gotten a little structure in my life: mornings I spent at Metropolis exploring the woes of retired chimps, inappropriate love for animals, and robots. Lunch was either Whitney's CSA box— a study in summer squash—or out with Heather, Amanda and Georgie. My afternoons and evenings were spent with Zoe or friends, flinging open that window of possibility and letting my curtains flail in the wind.

Still, sometimes I'd watch Zoe sauntering down the street to join me—her easy, bouncy walk, the effortless way she wore knits in the humidity, the sincerity with which she greeted strangers—and I felt so pleased it was me she was walking to meet. It was hard for me to ignore her potential. She was, as Heather, Amanda and Jurate had pointed out, the most promising crush I'd had in a long time. There were no complications, with the exception of her usual preference for dating men, which we kept neatly swept away and out of sight.

So of course I accepted when she invited me to go camping with her. "It would just be a night," she said, "I have to get back for a birthday party on Saturday evening, but let's spend Friday in the woods together." It was the last phrase—"spend Friday in the woods together"—which made me unable to resist. I had never been with someone who wanted to engage in regular dating practices with me. I associated flowers with funerals, and nice meals with my parents, but to go somewhere quiet with the intention of appreciating beauty and exploring a little, that was as romantic as anything I could imagine.

"You can't get gayer than camping," Whitney said. She stood with her arms crossed at the doorway between my room and the living room, and was eyeing me suspiciously as I packed up my things. "You're sure this isn't like a serious love affair?"

I shrugged. "How the hell do I know? Do I seem like someone who knows when a serious love affair is afoot?"

"You use words like 'afoot.' What isn't a serious love affair to you?" She bit off the end of a zucchini. That week we were trying squash as a carrot replacement.

"Hey, this is strictly good and no badness," I defended myself. "You should be impressed."

"You and Tutor Crush camping together. Oh, I'm impressed." Her smile was faint and mostly to herself. "You know, the weather is great, you'll have a lot of fun," she said, softening a bit.

"Thanks," I replied. "Now let me borrow a flask so I can be a proper camping lesbian."

"In the cupboard with the coffee mugs. There are several, as you would imagine." She watched me choose a standard silver one. "Be careful with Tutor Crush. I don't want to see you staring depressingly at the wall again," Whitney said. "And I know you won't be careful and it's not even like I believe it's good advice, but I want to be someone who said that."

I poured the last of an old Jim Beam pocket whiskey through a funnel into the flask. "You and me both."

Zoe drove a Honda Civic that we packed up with our tent and some blankets. She and I pooled what was left in each of our refrigerators, and went to the butcher shop on Paulina to pick up brats to roast.

"As a Midwesterner, I do not fuck around when it comes to sausages," she explained.

"I am always a proponent of discerning taste," I added in support. I was absolutely enticed by a woman who knew exactly what meat to cook and how.

We zipped quickly through the rest of our errands—gas, beer, firewood—and were on the road an hour after we'd met up. "How are we so efficient?" she asked me, as we took the highway north. "You're reading my mind, aren't you?" She shoved me in the shoulder a little. "Stop it. You're gonna find out how excited I am about those Pop Tarts you brought. And about being naked with you in a tent."

"Neither of which are secrets," I teased her. "Even for non-mind readers."

I was smiling and we were trading jabs, when I suddenly felt aware of how close I was to being consumed. It was like I'd casually walked by the mouth of a cave and only noticed because I heard my laughter echo in the hollow below. I had to keep it light, I thought. I could get out of this unscathed, and carry the sweetness out with me. It had turned out to be Zoe, my whim, who had been my most reliable source of joy these past few weeks, but I had to remember that this was just for fun. The last thing I needed was another crack in my porcelain heart to nurse through the dry winter.

"Why the long face?" she asked, gently.

I liked that Zoe was so upfront. She didn't avoid me when I seemed upset, she didn't pretend to care less for me than she did. It was open and freeing in a way I hadn't expected. Maybe it was because we knew that it was temporary, and there was no future to blight, no proverbial gun to jump.

"I was just thinking that I'll miss you when I'm gone." I smiled.

She put her hand on my thigh. "Oh, Aneesha, I'll miss you too. It's so easy to be happy with you. But then, clearly the whole of Chicago feels that way. I'm sure your grad school friends don't feel much differently."

I did wonder what my grad school friends were up to. They had all seemed content to see Riverside, and our MFAs, as a stop on the way to other, more real ways of living. For me, however, there was nothing more real than whatever I was doing in the moment. I considered Zoe's comment and thought that this year, I ought to make more of an effort to see if I couldn't make all of my Riverside friends happy where we were. I was fantastic at making other people happy, and there was no reason to be stingy with it.

We spent the afternoon splashing around the shallow end of a lake. Sparkling flecks of rock and sand billowed up each time I took a step into the water. A thick field of reeds and lily pads stretched out before us, undulating with the ripples of the water. At one point, Zoe and I stood beside each other staring up at the clouds. "Don't they look like pieces of torn fabric?" she asked. It was a very good comparison.

"Do you ever worry," I asked her, "that you already have all the things you want from your life, and the passing of time only means that you're going to lose them?"

"No," she said. "Nobody wants the same thing forever." She bent down and picked up a rock that she skipped across the water. "Anyway, sometimes you think you know and you don't even." She raised her eyebrow at me, and handed me a rock to skip.

I took it from her, and flung it so it hopped twice and sank. I thought she might be wrong. Not that I planned to want one thing forever, but there couldn't have been more than a few things that I did. This was one of them: standing in a quiet lake, doing a lot of nothing together with someone who wanted my company as much as I wanted hers. I wondered why we couldn't move through life like seasons in the year—there couldn't be more than four ways I wanted to live at once. It should have been possible, I thought.

I watched Zoe build a fire that evening, and relished the precision with which she placed each piece of wood, and how close she let her fingers get to the flames. We did get naked in the tent, and she slowly teased me into an orgasm that snapped me out like a crisp, clean sheet. Afterwards, I fell asleep with my head tucked into the space between her stomach and her curled up thighs, and I had never been less sorry that I wasn't careful with my heart.

⌁

The night of Heather's surprise party, Georgie and I got tipsy early. While Remi took Heather out for a drink, we haphazardly twisted and hung streamers, then stuffed the piñata and secured the bird's flap with layers of packing tape. The party was surely less of a surprise than Heather let on, but she made a point of putting on a shocked expression when the group of us jumped out from behind the couch. "You knew, didn't you?" we all accused her at various points, because it seemed impossible to put anything past Heather.

The piñata was the true surprise. When Georgie opened the hallway closet to reveal the chubby red bird, Heather gasped and held her chest. "How did you know I'm the best at this?" she gushed. I hadn't seen Heather so lighthearted since before the accident, and it felt good to be able provide her this tiny moment of relief. She posed for photos with the bird on her lap before Richard and Youngsu rigged it up over a tree branch outside.

We gathered on the sidewalk, and Amanda came over to compliment mine and Georgie's surprise party operation. "Great move with the piñata. Heather loves to destroy them."

"That sounds like the opening line to an awful porn," Georgie said.

"What? Who would even want to watch that?" Amanda asked.

"This is all news to me," I said. "I had no idea piñata parties were standard in Wisconsin, but if they're popular there, why not in porn?"

Amanda laughed. "Heather was always a weirdo, even when we were kids. She used to have a group with her friends where they tried to help old people take out the trash and mow their lawns, but everyone was too overwhelmed by her energy. She even made up a song."

I laughed. "Amanda, this is a really good surprise party, you're an awesome friend." I recalled my conversation with Georgie about the dissolution of our joint life, and I wondered if Amanda and Heather felt a similar unease over their separation. "Will it be weird when Heather is gone?" I asked.

Amanda was quiet for a moment. "Yeah, I think so, but everything is different now. Maybe it's just time for everyone to go their own way. There are still so many things I want to do." Before she died, was the implication, and I shivered.

Arthur stepped jauntily over to us with his beer in the air. "It's a reliable bunch," he said. "You act like a rag-tag group out in public, but look how wholesome this is." He was right. Everyone had done their part—nobody wanted to ruin a party for Heather.

Youngsu and Georgie were now leaning against the fence kissing, and nobody had made a single joke or snide comment. Somehow our dive bar crew had transformed into a group of responsible adults, grinning like idiots and preparing to swat at a piñata.

Heather began swinging her broomstick, and after making a few weak connections she grumbled. "You guys, I don't think I can do this with the blindfold on."

"Take it off!" Jurate shouted. "Swing free!"

I looked across the circle to catch Richard's eye, and he chuckled. "Yeah, Heather, take it off and swing free!" It was reconciliatory, and I knew that we'd already forgiven each other, but he was a close friend and I wanted to do better than that.

Amanda put out her hand to take the blindfold from Heather, and tied it up in her own hair.

Whitney wandered over to where we stood. "It's a good look," she said to Amanda. "Hey," she turned to me, "speaking of good looks, where's Zoe? I thought you invited her."

"We've all been dying to meet your mystery lady," Arthur added.

"I know, but she couldn't make it." I shrugged. "She also had a party tonight."

Arthur nodded and turned his attention to the dramatic wind-up that Heather was preparing. Whitney continued, however, to stare at me.

"What?" I asked her.

"I hear she's so cute and smart and funny. I want to meet her is all," said Whitney. "Yeah, I'm sure that's all," I said.

Whitney lowered her eyebrows at me. "Come on, Aneesha." She lifted her beer bottle in a way that seemed like it wasn't made of glass, but something lighter—she made everything look effortless. "I'm trying to share your excitement here."

"You are," I said. "You lent me your flask." "Well, okay, fine," she shrugged.

There was a muted thwack as Heather delivered a calculated blow, and a cheer rose up from around us. I continued watching Whiney. The faint smile lines at the sides of her mouth that darkened in her solemn expressions. The way her eyes met mine in a slow roll to somewhere else. I was afraid of losing her and not losing her, but my latest fear was that I'd hurt her. It seemed possible now. I had thought that because I was the one coming back to her life, because I found myself drafting long emails to her late at night, and missing her every time I sat down at a bar, that I was the one at her mercy. But her relationship with Logan was not a replacement for ours, and I saw now how equally devastating it would be for her to lose my friendship. I hadn't wanted to mix Zoe up with my friends because it would be easier for me when it was over, but I also wasn't prepared to lose Whitney in the way I knew I would one day when we saw how happy we could be with other people.

"Look," I said. "I'm excited, okay? I like her, but she's not like the paragon of woman or something."

Heather had put the blindfold back on and was smacking wildly, catching only pieces of the bird, a foot, the beak, a shoulder.

"No?" Whitney asked. "You know, you're my best friend. I want you to be happy."

I felt a twinge at Whitney's phrasing, at her removing herself from my happiness. "I know. Thank you. Same to you."

The stiffness of my response made her turn to look on me. "I'm serious. I made you a friendship bracelet."

As much as I didn't want to be won over by a friendship bracelet, I found myself smiling.

"What?" she asked.

"I can't wait to see it." I was awash with relief. "I made a million last summer for everyone, and all I wanted was for someone to make one for me."

"I know you did," Whitney said. "I just couldn't remember how to do it. I had to learn on YouTube, and then I made a few ugly ones that I just couldn't give to you. It was supposed to be a surprise, but oh well." She shrugged. "I still have the one that you made me attached to my work bag, and people ask about it all the time."

Heather finally ripped open the belly of the bird, and I watched the *Power Rangers* t-shirt fall out, followed by a glittery stream of plastic and candy. "Where did you get all this piñata stuff, by the way?" Whitney asked. "I want all of it."

"The dollar store. I know a good slap bracelet when I see one."

Heather bounced over to me with the t-shirt. "This is amazing! Thank you, thank you, thank you." She wrestled the t-shirt over my head. "Come on, Aneesha, show off the goods."

The party moved back inside where a dance-off began, and I showed down Arthur by using Blow Pops to drum on the counter and floor. Then we took a group bike ride around the neighborhood, from which it seemed only a few of us returned. I found Youngsu on the floor underneath the overhang of the island in the kitchen. He was putting together a puzzle of kittens wearing bows.

"Did you hear the news?" he asked me, without looking up.

I settled on the floor across from him, and tried to contribute to the puzzle, but I couldn't tell the difference between the fuzzy beige carpet pieces and the fuzzy beige kitten pieces. "No," I said. "I didn't hear the news. Well, which news?" There was Georgie leaving for China, and Heather leaving for Milwaukee, and Richard with his new love interest, and who knew what else.

"About the Heartland. They're selling it." He said this very calmly, and went back to picking up pieces of the bows. His fingers were long, and his movements were slow and methodical. "No guarantees they're keeping any of the staff."

"Oh," I said.

"I've been looking at other serving jobs, and wow," he looked up at me with the cartoon eyebrow arc. "We were getting way underpaid. I mean, figures. I'll still miss the people. How strange is it, just think," he said. "I'd have never met Georgie and you and everyone else, except for the Heartland. What would I be doing?"

I laughed. "I keep thinking the same thing. About who else I would have become if it weren't for the Heartland and who else I should become now, but I have to admit that I like this a lot."

Heather walked in and joined us on the floor. "Oh, I love kittens," she said, and immediately began to separate the pieces I couldn't tell apart.

"Youngsu just told me the Heartland's on the market," I said. "What kind of person will buy it, do you think?"

Heather had the puzzle about finished already. "I've heard Tim might buy it," she said.

"That would actually be great," said Youngsu.

Tim was a guy in a leather bomber who had spent much more of his life than ours posted at the Buffalo Bar, chatting away with everyone who passed through. Sometimes I'd see him just having a coffee and watching the weather report on TV before he went home.

"It has to be someone who already loves it," Heather said. "In some other lifetime, when we'd already gone off and accomplished as much as we could, it might have been nice to take on the Heartland."

Youngsu guffawed. "Heather."

She smiled. "Okay fine, but it's a nice idea, right?" She pressed the final piece in the puzzle and dusted her hands off. "Well, we knocked that out. You guys should all stay here tonight. We can have a sleepover and I'll make bacon in the morning. I want to thank you for such a great birthday, it really means a lot to me."

Georgie, Amanda, Sam, Whitney and Remi were in the living room, flipping through TV channels. We all shared the last couple beers and considered it, but in the end only Remi stayed. Instead, we rounded up the trash, and took it out to the alley where we tossed individual cans into the bins until none were left, and we finally got on our bikes to leave. While I rode Caliente slowly through the side streets of Rogers Park, I wondered who would take our place at the new Heartland, which creative directionless youngsters would find themselves waylaid for a period of time, and if they too would find it so difficult to separate at the end of each night.

✦

Amanda and I were both sweating in Sam's kitchen, stirring a pot of weed butter. He was out teaching a cartooning class to kids, but Amanda, Whitney and I were using his apartment as a base camp for our day at Pitchfork. We had gotten free tickets to the music festival, and we decided to go the good old-fashioned way: with pot brownies.

None of us, we had agreed, generally liked pot brownies or music festivals, but it was free and we figured we wouldn't not have fun together.

"So what's going on with Tutor Crush? Is she your girlfriend now?" Amanda asked me.

"Is Zoe my girlfriend?" I was unnerved. I couldn't tell if it was the excruciating heat, or the weed fumes, or the fact that Amanda's high-flame cooking style was making me nervous about burning the butter, but her question made me squirm.

I didn't want to say that things with Zoe had become routine because that made them sound boring. I took great pleasure in the lazy afternoons we spent lounging on each other, lost in our own separate books, wandering in and out of record stores, biking to beer at spots along the Chicago River. I had begun to rest easy in the fact that I was at least partially consumed by her.

"No, no, she's not my girlfriend. We're just enjoying each other's company."

"How do you make that distinction?" Amanda asked, and poked at the pot with a fork. "Because with me and boys it's really not that hard. They're either too annoying to spend quality time with or they're not, and they can be a boyfriend. You and Zoe are always doing fun interesting things together, you talk all the time, but you're not like together?" she asked.

It was not a distinction that I felt I was particularly apt to make. In my experience, a straightforward relationship that ended in the woman I cared for becoming my girlfriend, was not something I expected. Even when someone did want to be my girlfriend, it was generally with a few clauses and warnings that undid the value of it. With Zoe, it was that we understood she wanted to become a man's wife and the mother to children she'd obsess over. I figured she'd think of me as a crazy summer fling in the sunset days of her youth, a rebound, a tangent from the real things she wanted from her life, something with no pressure. One day we'd meet for wine, and she'd wear a matching sweater set, and we'd giggle together, in a friendly conspiring way—no mention of the way her left foot twitched violently right before she came. And so this, I explained to Amanda, absolutely prevented her from being my girlfriend.

"She's told you that?" Amanda asked, somewhat shocked, I

could see. I used this lapse in her cooking focus to quickly lower the heat on both the weed butter and the makeshift double-boiler where our chocolate was beginning to bubble.

"Of course not," I answered. "That's implicit. I doubt it would be much fun if we said out loud that we didn't expect anything from one another. But I'm leaving in a month, she's in a transition period, and I don't know." I shrugged and looked at Amanda.

She handed me a sieve, and I removed the saucepan from the stove. "I get it," Amanda said. "You're just taking it as it comes." She looked up at me suddenly, sharply. "You never worry you're wasting your time? Like what if all of this is for nothing?" she asked. "You're just throwing all of your eggs into a one basket and then it flies off. Poof." She smiled and shook a light cloud of flour at me.

"Just like that?" I smiled.

"Yeah, you know, just gone. Because people do that, and I really hate that," she said.

Amanda and I still hadn't talked about Zach's passing and I didn't want to push her into it. It seemed so clearly related, but she was guarded and I knew her feelings were cumbersome for her. I had also felt resentful of my emotions for most of my life, but I was coming around to the idea that if I didn't unfurl my cramped feelings and let them wave me around, there might not be anything else. Sometimes it felt like I had waited years of my life for the right moment to get serious and to give something my all, but so often my life was hanging together by tenuous, disparate threads. I wasn't sure I was a person for whom this moment would come.

Most people with whom I shared this feeling were confused. After all, I frolicked around with a passion for pleasure and more than enough to get by. I had a family who hoped the best for me, great friends, occasional achievements, and, every once in a while, a beautiful woman was taken by me. However, I knew that this was all a great and slippery piece of luck that came with no guarantees. I was familiar with the histories of my various people: artists, queers, women, people of color. Not that Amanda was entirely ignorant, but I got the impression that Zach was an awakening for her about just how cruel and lawless life could be. I had to say, it excited me to think that Amanda might join me on the side of the heedless and daring, that she might not have the arrogance—as it suddenly seemed—to hold out and toil patiently away for her hypothetical future self.

"People do disappear," I said, and cracked an egg on the side of a bowl. "The only sure thing is that the end comes. That's just the way things are."

Amanda put her hand on her hip and stared at me for a while. "And you won't be upset when you and Zoe split up?"

"Why would you say that?" I asked. "No, I'll be devastated! I'm falling over myself for her. I just won't be surprised. It's like when you go on vacation, knowing you have to go home afterwards."

Amanda pointed her index finger at me. I hoped this meant that I'd won her over a little. "That actually makes a lot of sense."

"What will you do about the impending doom?" I asked her.

"Something," she said. "I can't just sit around and wait for it to come."

My phone was ringing and Whitney's pop-eyed face lit up on my screen. "Let me in, I'm ready to do this thing!" she said. I imagined the running in place, and clapping like she did when she was excited.

Whitney came upstairs, tugged at the handkerchief around her neck and then gestured at my own. "Twins." She waved at the air. "I forgot how much pot smells. It's like high school all over again."

After a slightly burnt brownie, we rode very slowly from Logan Square down Armitage, towards Union Park. There were people everywhere, and if I hadn't felt buoyed by the brownie balloon, I'd have found the sticky droves of them repulsive. Whitney stood on her bike pedals and swooped left and right, taking the crowded street like a slalom. Amanda and I followed behind, weaving our way like pieces of colored ribbon through a braid. We locked up in front of some rank smelling port-o-potties, and I held my breath as I turned my key. "At least it smells too awful for anyone to stick around long enough to break our locks."

A few hours later, I had consumed a rainbow snow cone, a brat, two beers, and was lying face-up in the grassy infield of a baseball diamond. From this position I could hear the sets at three of the four stages, and if I focused on the clouds above me, relaxing into a sort of zombie state, I could simultaneously take them in together as one sound, one movement. It was like the aural version of when I relaxed my eyes and fixed them straight ahead, allowing me to perceive the full spectrum of my peripheral vision. I was stoned. The handkerchief around my neck had flapped up onto my chin, and was fluttering up and down with my breath. I felt perfectly open and alert.

Suddenly Whitney's face appeared above mine, her freckled forehead drawn. "So that's where you are." She looked around the mostly empty field. "Interesting choice of scenery."

"Shhh." I waved my hand at her. She was breaking my focused state.

"From far away it looks like something hit you, and you fell over." Amanda had joined us. The white frames of her sunglasses only emphasized the tinted squares where her eyes should have been, and it was like I had been discovered by a Storm Trooper in a sundress.

"Alright, alright, alright," I said, sitting up and adjusting my striped baseball cap. "You guys are ruining what I think is my 4D perception of this festival. Wait, how many dimensions is sound?" I asked them.

Whitney sat down beside me. "No, don't get up. It wasn't any better at the stage. Just a lot of dust and hay on the ground, why is there hay here?"

Amanda's storm trooper sandals were set in a wide stance, and her hands perched on her hips. "You guys really want to sit in the middle of a field? We're at a music festival. Let's just find another stage without hay."

"Where do you think they got the hay?" Whitney asked.

I looked down at the grass, and lifted a handful of brownish cuttings from the top of it. "Whit, it's just dried up grass from mowing the lawn."

She snorted and laughed "Well. That would do it, huh?" Whitney reached for a handful and sprinkled them on my shoulder. "Hay, girl."

Amanda put the schedule in Whitney's face. "Come on, pick a band, any band."

"How do I know? Ask Aneesha. She's the one hanging around

with hip college students, and high schoolers on websites and blogs and stuff."

"On websites and blogs and stuff?" I asked. "Are you like a hundred years old?" I snatched the schedule from Amanda and spotted an act I liked. The overly sentimental melodies layered over quick beats and nature sound effects had fueled my late-night writing sessions all year. "Baths," I said. "That one."

"Great," Amanda snapped her fingers, and handed us all a brownie refresher.

"Up. Let's go."

Whitney and I followed Amanda around another foreboding bank of port-o-potties. On stage a baby-faced man with curly muttonchops danced behind his mixing station, and occasionally choked the hell out of the microphone. I didn't expect him to be so round and womanly of figure, but then it made me feel more comfortable with his strained falsetto. It wasn't cool, like Morrissey or The Cure, it was urgent and unpretty.

"Mmm." Whitney bobbed her head and got into it. "Okay, so a little tinkly, a little swoony." Amanda seemed satisfied that we'd joined the festival, and I threw my head back, eyes closed, trying to get my 4D hearing back. I managed to catch some riffs of Deerhunter at the main stage, and then I caught a familiar lilt of laughter. I thought it was part of the music at first, some annoying child giggles for a touch of innocence, but then it was out of rhythm and I frowned.

"What's up?" Whitney asked.

I saw her perfect chestnut hair from across the stage, its waves gleaming beneath the low angle of the sun. She twisted and shimmied slowly to the music. "Oh, it's Zoe," I said.

Whitney whipped to her left, and took Amanda's elbow with her. "Who's the tall guy?" Amanda asked.

"I think—" I began, but then he leaned his bushy bearded face down and kissed her and it didn't seem like I needed to continue.

"She is so smart and funny and cute?" Whitney turned to offer me.

I laughed and cringed simultaneously. I had somehow assumed that I'd had until the end of the summer, that we were operating on my schedule. But of course that was wishful thinking. Hadn't I known that I could never have a whole woman—one worth wanting anyway? How fitting that the day Amanda asked, I was forced to confront the other half of my purposefully incomplete reality.

"I'm sorry," Amanda said, putting a hand on my shoulder.

"So you're not going to go over and say hi, I take it," Whitney said. Her voice was deep and sarcastic, but her eyebrows turned up in the middle, and I knew she felt bad for me.

A vengeful wave came over me, and I had already walked most of the way over to Zoe and the bearded man when I returned to myself. She was dancing blissfully, so at ease. Who was I to ruin this moment and for what? And so I stood remarkably close to Zoe and the bearded man, staring dumbly into the future I hadn't realized I might have wanted. Until now, when it was concretely clear that it would never be mine. The bearded man was wearing a well-tailored chambray shirt with beautiful red stitching, and he put his arms around Zoe from behind, holding her close so they swayed together. It was too much. I may not have wanted a commune or a baby, but I did in that moment wish that somebody, Zoe at least, would want to stupidly sway to this sappy music with me. I shifted my gaze up at the sky, to resign myself to the empty vastness of what it seemed I could expect.

That's when Zoe took notice of me. "Aneesha! I'd know that mug anywhere." She pulled me into a tight genuine hug, like nothing strange or unusual was transpiring. For her, I supposed, it wasn't. I shook the hand of the bearded man, who had a nice Jewish name that I forgot as soon as he spoke it, and hated myself for laughing so good-naturedly at his jokes about hipsters. As if it were possible to be at Pitchfork and also be exempt from these jokes. Had I cared about him, I'd have shared my working theory that being a hipster was comparable to being a racist, in that you did not get to decide for yourself whether you were one or not. I stood affably loose-limbed instead, pretending I wasn't me, blocking out the unrelenting pain this person who would be me later was going to experience.

"I'm here with my friends," I had uttered when suddenly Whitney shoved me into her armpit, and was holding me securely around the shoulders. Amanda wasn't far behind, scooting in on the other side. I lifted my thumb up to point at them with fake chagrin. "Whitney, Amanda. Zoe and," I said motioning to the bearded man. They all warily shook hands, and Whitney nodded her head in the direction she came from.

"We should get back. Enjoy your evening," I said to Zoe, who— to my complete and utter bafflement—winked at me.

Our three-across formation made an ungraceful turn to the left, and hobbled away from the stage. "What was that wink for?" I asked Whitney. "What's that supposed to mean?"

"Oh, forget about her. Come on," she said. "Don't you need another snow cone? Maybe a beer?"

I didn't want either of those things. What I wanted was to not be in front of a band that spoke to me in my most personal moments, and feel that in a crowd that contained my closest friends and my current lover, that there was nobody with whom to share this particular strain of beauty, nobody who would understand. What I really wanted was for somebody to love me the way I loved other people. Evening was starting to fall, and it was still humid, and I was feeling trapped because I couldn't imagine how this would ever happen. At best, I thought, I'd reach a golden age where somebody would be content enough to love me as their best friend, and I would be so exhausted by then I wouldn't know the difference.

"A hot dog?" Whitney was still trying desperately, and Amanda was looking at me with great confusion. Shaken, was how I'd describe her look. I don't think it had ever occurred to either of them that I might ever be deeply upset.

"Are you going to cry?" Amanda asked fearfully, which did the job of breaking me out of my downward spiral.

"No," I said, sharply "I am not going to cry."

"It's just that you're going home after vacation," she reminded me.

Whitney had no idea what she was referencing, but joined in all the same. "Yeah, Amanda's right. You'll go back to the desert where you have this great life, where you write, and drink beer, and enjoy less sweaty sunshine. And I'm sure Severine will be all about you when you get back. She's probably saving some IPAs for you in the back of her car right now. What are you losing here with Tutor Crush, really?"

They were watching me closely, ready to jump in and make me smile. Both of them were taller than me, and in another setting it would have felt menacing. Instead, their urgency, the way they leaned in over me—like a tree canopy, I thought—was sweet. They wanted so badly for me to be happy. If I'd told them to run out and find me a Christmas tree, to steal me a puppy, to slather themselves in fake nacho cheese, they'd have obligingly done so. That was the loyal friend love I inspired.

"Come on." I grabbed their elbows, and led them back to my spot in the baseball outfield. The three of us laid on our backs, our heads huddled in a triangle. Streaks of orange and purple were smeared across the sky. We listened to the polyphonic drone of TV on the Radio at the main stage, and the low bass buzzed in my chest cavity. It was like having feelings directly transmitted into me. I was upset that I had allowed myself to get my heart roughed up again, but even more disconcerted that maybe Richard had been right about me. I was wasting my time committing to not committing, when I knew what I wanted.

"Tutor Crush," Whitney said after some time. "Do you think we should make out in front of her? I'd do that."

"I think that would just be confusing," I said. "But thank you, really."

"Okay." She shrugged.

"Such high hopes." Amanda shook her head with disappointment.

"It's not her fault," I said.

"Aren't you glad I tried to tell you to watch out?" Whitney asked. "What a good friend I meant to be." She smiled, then frowned. "I really have to break up with Logan."

"You keep saying it," I replied. "When are you going to do it?"

"Wait, really?" Amanda asked. "I thought you were shooting for the long term?"

"I don't know what I'm shooting for, but it's not a ferret and kayak."

"Well," Amanda continued, "I've been doing some thinking, and I guess I should tell you that moving to France in October."

"Really?" Whitney asked.

"That's a big move," I said.

"It was something Zach and I always talked about doing. We wanted to take a lot of photos, drink wine, eat cheese. I got hired at a school in Lille, and I think I have to go."

I let that thought sit with me. We all carried so many people around inside of us. "You guys," I said. "We're not young anymore."

"Yeah," Whitney said. "But we're not mature either. Look at us."

Amanda rolled over on her stomach. "But think about how much more clueless we were when we first met. I didn't even know how to wear dresses that fit me, as you will all recall. Now we might actually be able to do the things that we want."

"Or we might finally have an inkling of what those things are," I agreed. Even I, who couldn't decide who I most wanted to be, could appreciate my own decision to send myself back to California, and invest in my writing.

"It doesn't feel good though," Whitney said. "It's only getting more lonely. You're going to France, Heather to Minneapolis, Aneesha back to California. I'm the only one sticking around. I'll just continue accounting and occasionally pretending to be alive." Whitney looked over at me. "You're really leaving all of my free time to soccer dykes?"

"Yes," I said. "You'll be free to fulfill your destiny of being a yuppie by day and a cargo shorts-wearing jock by night. I won't be around to say anything."

"That's what I'm worried about," Whitney smiled. "I won't even know that I've lost my crafty edge. I might buy a daybed at West Elm, you better watch out."

I put my head down on my hands, and let the music wash over me again. I was still disappointed by Zoe and maybe not just Zoe, but all bearded men, and sincere flighty women, and the general lack of permanence in my life. But as all of this came tumbling down on me, instead of the crushing loneliness I'd felt by the lake that night, I recognized the assurance I felt with Whitney and Amanda at my side. It was stronger than any strictly romantic feelings I'd yet to experience—and I was prone to heavy swoons— which wasn't a bad reminder to keep in my pocket.

Part 3: Departures

By the time August rolled around, the sun was already dropping in low angles that reminded me of the fall when Georgie got her cashiering job at the Heartland. I expected a whole new wave of nostalgia to overtake me—that the long, sharp shadows of fire hydrants would set me off—but instead, I was reminded of the opportunity that lived inside my daily interactions then. How I'd make friends with strangers one night, and help paint their houses the next day.

With a renewed sense of purpose, I spent the days following Pitchfork at Metropolis, adjusting and reworking my stories while the clatter of baking kept me company. I was only several days into a routine when I became aware that my work was unfamiliar to me. I didn't feel invested in the subtle twitches of language that suggested the origin of the ghosts tugging at Gloria from the bottom of the ocean. It seemed insignificant to infuse the architecture of a city with indirect allusions to my widow's bleak emotional landscape. I kept returning to my new piece about chimps in the Florida retirement home, and as much as I was entertained by the comical and heart-wrenching turns, I recognized that it wasn't more than a premise. I was tired of hiding behind a premise.

My short story collection was made up of pieces that felt like elaborate miniature houses that were designed—if you looked from just the right angle—to give you an obstructed and incomplete glimpse of the interior, where I placed my own beating heart. I had been convinced that this was the art of writing, but the whole process of creating these structures was exhausting, and it wasn't clear that anybody except me understood these glimpses. Now all I really wanted was to show-off the room within my heart. There were stories to write that were relevant to my world, involving characters I knew intimately, about questions I asked myself regularly. I was desperate to capture all the bits of my friends that I could, to preserve them now before they morphed into something else entirely. Why didn't I write about everyone and everything I loved? The idea seemed so obvious that I had to stand up, go to the bathroom, and return just to make sure this wasn't a false over-caffeinated revelation.

I decided it was genuine, and it wasn't only about my writing. I packed up my computer, and stepped, dazed, onto the sidewalk to give Zoe a call. I'd been friendly, but distant since The Night with the Bearded Man. I hadn't known what to say to her. Until this afternoon, it hadn't occurred to me that it would be easiest to just tell her the truth. Zoe showed some confusion that I was calling on the phone for a real-time conversation.

"So here's the thing," I began, and she cut me off quickly to ask if everything was okay. "What? Yes," I assured her.

"You're sure?"

"Yeah, I'm sure."

"So what's up?" Zoe asked tentatively. I imagined her chewing on one of her nails, putting aside the book I'd interrupted. "You know, you can tell me if you're not interested anymore," she said. "I know you always have girls hovering around your perimeter, and it's not a big deal, Aneesha. You don't have to be avoidant."

"The truth is," I said, "You're a big deal to me. So it's not that I'm not interested, it's that I've always been more interested than I should be." I told her about that night at Pitchfork, and how helpless I'd felt. "I don't have regrets. What I'm saying is that I'd like to take graceful leave of you while it can still be considered somewhat graceful."

Zoe laughed good-naturedly. "What happened to you?"

"What do you mean?" I asked.

"Since when does your kamikaze heart take pause to consider self-preservation?" Her tone was playful, but I had nothing light and witty with which to return. She was right, this was not easy for me. "I'm sorry, Aneesha. That's not what I meant. You've been wonderful this summer, and I respect this."

"Thanks," I said, because I couldn't begin to describe how unsatisfying it was to be summed up as 'wonderful,' how harmless and disproportional it felt to my own sharp sense of loss and longing.

"I really like you, Aneesha. Please don't be a stranger. Honestly," she added when I remained silent. "I just figured you were still so caught up in Whitney that I wouldn't even scratch the surface. Like, what would some guy possibly mean to you?"

"Oh." It suddenly seemed salient that my first reaction was to assure Zoe that she and Whitney did not exist in the same level of my heart. Partly I was feeling defensive, but it was also the truth. I had such a clear unfettered admiration for Zoe, and I hadn't yet learned all of the ways she could disappoint me. There was a murky quality to my feelings for Whitney, which only complicated the now-obvious fact that I didn't intend to be entirely without her. "You'd be surprised at how easily I scratch," I said. "But good for you and the guy. Shoot for the moon."

Zoe went on to encourage me to go to a storytelling event that she'd be at, but I knew I wouldn't go, and I politely told her as much. "Take care," I said formally when we were finishing up. The weight of an awful sadness was beginning to pool inside of me, and I thought about what Whitney's comment on how lonely it seemed to grow up.

"Don't pout," I scolded myself as I walked back to the apartment to report my sorrows to Courtney Love. "All this is for you and only you."

The night before I left for Iowa found me padding around Whitney and Logan's apartment in athletic shorts while the two of them got ready for a fundraiser. "Followed by drinks with colleagues," Logan announced with a smile. "Which is just a bunch of queers from my clinic, let's be honest."

"You should join us," Whitney tried to coax me. "You're not allowed to sit on the couch and stare at the wall all night, I'll feel too sad about that."

"I'm not only staring at the wall," I protested. "I'll probably go to the Buffalo Bar." Georgie and Amanda had asked me to meet them at the Heartland. Word was going around that my heart had been knocked askew, and everyone was being extra inviting.

"Maybe I should stay home," Whitney said, plopping down next to me on the couch. "We can watch something funny, and make collages with my vintage fashion magazines."

"Don't stay here because of me," I said. "I guarantee the queer homeless youth of Chicago need you more than I do."

Whitney held my hand in her thin fingers. Her dainty nails were painted a soft sea foam green. "You look like somebody knocked your ice cream cone on the sidewalk. Don't pretend you're not sad. I know how much you liked Tutor Crush."

Logan was on his phone. "Aneesha, why don't you call that girl from forever ago? The one who gave you that funny card, remember?" He was getting antsy, and I did not want to be responsible for ruining his night.

"Please go," I said, and took my hand back from Whitney. "Really, I'll be fine." If I were continuing on the path of good decisions it was Richard I needed to call, and not some girl I'd have to pretend to be enthused by.

"Well, look who is suddenly alive again," Richard said when he answered the phone.

"I know, Richard, I'm sorry. Can we get a drink?" I asked. It felt awful to have to ask, and to not be already built into his day. Richard had always been available to me, to throw his slanted logic on whatever I was doing, and to propose only slightly preposterous solutions.

There was a pause before he sighed, and I pictured him running a hand through his hair. "I'll tell you what we can do. I'm playing cards with some Heartland friends down at the bar. You may know that Jurate sprained her ankle the other night, and I'm going to keep her company, so why don't we go over there early. Just keep in mind, that these days, I like to be in bed not much past ten."

I was inclined to laugh, but he wasn't joking. "Okay, yeah, that's fine," I said. "I'll meet you at your place."

Richard lived in a two-story building on Damen that he shared with his aunt. The first floor and entryway were furnished in a cramped baroque style that Richard rushed guests through, but if you had the chance to look around a little it explained a lot about him. Everything was a little dandy and extravagant, like it was the pinnacle of style in another century.

Richard was wearing plaid shorts and a t-shirt when he answered the door. "Listen, doll," he said, stepping out to join me. "I know why you're here, and it's fine, okay?"

"It's probably not what you think," I said. "Plus it was a horrible way to talk to you, I'm sorry."

Richard started down the steps and seemed to smile. "It's not that you were wrong, exactly, and—" he clenched his fist in the air, "it was admirably ballsy. You just have awfully shit timing."

"I know, I know," I said. We walked the block to the Heartland in silence, and when he pushed the screen door open for me it was like he was inviting me back in. We sat at the bar, and Sally came over to take our drink orders. As she sashayed away to make our drinks, Richard nodded his head toward me.

"You know I've always thought—"

"Not Sally," I said.

"Oh why not? She's just so…"

"Perky?" I asked. "Chipper?"

"And those are such negative qualities, really just the worst." Richard was trying to play with me, but I could tell his heart wasn't in it. I had planned to tell him all of my stories of botched lady love— to start with Severine, move on to Zoe, and end with Whitney, but then I remembered the night we'd left the Heartland because the girls laughing at his jokes were either too stupid or condescending. This was not the same man. I wasn't sure what to share with him.

I cleared my throat. "Well, Georgie says your *Words with Friends* friend is coming to Iowa, so the visit must have gone well?"

Richard lit up. "You know, it really did." His own surprise was charming. "I had this moment where I was lying in bed, we'd had the most wonderful day, and I thought, this could seriously work."

"Like how seriously?" I asked.

"The thing is," Richard swung around on his bar stool with a limber quickness I hadn't expected. "You know, they always say for women it's about finding the right man, and for men it's about the right time. I think it's my time," he said, and smiled broadly.

Sally finally arrived with our drinks, and I buried the many levels of disgust I felt about this statement in my glass. I just wanted to be happy with him. I gulped at my gay-hound—it was a greyhound enhanced with lime and sparkling water, invented by Whitney's first and most embarrassing girlfriend. Maybe because of that I'd always had a soft spot for Lizzie. That was where I let my mind pause before considering that Richard had just told me he was feeling entitled to settle down. So much of our friendship had been intricate dissections of our interactions with women—so that we might identify and scheme to spend our time with the most magnificent ones—but it turned out none of this was very important once a man had decided it was "his time."

"Wow," I said, trying to sound neutral. "That sounds like a very successful visit. Tell me her name again?"

"Sherry." He sat up and put his hand to his chest like he was saluting a flag. "I'm very touched by her. And she's a funny girl, you're all going to love her."

I had the distinct feeling that I was not going to love her, and then he turned to me, his face brimming with the flattest, purest joy. No innuendo, no edge, nothing. He was shaking his head back and forth, like he didn't know how he'd gotten this lucky, and all I could think was that Richard was no more. He was going to have his own fucking baby, and he was gone now.

Jurate showed up a little while later, hobbling through the door on her crutches, and Richard ran to get the screen door for her.

"It's really okay," she said. "I know it looks bad, but I just stepped wrong walking. Who knew it was so hard sometimes?" I sat around with them joking, playing cards, and catching flack for my ineptitude with card strategies, but now I was the one whose heart wasn't in it.

I left early in the evening and wandered down Glenwood. I peeked in all of the bars along the way, remembering when Whitney and I couldn't not stop into each one on the way home. At Cunneen's I thought I'd go in for a beer, and ask Georgie and Amanda to meet me here instead. I ordered a tall boy, and was counting out my cash when a girl I used to go dancing with tapped me on the shoulder.

"How long are you in town, Aneesha?" she asked. "I haven't seen you and Whitney bouncing around here in ages." Lydia was nicer and blonder than I usually liked, and her fedora was a bit much, but I appreciated her goofy nature. I asked about her summer, and she sat and told me everything about working at the Giordano's on Sheridan. At the end, I was surprised and impressed when she smoothly segued into an invite to come home with her—ostensibly so I could enjoy the extra pizza she got for free and also partake in the air-conditioning at her apartment.

"I'm just saying," she began, when I gave her a suspicious look in return. "It's all very practical."

Lydia had a lopsided smile and a square forehead that I would have described as confident. After we went dancing, when Whitney would sloppily pull me off the train at her stop, Lydia used to touch my arm and say, "Be careful with that one." I felt touched remembering that. It made me think of how I felt with Zoe, and of Richard with his hand to his chest. I didn't want to believe in his time or anyone's time, but I was starting to understand that my own "time" was out there hovering around some dark corner, waiting to overtake me in one way or another. It was enough to compel me to act on my dwindling youth.

"Just for the pizza and the air, though," I said leaning into Lydia, as we stepped out of the bar. This seemed endlessly funny in the moment, but after the pizza and more beer, all we wanted was to fall asleep in a loose snuggle while the air conditioner hummed, and the movie *Elf* played quietly in the background.

And Then Came A Very Loud Truck

After our first run-in at the grocery store, Whitney invited me to have beers with friends at the Red Line Tap—a Heartland-affiliated bar that was located conveniently next door. There was a bluegrass band playing, one that despite seriously bad facial hair on the band members, everyone seemed to love. I was exhilarated when Whitney put her arm on my back as we ordered our beers, and held me close while we perched on our stools. "Walk me home," she said when we stepped onto our wobbly legs at the end of the night. That walk was spent trying out all possible configurations for putting our cold hands into the other person's various pockets, which ended in a riot of laughter. I still remembered the unexpectedly thin clinking of our teeth as we leaned in hard to kiss each other, and the satisfactory pull on the zipper that parted the thick wool of her burnt orange dress.

After that, we saw each other every day. It was easy. Even when I didn't mean to, I'd find her at Stella studying for her accounting exams or whipping around the corner on her bicycle. Though I firmly believed *The L Word* was an awful show, it seemed so integral to the process of becoming a lesbian that I wanted to watch it with her again. My first viewing experience had taken place on the moldy, beer-soaked carpet of the rugby girls' house in college, and I'd only gone because it was a scene—an incredibly uncomfortable, sexually charged scene—in which my jock friends and my jock-loving friends insisted we participate. So much of my time in queer circles had felt like a charade. Like, if only I could pretend that I cared about sports, or that I'd ever had a taste for Ani Difranco, or that I was moved by Ursula Le Guin's science fiction, I might manage to lure smart, funny, cool women into my life. As a result, my queer friends had rarely been my best friends—even the ones I'd dated, even the ones I'd loved.

With Whitney, it was different. There was no need to pretend or impress. The general approach to our lives was that we could try whatever we wanted, and even if it didn't work out, we'd have a good time. We embraced both the terrible and winsome qualities of everything from risky haircuts to the margaritas at Chili's.

"Listen, I want to say something," Whitney said to me, as we were dancing in our bar stools one evening at the Edgewater Lounge. She held up her index finger and I waited to see what was coming. "Just hear me out on this one, because I'm not sure if it's right or not."

I sipped from my beer uncertainly. I supposed it was time to discuss what we were doing, but I wasn't sure I was ready. "Okay, let's hear it."

"I think mini-backpacks are going to make a comeback." Whitney bit her lip for a moment. "Uh-huh. For sure."

I was relieved, and nearly spit my beer out. "Here I thought you were about to get philosophical on me."

"Oh hey, I'm sorry, deep writer person." She patted my shoulder. "This is just a superficial zone over here." Whitney held her hands up innocently, and shook her head. "No philosophy."

"But solid backpack theory that I want to hear. Please," I motioned for her to continue. "Tell me more about the comeback of mini-backpacks."

"We're gonna get some tomorrow and you're gonna see," Whitney proclaimed. "You'll say, 'this is the perfect size, not too much extra hanging off, and even fits in other backpacks.' You'll be hooked. Just like you were the first time." She put her beer carefully back on its coaster and held my eyes for a moment.

"What makes you so sure I was such a fan the first time around?" I asked.

"Please, Aneesha, you're not too cool for everything, okay? Though I'm sure you'd like everyone to think you were born wanting a vintage leather briefcase the whole time."

"A vintage leather briefcase? I'm still not ready for that. I need washable materials. Canvas is great for me."

"No?" she seemed not to believe me. "You're so sure about yourself, but let's see about that one in five years."

We spent strings of perfectly enjoyable days and nights like this—out on the lawn in saggy socks and ugly t-shirts, waving idiotically at the passersby. It came to a slow halt on a night in the early spring. There was still snow on the ground, but Whitney and I had taken to riding our bikes around town again. I savored the gritty crunch of the street under my tires. It was notable that I wouldn't later recall which bar we were leaving or under what circumstances. Only that it was well past midnight, and Whitney and I were riding side by side in the bike lane on Devon, a fairly well-trafficked street, when she suddenly turned to me and said, "So we should probably talk about this, right?"

"What?" I asked. Because it seemed like a bad time to talk about anything, and I knew I had more feelings than she'd care to know about.

"I don't know." Her left eyelid was on the verge of drooping, but wasn't quite there yet. "It's just that we're such good friends and—"

I couldn't decide whether it was a blessing or a curse that in that moment, my attention was intercepted by the massive, weathered semi that was approaching on the street. It blanketed everything in a deafening white roar as Whitney delivered something—which according to her face, was difficult to say or perhaps confusing or maybe she just didn't have the right words.

"Is that okay?" I caught at the end, when the truck had sped past us.

I wasn't completely unaware. I had been turned down in a dating context and simultaneously declared a great friend enough times to know what it looked like.

"Yeah, okay," I said into my scarf. There was never a graceful way to tell a lovely woman I was friends with that she was sitting on my heart, that I wouldn't be able to move until she got up and left. I was prepared to let go of the sweet way she held my hand to her chest when we slept, and the quiet mornings when the snow gathered in hushed piles outside of her window.

So I was surprised when Whitney smiled. "Okay, come on, let's go home," she said, and led us back to her place. "You'll have to warm my feet up, it's freezing."

I knew that a rational human being would have stopped Whitney before following her inside, and asked her to repeat herself. The fact that I'd missed what she said didn't mean it hadn't been said, but I was sure that none of this mattered. I felt sincerely that nobody had ever been so perfect for me. So I went in and warmed her feet, and let the snow continue to pile up outside the window. Even though I knew none of it would ever mean what I hoped it would, it didn't stop me from feeling a glorious, impermanent satisfaction.

We left for Georgie's sacred place the next morning. I was a little hungover and my tongue was a sour lizard in my mouth. I biked over to the Summertowns', and, with one glance at me, Georgie could tell that I wasn't at my best. "Don't just stand there," she said, motioning to the pile of blankets and towels at the foot of her parents' stairs. She hated doing laundry on the last day at the farm because she was afraid of breaking the dryer. As far as I knew this had never happened, but that was Georgie. Her solution was that we pack in and pack out all of the towels and bedding for the weekend.

Ryder was loading the back of his Prius with Costco-sized booze bottles, several 24-packs of cheap beer, and an equally large pack of toilet paper. "Boys," I said to him as I grabbed an armful of towels. "And since when do you drink vanilla vodka?"

"What do you mean?" he asked. "I love a vanilla cosmo in the afternoon. No, that's for my girlfriend." It was a nice gesture on his part, and since I was an avid user of toilet paper I had to half-rescind my disparaging mental note about boys' contributions.

I dumped a few piles of towels into the back of the white SUV that Georgie was loading, and got inside. She slumped into the driver's seat and hunched over her phone. Her face was pouty. Despite my sluggish start, I had managed to bring along a bag of chocolate chips to entertain Georgie on the drive, and I pulled them out of my backpack to present to her.

"Oh hey, thanks, Aneesha." She stuck her fingers in the bag and pulled out a few. "Sorry I was mean earlier. I just hate being the only person I can rely on." She paused to gather herself. "Richard and Sherry are running late, which means we might not have dinner for tonight, and I told everyone we'd grill because it would be easy, but they're the ones with the brats, which means we won't be able to."

"Georgie," I said. "Relax. Everyone can stop and eat when they want to, and if worst comes to worst, we can pick up frozen pizzas at the store. We probably want to have frozen pizzas on hand anyway." I closed my eyes and leaned back in my seat.

"Why are you so chill all the time? Stop it," she demanded. "Just join me and be irrationally angry."

I sensed her staring at me so I opened my eyes and watched a twitch pinch at the space below her left eyebrow.

"Look," I said. "If it makes you feel any better I'm still not looking forward to meeting Sherry, okay? I didn't realize when I told Richard to grow up that it meant I would lose my friend. I mean, who goes to bed at ten o'clock? That's not a real thing."

Georgie smiled calmly. "Oh that's perfect, keep going and we'll have a good drive." She started the car and checked her rearview mirror. "I hate when I'm the only one obsessing over my unimportant problems."

"Thanks, Georgie, that's just great." I threw a small handful of chocolate chips at her.

"Hey," she said sharply. "Don't waste those. What did you do last night anyway? I heard about Pitchfork, so I know you weren't with Tutor Crush." She was looking over me carefully, which worried me because there were several high-speed merges coming up ahead. "But of course you were," she said, and sighed.

"No," I jumped in. I was still aching over Zoe's absence, and I wanted some credit for that. "I just slept over with a girl I know. It was very PG. I feel kind of bad because now she'll probably think that I'm interested, when I just wanted to feel wanted for a little while, which, I know is incredibly selfish."

"Oh," Georgie sounded pleased. "Well yeah, but whatever, you're human just like everybody else."

"I know," I said. "But I aim to not do things that I wouldn't want done to me. I like to hope that's the way to get the right people in my life."

Georgie exited the freeway and pulled into a gas station. "I get it, but I mean, no guarantees, right? It's not like the Tutor girl doesn't think you're a good person. It's not like Whitney thinks you could be more awesome, but that doesn't mean they want to love you and stuff. So who cares if one rando girl thinks you're kind of an asshole?" Then she reached into her wallet and fished out ten dollars. "Maybe you should go buy a snack while I get gas."

I looked at the bill fluttering in her fingers. This was exactly the kind of post-breakup chat I'd have dispensed myself, and I resented that she was right. "Why does everyone keep wanting to feed me a snack, like that will somehow make my life fulfilling? Does it seem to you that I'm just hungry? Like I have a triangular Dorito-shaped hole in my life?"

"Don't we all have Dorito-shaped holes in our lives?" Georgie asked. "Isn't that how the junk food industry works?"

I snatched the money from her. "I'll get us snacks, but I'm serious."

"I know you're serious." She leaned down to look at me through both of our open car windows. "I just don't know what to tell you, Aneesha. Grow up, you can't have everything? Stop wanting more than you have? Find someone nice and forget the rest? I'm positive Sherry's nice." She grinned.

"You know I hate nice," I said. Richard and Georgie had hated nice once too, and now they didn't. So I was the only asshole left who hated nice people, and it felt unfair.

Georgie threw her hands in the air and twirled around. It was true. There was nothing to tell me. I wandered into the gas station, thought about buying a slurpee, but settled on the largest bag of Doritos I could find. Cooler Ranch. I liked that the comparison was mysteriously implicit.

It was nearing dark when we finally reached the Hill House. The drive was lined with elms silently awaiting us like butlers. Over the hills, bluish plumes of a storm were brewing. Georgie pulled into the driveway and turned off the engine. "Welcome to the Summertown Farm," she said grandly. Already her mood had lightened, and even if mine was only temporarily strengthened by chips, a calm fell upon us as we walked beneath the hissing cicadas into the house. Georgie immediately went to the fridge and tossed me a High Life. It smelled fishy, like it had taken a recent dip in the pond, but I popped the top anyway. "Get comfy, you know your way around," she said, and she began flipping switches, setting up fans, putting out towels: the work of an impeccable host.

Meanwhile I took my beer out into the backyard to wait for the storm. There was a pair of Adirondack chairs that faced the gently sloping hills of the farm. Cornfields and clusters of trees sloped downwards toward a set of train tracks. This spot in these peeling deep-backed chairs was where preciously romantic couples shared coffee and quiet exchanges in the morning. It seemed significant that I had never brought anyone here to sit beside me.

Usually I had a book and a beverage, some dreams to project onto the open landscape, and someone stuck in the riptide of my heart. For years, this had seemed okay. I was on the way to becoming, and I was looking for something larger, grander, and more meaningful than conventional adult life. As the curtain of rain quickly marched up the hills, however, it became clear to me that I was alone in that endeavor now. My friends, with the possible exception of Amanda, had all but abandoned our youthful hope of being something different in the world. I imagined this was an entirely un-unique experience, that generations of adults before me had weathered this same revelation. As Georgie said, I was human just like everyone else. That didn't make it any less disappointing that the happiness of my closest friends—even my own, I feared—might be so plain.

I wanted Zoe beside me telling me facts about fireflies I'd never heard before, reminding me that I didn't know all of myself and hopefully never would, but she wasn't mine to keep. All of my friends would fan out, and my beloved Chicago would dissolve, or continue on without me. I suddenly craved the bleach-bright Riverside mornings that shocked me into being each day. I missed staring at the rugged face of Mt. Rubidoux from my dining room table, and getting lost in a story. I wanted to sit in Severine's black Jeep, her cigarette cloud invading my space while we casually sipped beers and sped down the highway with the sunset bleeding behind us. I didn't care if she wasn't speaking to me. We could blast music and brood in complicit silence.

"You're not coming in?" came Georgie's voice from the deck. Shrill voices, door slams, and a rush of footsteps announced themselves from out of the darkness. Our friends were here. "You know I don't host well alone," she baited me.

Georgie didn't mention that the storm had arrived, that I was getting soaked, and lightning was shooting into the fields right in front of me. "I'll grab a bag of ice from the basement freezer?" I offered, but didn't feel ready to move yet.

"Good call, I haven't checked the trays. Where are those Doritos, by the way?"

"On the counter." I twisted around to look at her. I couldn't resist being needed by Georgie. "I'll cut up limes and lemons for cocktails. We should do it right." The rain dripped down my salty nose into my mouth.

"Okay, but can we pretend this isn't an ending?" Georgie called.

I finally stood up and squished through the grass to the patio, where Georgie's high-arched feet peeked down at me between the deck slats above. I felt immensely comforted by them. "No." I was momentarily sheltered from the rain. "I'm not pretending that. This is special."

Georgie looked down at me, and her hook nose seemed more severe than usual. "Well, then come inside, Aneesha." Her feet made little wet slaps on the deck as she turned and went back in. I stole one more look at the chairs and the hills and followed her lead.

❧

Richard and Sherry arrived later in the night. They attempted to quickly tuck away into a bedroom on the upper floor, ignoring the group's request that they join us for whiskey around the fire. By that time the rain had let up and Ryder, the fire master, had coaxed some dry logs into glowing warmly.

"Don't be selfish," Jurate pleaded. "Share your new friend with us."

"What about white Russians?" Ryder called out. "You want one?" He turned to me. "Can you use the vanilla vodka in that?"

"Sure," I replied. "Why not?"

Sherry yelled something incomprehensible from their room, and Richard smiled sheepishly, as if he, the man going around town smelling bicycle seats, had transformed into a demure Southern belle. He put up a polite hand to placate us, his fans. "Tomorrow you will see us both in the full light of day."

"What if the full light of day is too much light?" Heather murmured next to me. "There's always the shade of a strong cocktail," I answered. "Come on, let's set up our bedding before it's too late."

I put on my headlamp so that Heather and I could snap the poles together and put the pins in correctly. We staked a tarp down on a slight slope, in case it began to rain again, and I carried over the pillows, comforters and large pieces of foam that filled the trunk of Heather's car. I was always a minimalist camper, and my only contribution was a limp pillow and my sleeping bag. It seemed selfish once I saw the excess plush that Heather thought nothing of bringing along to share. It was clear to me that this was why she meant so much to all of us.

"Sorry I have nothing to add to our bedding cloud," I said as I zipped the front of the tent closed.

Heather grabbed my arm and put hers through it. "Don't be silly, Aneesha. I've always got you covered. Plus you brought the headlamp, an invaluable tool."

We walked down the slope to rejoin our friends at the fire pit, but Heather stopped at the Adirondack chairs before we got there. "You know what's so dumb?" she asked me.

"Tell me," I said.

We stood behind the chairs looking out at the same landscape that I'd pondered hours earlier. "I was so looking forward to bringing Remi here, sitting in these chairs together, and pretending for a minute that we could sit this way forever."

It was a surprise to hear that Remi wasn't coming. I felt a surge of empathy for her. "It's not dumb," I said, replaying my moment on the chairs. "That's too bad. I expected some great dancing and diving from him."

Heather scratched at her calf and then stood up again. "We broke up a couple days ago. I didn't say anything because I didn't want to mope this whole weekend, but I told him about Milwaukee, and he just got a research position in North Carolina for next year."

We both stood quietly. I could hear the gathering clatter of a train approaching. "I have to say I was surprised at how quickly he was out. Just done. No discussion about options."

"Heather," I said, pulling our linked arms tighter. "I'm so sorry."

She sighed and leaned her head against mine. It smelled like roses and something lightly clean. "I guess that's what happens," she said. "I just love him so much and we're such good friends. I know you think it's crazy that I want marriage, and kids, and a family, but he would have been so fun to do that with. I wanted to keep him forever."

"That's not crazy," I said. "If anyone can convince me that marriage and kids could be fun, it's you. But, Heather, you deserve to be with someone who appreciates you. You're so much better than the majority of people."

The train let out a low whistle and came rattling through the gulley below us. "That's what I've always thought about you," Heather said, and laughed. "I keep wondering if it's careless that I'm up and leaving everything for Vera, but then I'm not doing anything more important here. Sometimes I teach at the Jewish school, sometimes I sell my eggs, sometimes I'm at the Heartland?" she shrugged

"It makes sense to me," I said.

"I know, you'd do the same thing," she said. "Will you still come visit me in Milwaukee?"

"Yes." I didn't even have to think about it. "I'll visit you anywhere you go."

"Why do we love people so much?" Heather wondered aloud. "Do you think they know how much we care?"

I heard Amanda calling us from the deck. "Hey, you two tent loners, you need new beers?"

We both turned around. "I think they know we love them," I said. "Look how nice they are to us."

"Yes!" Heather yelled back to Amanda. "We need new loner beers."

"Loner brand only," I added.

"Good," Amanda said. "It's not bedtime yet, don't get any ideas."

"Loner brand only?" Heather asked me. She was already chuckling—with her flat bent 'ha.'

"Oh shut up, Heather, I don't want to hear it."

By the end of the night Whitney, Logan, Jurate and I were the only ones left around the fire. Even though our tent was well up from the fire pit I could hear Heather snoring loudly, and it gave me a cozy feeling. Jurate and Logan were having an in-depth political discussion that I hadn't been following. I'd had quite a few loner beers by then, and Whitney and I were deeply engrossed in making little men out of marshmallows.

"It's not that different from making snowmen," I remarked to her.

"Here, we need to add a little mouth." Whitney leaned close to me and, in the dim firelight, with great attention, she stuffed a chocolate chip into the head of our mallowman.

I was already kinked over with laughter. The chocolate chip was the wrong proportion, and her drunk hands, with all the elegance of a salami, had half-melted the chip. "Stop it," I said. "It's not the right size and you're smearing chocolate everywhere!"

"Just wait, you'll see," Whitney was saying. "It'll be a big surprised mouth, like somebody sat on him by accident."

"Sat on him by accident?" I asked. "That's your first example of a big surprise?" She laughed. "Wouldn't you be surprised? You would," she answered herself.

"You don't even have to answer."

"Hey!" I heard from the other side of the fire. "Earth to Aneesha!" I looked up, and Logan was standing with his arms wide open. His face was cast in orange and his features looked like a jack-o-lantern's. "I need you to back me up on this. Listen—"

I put my hands up and crossed them over my face. "No, I'm staying out of this. I'm an impartial party."

"No you're not," he said. "You're never impartial and you always have an opinion, even when it's none of your business. This is about gay marriage, just—"

"Logan," I said.

"Don't you think it's an important step in achieving equality?"

Jurate was staring blankly at me. She was done with their discussion. "That's not even my point," she said quietly. "I am only saying maybe not everyone wants marriage. It doesn't mean you don't want anybody to sit with you while you're in the hospital, you know? Doesn't mean you don't want kids. But marriage? Who decided that was the only way to have a family?"

"But for those of us who do, it's a meaningful gesture," Logan was gesturing emphatically at Jurate. "Equality is about having options. Aneesha," he said again to me.

Whitney and I looked at each other with chagrin. Gay marriage was not the issue that concerned us most.

"Oh, I'm sorry," Logan said in a huff. "Are you too busy making stupid art projects to contribute to an intellectual conversation? Why don't you two just go make out? It's obvious that's what you want." He gestured around the yard. "Seriously, what are you waiting for?"

I cleared my throat. "Do I think everyone should be able to have legal family benefits? Sure. Especially if you buy into the capitalist function of a family to acquire and pass on wealth. But is it mean-ingful to me whether or not heteronormative society is prepared to allow me the supposed privilege to model my relationships and values after theirs? No. I don't give a shit." I stuffed another chocolate chip into the belly of our mallowman. I didn't know how to address the make-out comment.

"And you agree with that?" Logan asked Whitney.

To my surprise Whitney engaged him. "I do, actually, and I've told you this before. But it's good to know that you're more interested in Aneesha's opinion than mine. Because who cares what I think, right? It's not like my opinions matter." She seemed to understand that she'd just started a fight and didn't feel like seeing it through.

"It's late, maybe we should go to bed." She began pushing herself off of the brick of the patio floor.

"You can do what you want," Logan said. "I'm going to bed. By myself." He threw his beer can on the ground and stormed inside.

We all stared at each other for a while. "Bed is not a bad idea," Jurate said finally, and walked quietly up the stairs to the deck. Whitney had our mallowman resting on the fire grate and was gently roasting him over the coals. There was a nice tan glow around his tubular extremities. "He's gonna be delicious," she said

"Whit."

"That wasn't good, huh?"

"That was bad."

"I'm sorry," she said. "For tonight. For that other night. For other other nights. For the whole summer, and everything else while we're at it." She squatted with her elbows at her knees, staring into the fire. I was sitting just enough behind her that I could feel her shielding the heat from me when the wind shifted.

"Don't be sorry, Whit. It's not about that."

She shook her head and steadily met my eyes. "No, I really am sorry. Because I know you have feelings, and I know Logan has feelings. Everyone has such strong feelings about things that they want, and I can't seem to stop fucking them up." She offered me the mallowman's lower leg.

I took it and let the crispy marshmallow skin crackle in my mouth. "What about you?" I asked.

She shrugged and said nothing.

I thought back to the cootie catcher and the secrets inside it. Those had just been the ones she was conscious of and willing to share. Who knew what other abstract ideas were floating around in her brain, yet to even register. "Well, I suppose there's no surprise there." I scooted over so we were sitting side by side.

Whitney started to roll her eyes, but stopped. "Okay, fine." She leaned closer to me. "Aneesha, you're my best friend. I could never stand to lose you. Never, okay?" The pleading honesty in her voice undid me a notch, and I quit judging her cool demeanor. "I don't know what else to say. I want you around all of the time. I miss you like hell every time you leave. I want you to move back here, and for us to do everything together, and talk about everything, and be friends like we were, like this, always, until we're dead. And that's it. I'm serious. I know you think it's selfish, but that's how I feel."

She'd never been this straightforward before. I sat back and looked up at the sky, which was now scattered with stars. She was still avoiding the heart of the mystery, which was why she wanted me around so badly. I needed to know. I wanted it to explain why we worked so well together. I wanted to understand who we were to each other, how it had happened, what it meant. That was impossible, I knew too. It was time for me to accept the mystery and let it go.

"You and I are exceptionally good at being not lonely together," I finally agreed.

"That's what I mean, it's the best." Whitney's enthusiasm grated on me. "We always have fun. I feel happy when I'm with you. That's special, right?"

"Yeah, of course."

"It's okay that we have different lives," she said. "But I don't want to lose you."

"Whit, lose me to what?"

"I don't know." She was shrugging over and over. "Who knows? To all the other people in your life, and all the places you go, and things you do, and you haven't even finished your book yet—"

"You mean to someone who wants to be with me?" I asked.

Her features twisted into tight a pout. "That makes it sound weird."

"I'm not going to stop being your friend. But you will lose me, even if just a little. I hope you do, anyway, for my sake."

"Of course, I know that," she said. "I've always known that."

"Well, if you've always known that," I said, "then I guess we have nothing to talk about." As the words landed I realized it had been a mean thing to say.

Our mallowman was falling through the grate and beginning to bubble in black pools over the coals. Whitney poked at the flaking ashes with a stick and started to stand up. "I'm sorry our friendship is so miserable for you."

"Wait, no, it's not that," I said. "It's just—" She seemed to settle back down. Just once I wanted for her to not be okay, to feel something with me in the moment. "I'm worried that I'll never meet anybody I get along with as well as you." I watched her squirm beneath my gaze. "I'm also worried that it'll never happen as long as we're around each other. And I'm especially worried that if we are, I'll stop hoping for it altogether and settle for someone fine. Someone nice. Which I know is melodramatic and shallow and a lot of things, but those are my actual fears."

"Aneesha, please." Whitney's expression was incredulous and she tossed her hands around emphatically. "You always end up around women who are scary and important, who have impressive hobbies, know how to coordinate outfits, and can get you into cool places I've never even heard of."

I felt devastated that she wasn't going to acknowledge my choice to be vulnerable with her. The time had come for me to go brood in my tent with Heather's calming snoring, but then she reached for the bag of marshmallows that was conveniently planted right next to my foot and patted me lightly. "I'm a way better friend than anything else I could ever be to you. And that's something we can do for as long as we know each other. Don't you think? Should we try mallowman again?"

This was along the lines of what I was hoping for, and I supposed if it was all I was going to get, it was fine. "How could you even think of making a stupid art project in lieu of an intellectual conversation about gay marriage," I asked her sternly.

Whitney laughed and handed me a bag of mini M&Ms. "See, you always have your sense of humor. You'll never settle and you'll never give up." She said this with such conviction. I wanted so badly to believe her.

"How do you know that?"

"You won't. You like to feel sorry for yourself, but you never let anyone else feel sorry for you. So I won't. You're the one looking for mysteries and surprises. You'll find them. You always do. And, by the way, good luck convincing someone nice to settle for you. Being nice isn't some debilitating weakness, it's a choice." Whitney smiled. She had won this round. It wasn't disagreeable.

"Whose t-shirt did you read that on?" I asked. She glared at me. "Oh, fuck you."

I chuckled and got to work lining up M&Ms in the belly of the new mallowman. I supposed that friendship was the guarantee that I needed. It gave us all the time in the world. I imagined us with grey hair and slippers drinking beer in rocking chairs somewhere in the mountains, silent, just like this. That's what I wanted to know was waiting for me. The draw of friendship, I thought, was that you already knew exactly what to look forward to—and not just with Whitney. I wanted Georgie, and Youngsu, and Richard,.and

Heather, and Jurate, and Amanda, and Jesse, and Zoe, and everyone to meet up with me again. None of us could promise that, but I could want it anyway. If nothing else, the summer was proof that I was not some inconsequential nobody flimsily blowing around town. I couldn't pretend that I was anymore. My wanting was a force of some strength and influence. I was a person who made things happen, even if they never turned out as I'd hoped.

"What are you thinking about?" Whitney asked me.

"I think it's going to be okay," I said. "I mean, yes, it was always going to be okay, but I think it might actually feel that way."

"I hope so." She nodded and we listened to the sudden wave of birds squawking above us in the trees. "Even if it's not, can we be okay?" she asked.

I shrugged because it seemed like a done deal to me, but to Whitney I must have seemed uncertain or uncaring.

"Please?" her voice cracked, and then all at once she was crying actual tears that fell and dripped off of the tip of her nose. I realized how wrong I'd been, thinking I wanted to see Whitney feel feelings. Her face hung low and her shoulders hunched so sharply.

I felt myself panicking. "No, yes, of course we'll be okay," I said and immediately grabbed her forearm. I didn't know what to say to make it stop. "It's always okay, you know that I love you. Please don't cry."

She sucked in a halting breath and pulled herself together. "I'm sorry. It seems to take so long to find out what I want, and I don't want to hurt anyone anymore."

"Whit," I said. "It's fine. You'll always have me as your friend."

"Oh man." She stood up and walked in circles around the fire, shaking out her hands. She had returned to herself when she sat back down again. "Alright. So friends for as long as possible, right?" she asked me.

I nodded. "Yes." This pact reminded me of a ritual eight-year-olds might perform in the woods, and I held up my pinky so we could swear on it.

Whitney smiled and linked her pinky with mine. "Maybe I can share yours and Heather's tent?" she asked. "I saw inside earlier. You guys have a lot more bedding than two people need."

I woke up smashed among Heather and Whitney's hair, and arms, and excess bedding. The air in the tent was musky and I immediately unzipped the flap, and stumbled toward the house. It was not yet unbearably hot, and I quietly closed the screen door behind me, thinking about how nice it would be to have a little quiet, alone time.

But as soon as I came up the stairs into the kitchen, I knew that wasn't going to happen. Richard and Georgie were harmoniously making coffee, and Sherry was seated at the long, ominously empty dining room table. She was all smiles and sweetness, fully made up, with her chunky neon sweater meticulously askew. It was all so intentional and underwhelming.

"If it isn't Aneesha," she said and patted the table across from her with an eager hand. "Come on, tell me all about you."

I was tender after a late night of drinking, and I liked the hushed numbness that fell over me the next morning. In this situation, however, it left me too weak to disagree. I felt compelled by a sense of fate to sit across from Sherry. "Fine," I said, in my low morning baritone, which I hoped came across like the cowboy who busted open the saloon doors in a Western. It seemed appropriate. Sherry was watching me with such keen attention as I sat down that I was tempted to ask her what she thought of my nipples, which were probably visible through my thin astronaut tanktop.

"Well." Sherry spread her fingers across the table and went about cheerily interrogating me. It began with all of my places of origin, types of schooling, family life, hobbies, professional experience. She paused before she started in on my love life.

And now the lion goes for the heart, I thought.

"So tell me about who you're involved with," she asked innocently enough.

I had no answers for her that weren't shrouded in ambiguity, confusion, and deep conviction with no logical foundation. So I began with the first of those tales. "It all began with an individual now called Zebra Silver," I offered. "I was immediately transfixed. I remember locking eyes with them in a bathroom mirror on our first day at college and knowing that I was unavoidably queer." Sherry had a glowing look of joy on her face. So I decided to continue. "I think it started to go sour around the time I shot a 16 millimeter movie in which Zebra wore dominatrix gear, and beat the shit out of me in a bathroom stall. It was painful to love someone who was both so self-involved and full of self-hate, but they taught me how alive I could feel," I said. "Everything is tranquil now. We talk on the phone to discuss art and hair and particularly good sex."

Sherry, I presumed, was someone for whom things were always crystal clear, and I was honestly curious what she'd get out of this story. She tapped her fingers on the table and then rested her round face thoughtfully in her hand. "So you don't want to have a family or be happy with somebody, huh?" was her follow-up question. To her credit, it wasn't the worst takeaway.

I looked over to the kitchen at Georgie and Richard. I wanted to see how much more of my life I was required to conjure and parade around for Sherry. I didn't want to share my actual, true self with her, but it was exhausting fending her off like this. Richard loosely tossed a bag of coffee in his hands. His fingers were outstretched in their childish way, and Georgie was carefully placing a filter in the coffee machine. She stood up proudly when it was done. Their banter looked light, unstrained, and I was happy to see them enjoying each other's company.

Sherry seemed to sense the growing warmth in me. "Ah," she said slyly, leaning her unrelenting smile closer to me. "So, did you and Georgie ever…?"

I cut my eyes back to her. "Did me and Georgie ever?" I wanted her to finish the question. It wasn't that it had never been asked before, but it was appalling to me each time, akin to asking whether I'd sexually considered a family member. I liked to make people ask the entire question because often it allowed them time to answer it for themselves.

"She's a very together, elegant, beautiful woman," Sherry was saying now. "I can see how that might be appealing, and you are such close friends."

"Right," I said. "People tell me that Georgie is attractive and I believe them, but that's not my personal experience of her." I glanced over at Georgie, whose face was locked in a deep frown as she pressed various buttons on the coffeemaker, trying to start it. I tried to blank my mind out and see Georgie as an elegant beautiful woman, but there were no features that jumped out and grabbed me. All of them offered me great comfort, and none encouraged me to wonder.

I returned to Sherry to see if she understood, but I realized she was still waiting for me to answer her question. "No way," I said. "Georgie and I do not interest each other. Never have. But you and Richard," I said, hoping to alight on something easy. "You seem to have hit it off fast."

"What's fast, really?" she asked me. "When you're an adult and you know what you want, there's no reason to mess around. It's all about making quality time for each other. You make a commitment and stick to it."

I nodded. I wanted to know how long she had counted Richard as an adult.

"I feel honored that you all invited me here," she said, and I was relieved that Sherry was almost done with me. "It's amazing and sweet, your little group of friends all gathering here to relive the past. It's kind of strange, for adults, but it's very cute."

I looked hard at Sherry. Her brown hair was impressively straightened, with just the right amount of volume so her face didn't look too big. Her smile continued to bear down on me. She was too insecure to bait into a debate in which I could cleanly destroy her—I had to admit that was disappointing—but she would not be allowed to dismiss my friendships and receive no resistance from me. "It's not at all strange or cute or sweet. It's what friends do. Actual adult friends, who grow and share and learn together. It's about making quality time for each other. You make a commitment and stick to it," I said.

Georgie must have caught the tone in my voice because she swooped over and placed a mug of coffee in front of Sherry. I hadn't even decided whether or not I would say anything more.

"Hey," Georgie said loudly to me even though her face was inches from mine. "Have you heard how Kristen Stewart cheated on her vampire boyfriend with an old dude?" She waved a celebrity gossip magazine in front of my face.

"No." I crossed my arms and let her hang the magazine out there for a while before I snatched it to take outside. I did want to know what this Kristen Stewart business was about. Whitney and I had always considered Kristen—KStew—a moody heartthrob. I was miffed that Georgie had cut short my defense of friendship, and that was what I fumed over as I galloped down to the patio.

Logan and Whitney were slung in canvas chairs by the firepit, and I had already thrown myself down in the lawn to join them before I recalled that the three of us were not on good terms. "Oh hell," I said, preparing to go away.

"It's fine," Whitney said.

I sat on the grass between them and waved the magazine. "Gossip from the big city." They gestured for me to read the article aloud. It revolved around a series of photos where it was impossible to tell whether KStew, with her face half lost in a black hoodie, was clutching at this older man with sure strong sex fingers or with desperate confused fear fingers—people were stalking her with telephoto lenses, after all.

"Who cares?" Logan asked after I was done. He sipped from a water bottle that somebody had left out the night before, and then tossed it back down.

"I just really wanted her to be queer," I said.

"She is," Whitney reassured me. Her sunglasses were resting crookedly on her nose and her head was cocked sideways. "She's just not ready to share. Just like Ellen Page. They'll all come around eventually."

"But why would it matter to you, either of you, if Kristen Stewart were queer? You don't even know her. It's not like you'd date her or something."

I didn't mind him asking, these were the kinds of questions that I enjoyed, but Logan was clearly still upset from the previous night. "If she came out, then I'd know when she wakes up in the morning and puts on her cut-off denim vest and shrugs her shoulders and puts up her hood up, that she means to look dyky and she knows it's hot. And everyone else would have to acknowledge that too."

Whitney put out her hand for a high-five. "Yep. Well said."

I pushed myself off my elbow to hit her hand because I didn't want to leave her hanging, but I knew it wasn't what Logan needed. I could tell from the look on his face that he knew it was over, and now he was waiting until it exploded. I didn't want to watch.

"What?" Logan asked me. He sighed. "Ugh, okay fine. You know I feel strongly about visibility."

"For good reason," I said. "You know you want KStew to be queer too." I didn't want to annoy him anymore, and I figured if I let them marinate in their own sour malaise, they might recognize the stench. "I'm going swimming," I announced, and to my surprise Whitney jumped out of her chair.

"Hey, me too. Great idea."

I turned to Logan, but he didn't move. He opened his arms in a limp shrug and continued to hang in his chair. "Maybe one of you can grab me a beer on your way out?"

"Just come," I said.

For a brief moment, he was my teammate again and I wanted to tell him to quit slogging, that the bog was no longer viable, but then he jutted his chin out at me. "Why would I want to swim with you? I let you live in my house, I'm nothing but nice to you, you even pretend to be my friend, and the whole time you're after my girlfriend. Why would I go swimming with you?"

He wasn't wrong about the chain of events and what it suggested about my character. I shrugged and turned to Whitney, who looked on calmly through her crooked sunglasses. She would not be ruffled. Regardless of how I answered Logan, regardless of my intentions, we had agreed to carry on as we always had: as the keeper of each other's secret plans and truer selves. Now, instead of letting it make me feel insignificant, I embraced the strength in that.

"Don't answer me with some avoidant philosophical bullshit," Logan was now huffing at me. "I'm asking you a serious question. Who the fuck do you think you are?"

"Honestly, that's not the right question," I said. "Who the fuck do you think Whitney is? She's just standing there watching this like it has nothing to do with her. Who invited me to live with you? Who allowed you to move in with her in the first place? Sure, maybe I'm not a good person. Let's say I'm deceitful, ungrateful, and overly involved in other peoples' lives. But the fact remains that I, the devious interloper, know more about what you and Whitney want from a relationship than either of you. That's something to consider. So, like I said, I'm going swimming."

"Well, that's just great," Logan called out behind me, and I figured he'd spoken for them both.

I jogged up the stairs to the house and grabbed a towel off of a stack by the fireplace. Heather and Amanda were splashing water on their faces side by side in the upstairs bathroom. I patted them each on the back. "Come for a morning swim," I said gently, and their heads bobbed around in agreement.

Georgie saw me digging around in my bag for my swimsuit and the next thing I knew, she was regally strutting around the kitchen, packing up a cooler with ice and beer. "Aneesha, grab the opener, will you?"

Richard sauntered into the kitchen and mussed my unwashed hair. "Well, there you are, Little A. I was wondering where you got off to."

I briefly leaned into his side hug, and opened the squeaky utensil drawer. Even after watching him this morning, I wasn't convinced that this was the Richard I knew and loved. "Come swimming," I said. "You don't have to go in. Have Ryder or Georgie tow you around in the paddleboat. Georgie loves being a tour guide, am I right?"

Georgie took the opener from me and smiled. "I really could give you and Sherry a tour of the pond. There are a lot of turtles out this time of year." She adjusted the towel around her waist and crossed her arms. "We won't take the boat with the mouse."

Richard cast a look beneath the kitchen cupboards, to where Sherry sat in a low chair, looking rather alertly at a magazine in her lap. "I told Sherry we'd go into town," Richard said softly. "She wanted to go look at antiques. She'll want to explore a little, go to the grocery store. I think that's more her style."

"What are you talking about all quietly over there, sweetie?" Sherry called.

"Oh, honey, I was just telling the girls about our plan to go to town."

Sherry got up and walked into the kitchen. She looked at me strangely, and then stood on the other side of Richard, lifting his arm from the counter and placing it around her shoulders. "Well, we do like some small-town antiquing," she addressed Georgie. "You never know what treasures have gone overlooked. And sweetheart, you don't need to be putting your hands all over everyone, I'm your girl." She pulled him towards her, so his arm fell off of my shoulder and on to the counter.

I raised my eyebrow at Richard as he glanced my way. "We better get a move-on then, huh?" he said, and turned to smile at Sherry.

"You're really going into town instead of enjoying the farm?" Georgie asked. "This place has acres of forest, a beautiful creek, the pond, and there's the observation tower down the road, named after my grandma."

"I don't like bugs," Sherry said apologetically. "But I'm sure you give a wonderful tour, Georgie."

"Alright, suit yourself." Georgie nodded her head at me, and I left my post at the counter to take the opposite cooler handle. "We're swimming," she announced indignantly, and I followed her down the stairs, outside past the firepit, and down the grassy hill to the pond. Logan and Whitney were nowhere to be seen.

"Stupid people," Georgie muttered. We rounded the bend and found that Ryder and his girlfriend, Claire, were already fishing on the far side of the pond. Meanwhile, Heather and Amanda were sitting on the wooden steps of the screened-in picnic hut, blowing up red and blue tubes.

"We brought extra," Heather explained. "Every year I bring noodles and every year they disappear to places unknown. Maybe these will fare better."

"Maybe the mice eat them," I said, and Georgie looked at me like this was a rude suggestion. "Okay, maybe they don't."

The pond was dark and glassy. A tall fence of reeds shot

up around the edge of the water at various angles. In front of the floating dock, a small bubble floated to the surface and made a small gurgle.

"I'm so mad at Richard," Georgie said. "I invited him here to spend time with us, not so he could use me for a lovers' weekend."

We dropped the cooler into the back of the paddleboat.

"How's Sherry?" Heather asked. "That's her name, right?" Heather must have been a little jealous, I thought, or maybe a little disappointed.

"Aneesha," Amanda called, and tossed me a plump blue floaty tube. I caught it by putting my arm through its middle.

"Oh, Sherry's just fine," I said, trying to compensate for what suddenly seemed like a full morning of dubious friend behavior, and I'd only been up for a few hours.

"You were about to bite her head off at the breakfast table," Georgie said. She was amused now, and I saw that familiar, evil sparkle in her eye. "You were just itching to do it, I saw you pulling back so you could decide how you'd like to torture her later."

"I was not," I said. "Don't do that."

"Do what?" she asked cheerily.

"Everything is too fragile. I shouldn't be mean."

"You're being dramatic. Nothing is as fragile as you think." She patted the seat next to her in the boat, but it was covered in streaks of mud.

"I don't want a mud butt first thing," I said, "I'll give you a push." I leaned into the boat, and sent her jerkily into the water. I worried that I'd pushed too hard when she and the cooler sloshed side to side, but then the paddles started splashing and Georgie was off.

"Was she really okay?" Heather asked me.

"No, she's not okay."

"She seems a little high maintenance," Amanda added.

The three of us waded onto the sandy part of the beach, and slipped onto our tubes.

I rested my chin on the bouncy blue surface of my floaty. On this side of the pond, with the trees shading me, I could see my reflection in the water, and it struck me that I never looked the way

I thought I did. On some days I was much better-looking than I expected, but today my hair was flat in places, I had bags under my eyes, and my nose was wider and less pointed than in my mind. I was not everything I imagined. "Sherry's not like us," I said, "but none of us could love Richard like that, so what would we expect?"

We acknowledged this with a little chuckle.

"Hey! What are you laughing about over there?" Georgie demanded from the dock.

"Oh, you already know," I yelled back.

"You're going to sabotage them, aren't you?" She grinned.

"No I'm not," I said, but I had it in me, I was feeling severe.

"Have you seen Whitney and Logan?" It was like Amanda had read my mind.

"We talked about going on a little creek hike today," she said.

"Maybe they took one early," I offered, and I suddenly worried for Whitney. My heart lurched outward and I had to smack it back. This was her business. I couldn't go around feeling so deeply for her all the time.

Eventually Jurate jogged around by the pond, and pulled a kayak out to join us. "Hey, so who is going to be the brave one and jump?" she asked.

"Heather," we all said together.

"Really?" Heather asked. She swam over to the dock, hoisted herself up on the rickety diving platform, and knifed beautifully into the pond. When she surfaced, she knocked some water out of her ears, and eased back into her floaty. "Well, there you go," she said and cracked open a new beer. "Who wants to follow my dive?"

We spent the afternoon floating around the pond, drinking beer, taking turns diving, teasing each other. Heather told us her breakup story. Georgie aired her misgivings about her future. Amanda worried over whether she'd ever have strong feelings for anyone, and I lamented my continual strong feelings for all the wrong women. Jurate listened. And just as Sherry said, the past was shoring up with the present. When we were together there was such a balance and ease. It didn't feel like there was anywhere else: no place to return to, no place to move towards. The beer started to catch up with me, and

I realized we didn't need the Heartland anymore. We didn't need Chicago—they weren't the reason we were here together.

Georgie was sitting on the dock with her feet in the water, looking around wistfully. I figured the beer was starting to catch up with her too. I nudged Heather who was also watching Georgie.

"You okay there, Summertown?" I asked.

"Yes," Georgie said finally. "I'm having a moment that I want to keep. I feel like we should make a toast. You do it," she said to me, and raised her can in the air.

"Okay," I said, and raised my own can. "Here's to friendship. The grandest promise I know how to make, and I couldn't be more pleased than to share it with you. I like to think that even when we're apart, off in our own lives, getting farther away from the circumstances that brought us together, that this pond will continue to exist, waiting for us to jump in again. That's my cheesy toast, I hope you treasure it forever."

"Hear, hear," Heather said. "Who doesn't like some cheese?"

"That's perfect, you know," Georgie said. She had snapped to attention. "Because not all of us are here in the pond. Some people could not pull it together, and others are too busy attending to matters which they have deemed more important." She paused to raise an eyebrow. "I think you're right, Aneesha. There is something to be said of being capable of making a commitment to your friends. That makes this important."

"You guys are going to hate this, but you know who brought this to my attention?" I asked.

Amanda knew. She looked at me and shook her head.

"Yes. Sherry. Not intentionally, but the credit is hers."

"So you're going to be nice, then?" Georgie asked. "Because you're not actually allowed to intentionally ruin anybody's relationship in my favorite place on earth."

"Well, it's too late for that," I began, and launched into the Whitney and Logan events of that morning and previous night. When I was done, a steady stream of clouds was passing overhead, and we all looked up from beneath the cool shadow. I heard someone's stomach growl.

"Oh, poor guys. But who didn't see that coming? I'm ready for lunch," Georgie announced.

I saw Whitney sitting alone on the deck as we came up the hill. She had her embroidery box on her lap and was pulling at squares of thread. When I got up there, I took the chair next to her, and we both looked down over the pond.

Georgie stopped on her way into the house. "We're making sandwiches, you want one?"

"Yeah," I said. "Bring two."

"I saw you guys swimming down there," Whitney said. "Looked like fun."

"It wasn't bad," Georgie offered, and closed the screen door behind her.

I watched Whitney tie knots on her friendship bracelet. "I'm sorry about what I said earlier to Logan."

"It's fine. It wasn't like you were the actual problem. But yeah, thanks for throwing me under the bus."

"I admit it was a desperate move," I said. "Where is Logan now?"

"I'm pretty sure I heard the car leave." Whitney kept her gazed fixed out over the trees.

"Ah," I said. "I'm sorry, Whit."

We sat in silence until Georgie came out carrying two plates with turkey sandwiches and large mounds of potato salad. "Warning. I've never been known to go light on the mayo." She smiled and went back inside.

"You must think I'm an idiot," Whitney said.

"Nah," I said, and bit into my sandwich. It was satisfying in the way of Georgie's food: unsubtle, powerful, long-lasting, all of the qualities of a good pickup truck.

Whitney laughed. "You're so not like anybody else. Most people who don't like people for their flaws would think I'm in idiot."

"Oh burn," I said. "How awful that I like people for being human, how embarrassing for me. And how embarrassing for you, Whitney, that you're not a robot, and have mixed feelings sometimes. What a major bummer."

"Alright, stop it, you made your point." Whitney pulled out a few chunks of red onion. "This sandwich has a lot going on."

"Very heavy on the condiments," I agreed. "Hooooo, big spot of hot sauce."

"Ketchup too?" she asked.

"Are you okay?" I asked.

"I'm relieved," she said. "It makes me feel guilty. I know there are things I'll miss. I just—" She winced and shrugged.

"You didn't want to have kayaks together."

"I think I was a horrible girlfriend to him."

I nodded and continued to eat.

"Really?" she laughed, and punched my shoulder. "You are seriously awful at post-breakup friend duty."

I threw my hands in the air. "You said it first, I just don't disagree with you!"

"Say it, don't spray it," she said, and handed me my paper towel, which had fluttered to the floor of the deck.

"Thanks," I said. "Now you can finally make it happen with Peach Tree."

She had food in her mouth. I watched her laugh and try not to spit it out. "You know," Whitney said after she swallowed, "I may have missed my chance. I saw her not that long ago, and I think she has a wife now. She was complaining about how their TV is on a cooler or something. I was drunk, I wasn't paying attention."

"I guess even Peach Tree wants to settle down."

"I think that's all Peach Tree ever wanted, lesbe honest."

"Oh, Whitney," I said.

"What?" she asked sheepishly. "Bad?"

"No, perfect."

I tried not to imagine Logan on his long solo drive home. I was selfishly happy that he was gone. As I carefully watched Whitney throughout the evening, it was undeniable that she laughed harder and freely snarked, that she wasn't waiting with a frowny cringe for something to rub her the wrong way. Her relief was mine, because

it also confirmed that I knew Whitney's authentic self, an idea that
had felt shaky all summer. When we all sat down to make our own
Apples to Apples game, Whitney had a mischievous grin on her face.
Heather handed us 15 index cards. "Remember, 10 nouns, 5 adjec-
tives and, yes, you can use proper nouns."

"Aneesha always puts me in," Jurate complained. "I'm getting
her back."

"Dyky is an adjective, right?" Whitney asked.

Then I heard the front door close. "I hope people need a drink
because I think I might have brought too much."

I turned around and Youngsu was standing in the doorway, a case
of beer under each arm. He was wearing a worn green baseball cap
and a faded blue t-shirt that made him look like the quintessential
summer dad.

"You made it!" we all exclaimed.

"You're such a good guest," I said, taking a pack of beer from
him. He laughed and patted my shoulder. "I'm hoping."

Georgie walked up to him cautiously. "You're here. I thought
you'd decided not to come. Did you get lost?"

Youngsu smiled and crossed his arms triumphantly. "Only for
one hour. I stopped to consult my map and corrected the situation."

"Hmm," Georgie said, but I knew she was pleased.

"I know it seemed touch and go," he said.

"Yep, very touch and go." She nodded, and put her hands on
her hips.

"But I wouldn't have missed this for the world," he said. "I can
pull it together sometimes, Summertown, it just takes me a while.
Better late than never, I hope."

"Better," she said, relenting a little, and put her arm around his
waist. "Come on, we're making a game, we need some strange nouns."

"What else did I miss?" he asked.

Amanda shrugged. "A few breakups, a girlfriend we don't love,
and two cases of beer. Nothing you can't catch up on."

"That's a lot," he said. "I didn't miss the dancing, did I? Because,
Aneesha, I have some jams you might like."

"Oh, oh, dancing!" Whitney was already hopping around the

living room. Jurate suddenly appeared with a glass of Jameson for Youngsu. "Drinks first, dancing second."

"I'll take what the gentleman is having," Georgie responded.

That was how, as the sun was setting, we ended up on the patio dancing to a playlist that Youngsu had been secretly compiling all summer. I was in the midst of a dance with Amanda and Youngsu that included pretending to be models on a yacht, when Richard and Sherry came sauntering down the hill into the yard.

"You didn't wait for us?" Richard asked. He stood motionless against our oscillating group, and held his arms out helplessly. "You could have called at least."

"To say what?" Georgie asked bitterly. "Hi, it's us, we're having a good time? That was the whole point."

Richard continued to stand still, and his silence told me he was incredibly angry.

"Come on, baby, let's put on some evening clothes." Sherry gently tugged his elbow. "Or at least pour us a drink and join in, there's no point in pouting."

Richard didn't move. "Well, did you eat yet?" he asked, his tone growing more accusatory, more insistent.

Sherry let go of his arm. I left my dance, picked up my glass and walked over to stand in front of Richard. His nose was pink from the sun and his mouth was set firmly. I could tell he was upset because he had missed out while he was in town, and that had been his very own choice. This was nothing but some hapless drunken fools in a pretty setting. It was only significant if you cared about the company, and I liked to think he still did.

"Have my drink," I said. I took his hand and used my own to close his fingers around the glass. It still had ice in it and he jumped from the chill.

He sighed. "I don't want—"

"Richard, I miss you. For old time's sake, quit nagging and join us. We're all here, exactly the same as you left us."

A breeze blew the part in his hair the wrong way, and he seemed flustered by it.

Sherry reached over to brush his bangs off of his forehead. He took a gulp of the whiskey, swallowed and coughed. "Listen, doll, in the future," he began. He was holding back a smile. "More ice, less water. Work on it, Aneesha."

I smiled and took my drink back. "Work on it yourself, asshole. And Sherry," I said, "you're welcome to drink anything that's up there."

Richard chuckled and patted the top of my head. "Be careful what you offer Sherry. Her sunny demeanor does not betray her capacity for the drink."

"Well, she's dating you," I said. "I'm making some assumptions."

I winked at Sherry who seemed tickled by this. She laughed and patted my arm in a conspiratorial fashion. It was a delicate touch that made me think of PTA meetings.

There was a hungry wholesomeness to her. Her heart wasn't a piece of hard jerky, it was shiny, and gold, and full of hope. Sherry was in no way afraid that her best days were behind her and, regardless of what I thought about it, Richard needed that.

He followed Sherry up the stairs, and opened the screen door for her with an over-the-top flourish that said, "No, no, after you, my darling." I had spent so many nights watching his excessively chivalrous behavior wasted on drunk girls with no sense of nuance, or older women who thought it was an act, or people like me, his friends, who rolled their eyes and wished this fountain of affection had another outlet. So when Sherry delicately curtseyed and put her hand out for a kiss, I was both wholly disgusted and utterly pleased.

"Get back over here, it's our song!" Whitney had her hands on my shoulders and was guiding me back to the patio. I recognized the leisurely guitar riff that opened Miley Cyrus's "Party in the U.S.A." It called to mind all of the nights I had feverishly danced beside Whitney in her living room, at the Heartland, at gay clubs—both the hip kind and the kind that stunk of sticky gummy bear drinks even before they opened. I recalled the way my bandana flapped up and down on my neck as she and I jumped higher and higher and higher, and how that was the kind of thing I could keep with me forever. Only I didn't have to keep it alone. I had forced this song on everybody, it turned out. Because suddenly there were 10 people on the patio, people with more discerning taste than myself, who were excited about this bad song, who were so connected to my happiness that they loved it too.

Richard hurried back down to the patio to share this dance with me. He switched his hips and grabbed my hand and we whirled over the brick. We folded in and out of each others' embraces, knees kicking, backs jerking in hexagonal patterns, arms like hypnotic snakes, until the two of us were on the ground butt to butt, our legs meeting in the air like a strange water ballet. As if they weren't connected to us, I watched his and my feet flex and flutter, our legs arcing and braiding, and suddenly it occurred to me only Richard and I could dance this way and mean it. The song ended and we lay panting on ground, encircled by our friends. They clapped and cheered—from what I imagined was as much shock as entertainment. Then the next song started and everyone went back to dancing. Richard and I remained, our sweaty backs to the brick, staring at the blackening swath of sky. I was aware that this kind of dancing was done for us. I already dreaded the moment I stood up, when we'd be different people.

"You did it," I said.

"What you say, Little A?" Richard stretched his leg sideways, and leaned his head closer to mine.

"You got serious. You're becoming the adult you want to be."

"Oh, quit fucking with me," he said. "It's already scary enough without your sarcasm."

"I'm serious." I squeezed his arm. "I'm full of admiration for you. I know it looks and sounds like disgust—it's that too—but this takes guts. You're gonna get married and be a dad and have a life."

"Well, thanks, but you better know it's going to happen to you," he said. "One day you'll go get something, Aneesha. When it's in your sights, and you're ready to drop everything for it, and you're about to shit your pants, you can be sure I will be waiting for you at the bar with a scotch and a Xanax to say I fucking told you so."

We both cackled for a good minute or two. "I'm sure I'll need it," I said.

Richard got to his knees and pulled me up so we were both

standing. "Now, if you'll please excuse, I'm going to dance with my foreseeable future," he said. "It looks like yours is awaiting you too."

I looked over to where Georgie, Whitney, Heather, Amanda and Jurate were adjusting each other's floppy sun hats.

"Ready for yours?" Heather asked. "I forgot that I brought these, aren't they great? I thought we could use a more mature matching summer look."

"Calm down, Heather!" I yelled as she plopped the hat on my head.

"Calm down yourself!" she cried, and slipped the knot on the string all the way up to my chin.

※

I was over-sunned, greasy and limp by end of the weekend. There was a deep smoky odor that seemed to be emanating from my scalp, a layer of pond scum on my swimsuit, and all of my t-shirts smelled sulfuric from the fireworks we'd lit every night, but I felt spent in a positive way. I had given my all to these friends of mine, and it seemed enough to sustain us into our foreseeable futures, as Richard had put it.

We watched each other go, the dust clouding behind each car that made its way down the gravel drive, and made plans to see each other before we all split off in our own directions. Georgie and I were the last to leave. We closed all the blinds, unloaded the dishwasher, and packed the piles of extra towels and sheets into the trunk of the car. Georgie made sure to point out to me how nice it was that we didn't have to wait for the laundry to get done before we left.

"You're right," I said. "You always are the most excellent host."

"Nobody said hosting was easy," she replied. "But I do love it."

When we got back to the city, she offered to drop me off at Whitney's, but it wasn't terribly late and the wandering part of me, which never seemed to sleep, wanted to get on Caliente and ride around.

Georgie looked at me like I was crazy. "Okay. Well, it's been a long weekend. I hope you know that I can't come with you."

"Don't worry, that's okay," I said. "I'll be fine on my own."

The night air was heavy and warm as I sped off on the clear streets. I found myself taking a hard left turn, swooping down the middle of Glenwood. Already, I saw the red screen door of the Heartland flapping loosely, the lights of the Buffalo Bar glowing behind it. Sweat beads blossomed on my nose, and the streetlights blurred into a streak in my peripheral vision. The full trees huddled over me, breathing sweet maple gusts into my face. As I pedaled hard over the speed bumps, leaning forward into each lurching lift, a balloon of nostalgia expanded inside me. "Remember this," I whispered to myself. The windows of the stacked brick buildings were open and ready. I threw my arms in the air, took a deep breath, and prepared to holler my goodbye.

Acknowledgements

I had the pleasure of beginning this book during my MFA program at the University of California, Riverside. I am forever grateful to Michael Jayme and Andrew Winer for showing me that short stories can be stretched into novels, and assuring me mine was worth writing. The Vermont Studio Centers gave me the gift of time in a beautiful place with extraordinary company to finally finish it.

An earlier draft of this manuscript very graciously and meticulously edited by Joy Johannessen, whom I was lucky to meet at the Community of Writers, and the strangely formatted version of the final one was smoothed out by Safia Elhillo.

My readers, Amanda Ruud, Samantha Lamph, Emily Wells, Daniel Suess, and Vinh-Paul Ha, encouraged me and pointed out my mistakes, large and small — thank you for cleaning me up. I am forever grateful to Amy Wilder and Sophie Grimes for letting me take ownership of this version of our loves and lives, and for opening up your homes to me in all of the senses of the word. The biggest thank you to everyone who shared time with me in Chicago, to all of my friends, who make me feel supported and loved every day, and to my family, who will always pitch in to help me succeed.

Photo by Lara Kaur

Kamala Puligandla is a writer and editor from Oakland, who lives in Los Angeles, CA. She has writing degrees from Oberlin College and UC Riverside. Currently, Kamala is the Editor-In-Chief at Autostraddle.com, the world's largest website dedicated to queer women and nonbinary people. *Zigzags*, is her first novel, and her novella, *You Can Vibe Me On My FemmePhone* is forthcoming in Jan 2021 on Co — Conspirator Press. She is well-known for her contagious laugh, her willingness to have one more drink, and her easily undone heart. Find her at kamalapuligandla.com.